FRIENDS *of the*
Livingston Public Library
Gratefully Acknowledges
the Contribution of

Constance McGoff

For the 2017-2018 Membership Year

RED SWAN

RED SWAN

P. T. DEUTERMANN

ST. MARTIN'S PRESS ⚏ NEW YORK

RED SWAN. Copyright © 2017 by P. T. Deutermann. All rights reserved. Printed in the United States of America. For information, address St. Martin's Press, 175 Fifth Avenue, New York, NY 10010.

Designed by Jonathan Bennett

The Library of Congress Cataloging-in-Publication Data is available upon request.

ISBN 978-1-250-11408-2 (hardcover)
ISBN 978-1-250-11409-9 (e-book)

Our books may be purchased in bulk for promotional, educational, or business use. Please contact your local bookseller or the Macmillan Corporate and Premium Sales Department at 1-800-221-7945, extension 5442, or by e-mail at MacmillanSpecialMarkets@macmillan.com.

First Edition: August 2017

10 9 8 7 6 5 4 3 2 1

This book is dedicated to the memory of my older brother,
David Ward Deutermann, a Navy submarine officer,
mechanical and electrical engineer,
master woodworking craftsman, patient parent,
and devoted husband, whose dry wit was always sufficient cause
to seek his company and advice. He is missed.

ACKNOWLEDGMENTS

I did not consult any books or persons while writing this story, but I do wish to acknowledge and thank the website Google, which has revolutionized the process of researching the information that makes us authors look like we know what we're talking about.

Quis custodiet ipsos custodes?
Who shall guard the guards themselves?

(JUVENAL, FIRST CENTURY AD)

I

THE BLACK SWAN

ONE

Dr. Preston Allender examined the woman standing in front of his desk. According to her service record, she was thirty-three. Pretty, brunette, well made, and obviously fit. Her expression seemed a bit haughty, as if she was here only because she had to be. She wore a gray linen skirt and jacket over a white silk blouse. The skirt ended demurely just below her knees, and her shoes qualified as more useful than fashionable. Her hands rested on her hips and her head tilted slightly to one side. Allender continued to examine her, his gaze partially obscured by large-framed eyeglasses with smoky lenses. He waited until she gave a small sigh of impatience. He had not invited her to sit down in one of the straight-backed chairs in front of his desk.

He glanced at her file. "You're Melanie Sloan?"

"Yes," she said. She had the throaty voice of a smoker, or an ex-smoker. Her suit jacket was a little big for her. He wondered if she was trying to conceal the size of her breasts. It didn't much matter—she exhibited an almost electric sex appeal, and that had been the number one criterion on his internal staffing call list. He was about to do a somewhat delicate dance here, because the operative for this particular mission *might*—his word—have to engage in intimate physical relations with the target of the operation. She was attractive enough, in an edgy way, but right now he had to see if she had the salt to take this on. He hoped so—her face was the closest match yet to the picture in his desk drawer.

"You've just finished your first overseas assignment in"—he glanced down at her record again—"Lisbon, and now you're back for specialty training, correct?"

"Yes." Her tone of voice indicated growing impatience, as if she were saying, *If that's my record you're looking at, then we both know all this. Why are you wasting my time?*

Good, he thought; she had a high opinion of herself, and that was going to be a vital trait. *If* she was the one. So: Time to confirm that.

"And you do understand that if you are approved for this mission, you might be required to consummate a physical relationship with the target individual?"

She hesitated. "I read that, yes," she said. "But I do have standards. I'll do that only if the target is a reasonably attractive man and not some drooling old troll with an enormous belly and bad teeth."

Allender didn't miss a beat. "What if the target is a woman?" he asked.

She blinked at that. "I suppose so," she said. "Although I'm not that way."

"I understand," he said, closing her file. "Now: Will you please disrobe."

"*Wha-at!*" she exclaimed.

"Will you please take off all of your clothes," he said, looking up and directly into her face now.

"In your dreams, Mister Whoever-the-hell-you-are."

"Not in my dreams, Ms. Sloan," he said, mildly. "And besides, why not? Are you embarrassed by your body?"

"I'd be embarrassed to have some perfect stranger gawking at me like some Peeping Tom, that's what. Any woman would. Are you *nuts*?" Her voice was shrill now and her hands, still planted on her hips, were balling into fists.

"But that's just it, Ms. Sloan," he said, keeping his tone as mild and reasonable as he could. "You're squawking about some stranger staring at your naked body, but what you said was 'gawking at *me*.' If you can't mentally separate your naked body from the inner you, the woman and the clandestine operative, then we can't use you for this mission."

She opened her mouth to reply but then closed it.

He reached for his phone, hit the intercom switch, and told his executive assistant that Ms. Sloan was leaving now.

"Wait," she said. "I'll do it. If that's what I have to do, I'll do it."

"No, Ms. Sloan," Allender said, with a faint smile. "I need someone a whole lot tougher than I think you are. Don't worry—none of this will affect your performance record. I'm sure you're an excellent operative, just like it says in your record. Thank you for coming in. Oh, and I'd appreciate it if you do not speak to anyone about your interview with me."

A calculating look crossed her face. "I should think not," she said. "That was a highly inappropriate request and you know it. You're lucky I don't file a sexual-harassment grievance against you. See how that would affect *your* performance record."

He sat back in his chair and removed the smoky glasses. He saw her react to his eyes. "Do what you must, Ms. Sloan," he said, softly. "Although you should understand that I don't have a performance record. I'm just a consultant here."

Carol Mann, Allender's executive assistant and a plain, plump woman in her fifties, stepped into the office at that moment and indicated to Sloan that she could leave now. Once the obviously still upset candidate was gone, Carol stuck her head back through the door.

"Told you," she said. "That's five bucks."

"It's unseemly to gloat," he said, reaching for his wallet.

"Put those glasses back on," she said. "You're disturbing my pacemaker."

Once Carol had left, Allender leaned back in his chair and rubbed his eyes before remounting the smoky glasses. This was going to be harder than he'd thought. Sloan had been the single most promising of the three candidates sent over from the training directorate. He'd rejected the first two based on their records alone—competent, but lacking that certain edge Sloan exhibited. Plus, she had done exceptionally well during her basic training period and her first overseas assignment. Mark Hannigan, chief of the Lisbon station, was not known for handing out effusive praise, especially for first-timers. She had impressed him somehow; maybe it was just that sex appeal, although her personality seemed more challenging than flirtatious. That could have been nerves, he thought. Or maybe she'd figured out who was doing the interview and clutched up a little. Nothing new there.

He was thumbing through her file again, wondering how to recast the staffing call, when Carol reappeared. "May have to give you your fiver back," she announced. "Sloan's back in reception and wants another try."

"Really."

"Yup. Send her in?"

"Let's wait five minutes," he said.

"Don't be mean," she chided.

"I'm being me," he said.

"Well, whoop, whoop," she replied, dryly. "Dragon Eyes *is* in the building."

He took off his glasses again and glared at her. Carol pretended to quail in terror, but then closed the door.

Preston Allender was something of a gray eminence within the Agency. A psychiatrist, he was technically assigned to the operational training directorate as a medical consultant at the rank of assistant deputy director. All candidates for the Clandestine Service went through two years of intense preparation, much of it right there at Camp Peary, known throughout the Agency as the Farm. It was located in the Tidewater area of Virginia, near Williamsburg. During the candidates' two-year syllabus, every instructor involved in their training and qualification process carefully evaluated each candidate for weaknesses: technical incompetence, mental or emotional instability, latent psychological fears, and hidden physical limitations. And, of course, they'd been briefed to constantly probe the possibility that the candidate might already be a spy—for someone else.

In order to ensure that the instructors themselves were competent to perform this constant analysis, everyone who had material contact with CS candidates had to spend some quality time annually with Preston Allender, whose unique physical appearance and surgically incisive mind could deconstruct an individual's psyche over the course of a single morning. "Everyone" meant just that: departmental bosses, midlevel supervisors, right down to the individual hands-on instructors, the people who taught close-contact fighting, shooting, intrusion, disguise, communications, and escape and evasion. Once a year they had to endure an office call on the man they called, well behind his back, Dragon Eyes. Allender's brief was not so much concerned with internal Agency security as it was with each faculty member's psychological suitability for the stressful work of shaping a clandestine operative. That skill could atrophy over time, and so the supervisory operatives who trained and evaluated the newbies were universally wary of him. Part of that wariness stemmed from Allender's physical presence.

He was exactly six feet tall, slender, and so entirely composed that people meeting him for the first time were intimidated. He was physically fit, having adopted the habit of taking long walks after dinner each evening through the precincts of wherever his duties brought him. A long face, jet-black hair brushed straight back, a broad forehead, arching eyebrows, prominent cheekbones flanking a faintly hooked nose, and a mouth that seemed to hint at a set of steel teeth. His most striking facial feature, however, was the color of his large, deep-set, and faintly Asiatic eyes, which were bright amber, if not outright gold, with glistening, black pupils that seemed to change shape depending on the tone and tenor of the conversation. Whenever he came into a room he seemed to loom, even if he didn't happen to be the tallest man in the room, prompting one wag to call him the Agency's version of the specter at the feast.

Because of those golden eyes, people would literally stare at him, so long ago he'd taken to wearing large, square-framed European glasses, the kind favored by European movie directors, the lenses lightly tinted to obscure the color of his eyes. He moved through a room carefully, as if unwilling to make physical contact with anything or anyone. He was not one who shook hands; when introduced to someone else he would put his hands behind him like a solicitous undertaker, bend slightly at the waist, look down as if from a great height and just nod.

He was also the dean of the Agency's interrogation section. Whenever the operations directorate had a seriously tough nut to crack, they summoned Allender from his Washington office to the Farm or one of the isolation centers out in the countryside around Washington. Summoning Allender was never a trivial decision. Over the years they'd learned that he would either break the subject's resistance to sharing whatever he knew, or drive him into some kind of mental breakdown state, using techniques of spatial disorientation, those disturbing eyes, and what looked to some an awful lot like an ability to read their minds. He would have smiled at that fantasy, but he did have the ability to anticipate what the subject would say next, sometimes right down to the exact words, and when he enunciated some or all of those words just before the subject did, people watching on the monitors would become just a little bit anxious. The subject would often become very afraid.

He pressed the intercom button and said, "Okay."

Sloan came back in and stood before his desk, looking much more composed this time, although he could see tension in every visible muscle of her body.

"You wish to start over?" he asked.

"Yes, sir."

"Sir" this time, he thought; she must have figured out who I am. He took off his glasses again and saw her swallow when she saw those glowing eyes. "Very well," he said. "Disrobe."

She hesitated for a long moment. Then, looking straight ahead, she took a deep breath, and began unbuttoning her suit jacket. She draped that on one of the chairs and then unbuttoned her blouse, revealing a plain, unadorned bra. The blouse followed the suit coat, and the bra followed the blouse. Allender took care to stare directly into her face the entire time, forcing her to maintain eye contact though she clearly didn't want to. No one did. She kicked off her shoes and then undid a button on the back of her skirt, slid down a small zipper, and stepped out of it, holding on to one of the chairs to keep from toppling over. Beige pantyhose and cotton hipsters remained. She paused for a moment, and then sighed. She thumbed the pantyhose and her panties down in one smooth movement. Finally, everything was off and she stood in front of him in all her glory. She didn't seem to know what to do with her hands and arms, so she simply folded them under her breasts. Then her personality reasserted itself and she cocked her head to one side, raised her eyebrows in an expression that fairly shouted, Do you *mind*?

Now he did look. He examined her body, which was indeed well made. She was not quite voluptuous, but rather somewhere between the California ideal of a boy with breasts and a Modigliani nude. Her breasts were in proportion to the rest of her body, and her hips were rounded in a pleasing, promising shape. Her pubic area was whiter than the rest of her skin but not yet ready for a summer bathing suit. He kept his expression neutral during his inspection and tried to convey the impression that he was examining a side of beef. He needed the situation to be asexual. She hadn't done any kind of a striptease, and his interest was, for the moment, entirely clinical. After a full minute of inspection, he was pleased to see that she was starting to relax just a bit. He also noticed that her nipples were erect.

"Please be seated," he said, finally, looking away while reopening her file. She sat down in the second chair, the one without the clothes, and once again folded her arms over her chest. "Are you cold?" he asked.

"No," she said.

"Are you embarrassed?"

"You think?" she said.

"I don't know," he replied. "That's why I asked. Do you know who I am?"

"I know—I think that you . . ." She ran out of words, unable or unwilling to say that she'd heard of the boss with the unholy amber eyes.

"Let me tell you what *I* see," he said. "A standard naked lady. A pretty if somewhat outraged face. Two breasts, one a bit larger than the other, taut abs, two thighs, two legs, a patch of hair where all that intersects, a small black mole above your navel, a brown one between your breasts, eyebrows that are naturally shaped and not altered by cosmetics, hints of gray in the roots of your hair, a small scar on your right cheekbone, two fingernails indicating that you sometimes bite your nails, a knee, your right one, which is giving you some pain, probably because your right leg is longer than your left, evidence of a recurring cold sore on your upper lip, right side, and, yes, Ms. Sloan, I think that you *are* just the slightest bit cold."

"Well, shit," she said, as bravely as she could. "That good?"

He let the hint of a smile flit across his face. "Good enough," he said. "Now look: The point of this exercise relates to the mission. If you are selected to take this on, you are going to have to be able to divest yourself of that intimate relationship a woman has with her body and her underlying psyche. When you, the woman, are in love or even just in lust, you are ready to give your*self* to your lover. By that I mean you make no distinction between self and body. In the game being contemplated, you will not ever give your*self* to anyone except your controller, and there will be nothing sexual about that connection. Your body, on the other hand, may be subject to different rules, but in a way you can't yet appreciate."

"So we're talking—what?" she asked "A honey-trap mission?"

"No," he said. "If anything, it's a *no*-honey trap. But let's not get too far ahead of ourselves."

He looked over her shoulder. In deference to Company rules, Carol Mann had come in surreptitiously when the interview began and had been sitting in a chair at the back of the room throughout. "Carol," Allender said. "Take over for a few minutes, please."

Then he turned back to Sloan. "I'm going to step out while you get dressed. Once you've done that, Carol, who is my executive assistant here at the Farm, will conduct a short interview with you. She will be asking you some questions which I have prepared, and possibly some of her own."

Sloan cocked her head to one side again and gave him an appraising look. "Why aren't *you* asking them?" she said.

"Because I've seen you naked, Ms. Sloan, and I don't want that fact to color your answers until I know you a lot better."

Allender got up without another glance toward Sloan and walked out. Carol came forward from the back of the room, pretending not to notice that Sloan was sitting naked in a chair in front of her boss's desk. Sloan turned in the chair to look up at Carol, who had a folder in her hands.

"Okay," Sloan said. "So maybe *you* can tell me: What the *fuck*?"

"Never a dull day with Preston Allender," Carol said. "You want to put your clothes on now, dear? And if it makes you feel any better, I was in the room the entire time that you were, um, déshabillé."

"Oh, great," Sloan said, hustling back into her clothes with as much grace as possible, which wasn't much. "That's truly comforting. Stereo voyeurs. And how many cameras, I wonder."

Carol ignored the sarcasm, went around Allender's desk, and sat down in his high-backed chair. "No cameras, Ms. Sloan," she said. "And it's *Doctor* Allender, not Mister. He is actually a medical doctor, and, for what it's worth, I'm not much interested in seeing you or any other woman naked. I don't think he is either, although no one is too sure about that."

"What kind of medical doctor?" Sloan asked, tugging her skirt up around her hips.

"He's a doctor of psychiatry. He also happens to be the assistant deputy director for psychological assessment for the entire Clandestine Service directorate."

Sloan blinked. "Assistant deputy director? That's pretty senior, isn't it?"

"Yes, it is," Carol replied. "So you might want to rein in that 'what the fuck' tone of voice. You do *not* want to get on the wrong side of Preston Allender."

"Oka-a-y," Sloan said. "But you have to admit: 'Hi, there. Nice to meet you. Strip down.' Seriously?"

Carol sighed. "Ms. Sloan," she said. "You're new to this intelligence game. You've been through basic training and one overseas assignment. In the Agency's view you've just finished your apprenticeship. I'm not privy to whatever operation Doctor Allender is staffing but I can guarantee that there will be a significant psychological dimension to it, as well as some real danger for the operative. He needs to know what you're made of, and that doesn't involve voyeurism. And, for what it's worth, you *do* want to think long and hard about acceding to any mission Preston Allender is supporting."

"I see," Sloan said, visibly taken aback.

"I doubt it," Carol replied. "Look: I've worked for him for fifteen years, and there are two things about him which I'll share with you. First: People think he's a mind reader, and while I think that's a carnival delusion, when he trains those dragon eyes of his on you and begins to ask questions, you're soon going to realize that he seems to know the answers right about the time you frame them in your own mind. On three occasions in the past fifteen years he's uncovered people in the training directorate who were playing for some other team."

"What happened to them?"

"Each one was taken to a special facility here on the Farm where Doctor Allender himself trains senior operatives to conduct interrogations. They got to spend several hours with him, one-on-one, in what's called a 'quiet room.' In terms of optics, that's a cross between a sensory-deprivation chamber and a fully staffed surgical suite. Of the three, one hanged himself rather than face Allender again. Each of the other two are currently in federal institutions with a diagnosis of profound protective catatonia."

"*Je*-sus," Sloan breathed. "How—"

"Think of him as the high priest of mind fuck in the Agency. In the *entire* Agency."

"Tell you what, lady," Sloan said. "You guys are starting to scare me."

"Well, good," Carol beamed. "Thought for a moment you weren't getting it. Ready to go back to your day job? That would be my recommendation, you know."

Sloan's eyes narrowed. "What was the second thing?"

"Ninety-nine percent of the Agency's missions in the world of human intelligence involve fairly straightforward tradecraft. You remember: informed patience, planning, intense attention to detail, dogged persistence, and the ability to convince people from other nations and cultures to tell us what we need to know."

"I think I knew that," Sloan said.

"Well, that last 'thing' is called recruiting, and if you can recruit, you are considered unusually valuable to the Agency. Your record says you have the makings of a recruiter, which is one factor that brought you to Doctor Allender's attention. That and your physical appearance."

"The world's *second*-oldest profession," Sloan said. "And the other one percent?"

"The other one percent are the intelligence games played at the nation-state level in what's called informally the serious-shit arena, where mistakes cost agents their lives and senior Agency officials their jobs."

"In that order?" Sloan asked. "Somehow I don't see those as entirely equal consequences."

Carol sighed. "They aren't, Ms. Sloan," she said. "We can replace inexperienced agents fairly easily."

"Hah!" Sloan exclaimed. "Somehow I knew that, too."

"We have four years invested in you. That's trivial when compared to senior people with *decades* of experience in intelligence and counterintelligence. It's just that the big dogs don't take prisoners when things get dicey. It's a pretty simple calculus. Shall we continue?"

Sloan shrugged and made a "sorry I asked" face.

"Okay," Carol said. "Doctor Allender is not an operational player, but when he gets called into that arena, anyone working for him or under his control had better be damn good. That's the bad news."

"There's *good* news?" Sloan asked.

"Yes," Carol said. "For the really consequential missions, there's a two-hundred-fifty-thousand-dollar bonus for the operative. Tax-free. As long as the mission succeeds, which really means if *you* both succeed and survive."

Sloan sat back in her chair and adjusted her skirt. "Well, now," she said. "And when it's all over, what happens then?"

"Because you will have inflicted grievous damage on our opponents, you will have to begin a new life, most probably with a new and improved face, and maybe even a new profession. You will no longer be able to assume duties as second cultural attaché at one of our embassies because there will probably be an entire foreign intelligence service looking to T-bone you with a cement truck at the nearest intersection."

"Wow," Sloan said, and this time the sarcasm was gone. "And if I *don't* succeed?"

"You won't care," Carol said. "Because you won't be with us anymore. You want time to think about this?"

"If I say yes, would that disqualify me?"

"Absolutely," Carol said, approvingly.

Sloan obviously didn't know what to say, or do.

"I was kidding," Carol said. "You'd be a fool not to think and think hard about whether this is something you want to get into. As I said—you're new. That's an advantage. Doctor Allender likes that because his team won't have to purge you of operational bad habits. Plus, with any luck, the opposition won't have noticed you yet, especially in a quiet station like Lisbon."

"May I ask who the opposition is?"

"Not yet," Carol said.

"And how will Doctor Allender know if I'm the right candidate?"

Carol smiled. "Shrewd question," she said. "But I have no idea. That's *his* specialty. Tell me something: Why did you want to be an operative in the first place?"

Sloan sighed in frustration. "I'm sorry," she said. "But that sort of stuff's all in my record, from applicant to candidate to intern to first posting—what part of all that don't you have right there in that folder?"

"The part about your weekends with Mark Hannigan, for one," Allender said from the back of the room.

They both watched Sloan's face go bright red. Allender came back to his desk and Carol got up to leave. "I'll take it from here, Carol," he said, sitting down.

Once Carol had left, he leaned back in his chair. "I called Mark. Asked him about you. He parroted the praise he'd put in your performance evaluations. I let him blather on for a full minute and then asked him if you were a good lay or a great lay. The silence on the line was palpable."

"Oh, shit," she whispered.

"To your credit, he finally said, 'great'. He then asked me if he could know what had happened to you. I told him to buy his wife some flowers and to forget that I had called."

Sloan swallowed and then looked away.

"Did you seduce him or was it the other way around?" Allender asked.

"It was sort of mutual," she said, finally recovering her composure. "He was the station chief. *The* boss. I was a newbie. He took me under his wing. He was nice. He was acting as a mentor, not like a—not like a married man looking for something on the side."

"So: Who made the first move?"

She thought about that for a moment. "You know?" she said. "I think it was just mutual. He's an attractive man, as you must know, and I . . . well, strange town, new job, first real assignment . . . I was lonely, and hanging out in Lisbon bars was out of the question."

"How long did it go on?"

"A few months," she said. "Then something happened—I'm not sure what, but he told me we had to stop."

"How'd you feel about that?"

"Just fine, actually," she said. "I'd never expected there to be any kind of future in it. Saw lots of Portugal. It was nice, but nobody got his heart broken."

"You don't know that, do you," he said.

"You mean Angela, his wife? The only thing she cares about is her show dogs. She and that bratty daughter of hers. Twenty-four seven, dogs, dogs, dogs. Training, showing, feeding, grooming, even breeding, I think."

"What breed of dogs?"

"I don't recall. It wasn't something Mark wanted to talk about, ever. They seemed to lead entirely separate lives."

"Refresh my memory—you've not been married, correct?"

"That's right."

"Marriage not for you?"

She sighed. "I've lived and worked in academia, the sweaty halls of Congress, and the so-very-precious world of the State Department. I didn't see many marriages that seemed worth the candle along the way."

"And you came to the Agency later in life than most applicants. Get bored with regular civilian life?"

"Pretty much. I started with a professional lobbying firm after getting an MA from the Fletcher School. Two years of that and I began to feel like my work was sticking to my clothes, so I moved over to State and got a staff slot in INR. Enjoyed the work and some of the people, and met several Agency staffers over the next four years."

"Would you call yourself an adrenaline junkie?"

"No, not really," she said, giving him what looked a lot like a challenging glare. "But I don't mind being on the edge occasionally."

"Did one of us recruit you or did you just apply out of the blue?"

"I met Mister McGill at a diplomatic function. He told me that with my background in congressional relations and INR I could probably get into the really interesting side of intelligence work if I cared to apply."

Allender smiled inwardly. Carson McGill was the current deputy director for operations at the Agency, known as the DDO. Twice divorced, he was also a well-known ass bandit, which was almost comical, given what he looked like.

"There was no quid pro quo, at least not that I was aware of," she said, mirroring his smile for just a brief moment. "Not quite my type."

"The exception that proves the rule, I suppose," Allender said, smoothly, declining to follow up with the question that usually followed that assertion. "You came down here from D.C., what, two weeks ago?"

"Yes. I have two weeks to go and then they're talking language school, once my next assignment reveals itself."

He thought for a moment, and then asked an important question. "Was your relationship with Hannigan known within the embassy? Or even just within the station?"

"I don't think it was," she said. "We kept it professional during the working week and at functions. Lisbon isn't a big operation, as I'm sure you know. I went out with the assistant defense attaché a couple of times, but he was a colonel and rather too full of himself."

"You make it sound as if your relationships run more along the lines of a sporting event than a search for a soul mate."

She shrugged. "That's pretty much true," she said. "I'm not against marriage or anything, but I wasn't cut out for the wife and kids role."

"Very well," Allender said. "Thank you for coming back in. I apologize, a little bit, anyway, for putting you through the disrobe routine. Your womanly attributes are vital to what's being planned. I had to see if your interest in doing something unusual, even for us, could overcome your outrage. If we decide to bring you onboard for this operation, I promise not to embarrass you like that again. Now, having said that, I need you to have dinner with me in town tomorrow night."

Her eyebrows rose.

"Specifically, I need you make an entrance, wearing something sexy but stylishly sophisticated. I will be at the table before you get there, and I want to see what the reaction is when you walk across the dining room. The place is called Opus Nine. The clientele is upmarket. If nothing else, I promise you a really good steak."

She gave him an appraising look. "Will I have to disrobe?" she asked, finally, with a perfectly straight face.

"No," he replied. "If you do the strut right, every man in the dining room will be doing that for you in his mind's eye." He passed across a card. "Call this number in the morning and ask for Twyla. Think of her as the Agency's version of Angels Costumes out in Hollywood. She'll have makeup artists, a hairstylist, and a selection of clothes that may surprise you. We'll even provide a car and driver."

"Is there going to be someone important there?"

"Oh, yes," he said. He paused. "Me."

She tried not to roll her eyes.

TWO

The following evening, Melanie Sloan found herself in the backseat of a large, silver-colored Mercedes sedan, headed for the Opus Nine restaurant. Her driver was an equally large man decked out in the traditional black uniform of a chauffeur, right down to his black cap. She'd recognized him from her training days as one of the scarier hand-to-hand combat instructors at the Farm. When he'd come to pick her up at the operatives' billeting building he'd been completely in character, insisting that she ride in the back when she'd reached for the right front door. She'd wondered what the desk people in the lobby must have thought, having seen her come back with the garment bags from the session with Twyla's costume people wearing shabby jeans and a sweatshirt, but made up like a movie star.

Now she was decked out in a high-thigh-slashed dress from Alexandre Vauthier with net stockings and a black waist sash, with makeup, jewelry, and a hairstyle to match. She felt hugely self-conscious. On the other hand, she thought, this was a whole lot better than sitting bare-assed naked in a straight-backed wooden chair in front of Dragon Eyes. She hadn't recognized him until he'd taken off those French movie director's glasses. The instructors on the newbie courses had told stories about the doctor who could purportedly see into people's minds. Their description of those penetrating eyes hadn't done them justice. She shivered despite herself.

She forced herself to sit perfectly upright so as not to disturb her elaborate costume or her hairdo. With her left hand she held some slack in the shoulder strap of the seat belt to keep it from mashing the dress's delicate if daring lace bodice. As she thought about her séance with Allender yesterday she mused on her life and career with the Agency so far.

She'd grown up in Boston, the only child of two extremely successful parents who'd married later in life. Her mother was an eminent cardiologist at Mass General, specializing in women's coronary care. Her father was a professor of molecular biology at Harvard Medical. Both her parents had been fully booked and professionally self-absorbed while she was growing up, leaving Melanie eventually to feel more well-polished than cherished as a child. Loving and doting parents they were not. They had, however, done their duty with regard to her education and appropriate social grooming in the rarefied atmosphere of Boston's academic universe. It hadn't hurt that she'd inherited her mother's good looks, and she herself had managed an undergraduate degree from Boston University and a master's from the Fletcher School of Law and Diplomacy.

"Almost there," the driver announced.

"Right," she said, taking a deep breath. Now she was wearing a few thousand dollars' worth of clothes and shoes, not to mention jewelry. While it all felt wonderful, she still wondered what Allender wanted her to do when she did The Walk across the restaurant. And how was she supposed to know where he was seated?

She needn't have worried. The maître d' *and* a waiter were standing at the restaurant's front entrance when the big Merc came swooping up. The driver got out and hustled around to open the right rear door, and then the maître d' was making effusive greetings as the driver handed her out of the car. With the maître d' leading and the waiter in tow, they made their way into the main dining room and then turned to head for a curved upholstered booth just beyond the piano, where Allender was sitting in isolated splendor. He was wearing a luxurious-looking dark burgundy smoking jacket over gray slacks, and instead of a shirt he wore what looked like a silk turtleneck sweater.

Melanie concentrated on not tripping over those incredibly narrow heels she was wearing and looked straight ahead with as regal an expression as she could manage. She saw Allender incline his head in an approving nod and then start to get up as she approached. If other people were watching, she didn't see them, because Allender had now removed his shadowy glasses and was giving her the full-on dragon-eyes treatment, but with a wholly different blaze this time, one of visible admiration. She found herself mesmerized for a moment by those amazing eyes, and then the maître d' was pulling the table to one side so she could sit beside him in the plush enclosure while the waiter fussed with the glasses and cutlery.

"Welcome to Opus Nine, Ms. Rockefeller," the maître d' gushed. "*Such* a pleasure to have you join us for dinner."

This time Melanie did see reactions from other diners nearby at the mention of that fabled name. She nodded and smiled at him but didn't say anything. Menus were placed discreetly on the table and then they were left alone. Melanie surveyed the room, which was crowded and somewhat noisy. She looked sideways at Allender as if to ask, Well?

He'd put his glasses back on but it was obvious he was impressed—and pleased. "Stunning," he said. "I saw one poor guy miss his mouth and drop a forkful of mashed potatoes into his lap, and another one poured wine all over his table. The bartender overfilled a glass of beer and two waiters tried for the same door at the same time, fortunately with empty trays. Well done, indeed, Ms.—Rockefeller."

"What *did* you tell them," she asked, as the waiter approached with an ice bucket and some champagne.

"Only that I had an important guest coming for dinner who would appreciate some discretion because she was a Rockefeller. Twyla certainly did you justice."

"I'm terrified I'm going to spill something on it," she admitted quietly, after the waiter had poured out the champagne and backed away.

"Don't be," Allender said. "After all, this little Kabuki certainly beats sitting bare-assed naked in a straight-backed wooden chair in my office, yes?"

She almost dropped her champagne flute, although he didn't appear to notice. Good *Lord,* she thought. Those were her exact words. In the car. She'd thought exactly those words. No way. No. Freaking. Way.

The waiter returned, took their orders, topped off the champagne, and set the almost empty bottle to one side. He'd ordered the fish of the day; she'd gone for beef. After two years in Europe, she craved American beef.

For the next ten minutes he led the conversation, mostly asking her about her life in Boston and then in Washington, before the Agency. She realized he was trying to put her at ease. She wondered how old he was. If he was an assistant deputy director, fifties, probably. He was entirely composed, with no fidgeting or adjusting of his body's position on the banquette. One elegantly long hand for his champagne flute, the other in his lap, reminding her of one of those sitting Buddha statues. Since they were sitting side by side in the European fashion, they made minimal eye contact, especially with those Onassis eyeglasses. His voice was calm and devoid of any identifiable accent, pleasant but professionally neutral. He was making no attempt to initiate intimacy between them, remaining well out of her personal space. It was almost like talking to someone you happened to sit next to on the bus, she thought. She was tempted to ask him about *his* background and service with the Agency, but then thought better of it. It wasn't a date, not with all the Ms. Rockefeller

BS, or Kabuki as he'd called it. What *are* we doing here, she wondered?

"Do you see the Chinese family, third table on the left from our vantage point?"

Not moving her head, she looked. There were four of them. One older man with an authoritative bearing and obviously the paterfamilias. Next to him was a plain, round-faced Chinese lady, probably his wife. The other two were younger, looking like son and daughter-in-law, or vice versa. As she looked away, she thought she saw the older man stealing a surreptitious look in her direction.

"Yes," she said, looking now into the middle distance, as if unaware there was anyone else in the busy restaurant.

"Depending on who leaves first, us or them, I want you to give the older man a secret smile. Just a quick look. Acknowledge his interest. Let him know that you're aware of him. That's all. If his wife is watching you or him, don't do it, but *do* look for an opportunity to make eye contact without her seeing you do it. Even if he just takes a last look as they're going out the door."

"Okay," she said.

"Try it on me."

She did.

"A tiny bit too long. I want him wondering if it even happened. Again."

She looked away and then back.

"Much better, but don't let your gaze linger like that. A quick flash, then a demure look away and down."

The waiter showed up with dinner. Allender asked if she'd like some wine, but she said no. The champagne had gone to her head a little more than she would have liked in these circumstances. He ordered a single glass of red and then they enjoyed Opus Nine's justifiably famous cooking. As they were finishing, the Chinese family got up and headed for the door. The "wife," chattering away with the "son," was paying no attention to her husband, and just before the group entered the hallway to the front door, the older man looked back at Melanie. She managed a quick glance in his direction. There'd been nothing subtle about *his* look, and then he was gone.

"Contact?" he asked.

"Oh, yes, I'd say so," she said, with a small smile. Like an eagle looking at a baby bunny, she thought.

"Good. Now describe him to me, please."

She waited until the plates were cleared and coffee ordered. "Mainland Chinese, I'd think," she began. "Bigger and taller than the average Chinese I've met. Early fifties. Military bearing, lots of authority, so I'd guess PLA, probably a general or maybe even a commissar."

"What's unique about the face?"

"Those black, flyaway eyebrows that make him look like he's about to pounce. Not the usual round, fleshy face I associate with older Chinese party officials. More oval, with a strong nose and cheekbones. Thick, black hair. No eyeglasses. Not a man who smiles much."

"Very good," he said. "Especially from twenty feet away. You must have excellent distance vision. What was he wearing?"

She drew a complete blank. She simply couldn't remember. How odd.

"You can't remember because you were focused on his face, which, admittedly, is his most interesting feature. I can relate to that."

She turned her head to look directly at him and thought she saw the trace of a smile, although with those birth-control glasses she couldn't be too sure. It was the first thing he'd said to her that was even remotely personal, but if it had been a "moment" it quickly passed.

Coffee came and dessert was declined.

"So," she asked once the waiter had withdrawn. "May I ask who that man was?"

"I've determined two things this evening," he said, appearing to ignore her question. "One, you can rock a room just by walking in, especially when you're properly adorned. And, two, the chief of the Ministry of Security Services office at the People's Republic of China embassy in Washington, Major General Chiang Liang-fu, was at least somewhat smitten."

Wow, she thought. "What in the world is someone like that doing in the Williamsburg area?" she asked.

"Vacation? Seeing some of the United States with his family? Meeting with whatever network they have in place in this area that covers the Farm or the military bases here in the Tidewater area? Possibly all of the above, although I doubt it's really an operational visit. We know who he is, what he is, and *where* he is at all times. It's not like he sneaks around undercover. He doesn't have to."

"Does he know who you are?" she asked.

"Probably," he said, but did not elaborate. That surprised her.

"And he likes the ladies?" she asked.

"Indeed he does," he said. "And, of course, official Washington is positively a groaning board of attractive women. Or so I've been told."

She laughed out loud. The purported ratio of nine attractive women to every eligible man was a well-known urban legend in Washington. "Or so you've been told?" she teased.

"Time to go," he said, glancing quickly around the room. "You go to the powder room; I'll wait out front. When you come out walk directly to the front door. Your car will be ready. We'll say our good-byes, and then you'll leave. The cultural-indoc section will expect you at nine tomorrow."

"Got it," she said, beginning to slide sideways on the banquette. The waiter, who'd been hovering nearby, rushed to move the table aside and offer a hand up. She had a thousand questions, but realized that he'd tell her what she needed to know when she needed to know it. It would be unprofessional to get ahead of that curve right now.

Five minutes later she was escorted by the maître d' through the front doors to the waiting Mercedes. She saw one of the dark-windowed Agency Suburbans parked nearby. Allender was standing by the Mercedes. He took her right hand and helped her into the sedan, babbling something about a delightful evening and hoping she'd enjoy the rest of her time in Williamsburg. As she put on her seat belt, she resisted an urge to look back as the big Merc rumbled away from the restaurant. This time she didn't bother to hold off the shoulder strap.

She'd had some fun tonight, a nice change from the tedious business of yet more training. The clothes and the rest of her costume had been a treat and she was proud to have been able to pull it off. And Allender: What a fascinating man. When he'd had those protective glasses off, anyone who could see his face had been staring. She could well believe people thought he was a mind reader. And yet, he wasn't a cold fish. She'd gotten the impression of tight control more than intellectual arrogance. She felt herself blushing at the thought of going to bed with a man like that. She saw her driver glancing back at her in the shadow of the backseat and composed her face.

THREE

Preston Allender relaxed in the backseat of the Suburban as he was driven back to the Farm through the dense evening traffic. So far, so good, he thought, fairly sure now that he had his candidate. She'd dropped into character without a hitch and she hadn't badgered him with premature questions. She was being surprisingly professional for just two years in the field, and she'd certainly had the desired effect on Chiang Liang-fu. Carson McGill would be pleased. Hell, even he'd felt like a teenager who'd scored a dinner date with the best-looking girl in school.

There had been that one question about his knowing Chiang. He smiled mentally at the memories that inquiry had provoked. His father, an electronics engineer, had been a rising star at Westinghouse in the field of medical imaging when he'd met and married Allender's future mother, an exchange student from Taiwan, who was finishing a Ph.D. in molecular biology at MIT. Young Preston had been five when they left the Boston area for Taipei.

They rented a house in the Songshan District and Preston attended the prestigious Taipei American School in the Shilin District. In the twelve years they spent in Taipei, Preston grew up as an only child in a household that spoke both upper-class Mandarin and English. Following a management shakeout at Westinghouse after a big contract went to another company, Preston's father had left the company and brought the family back to America. They bought a house in the prestigious Kalorama neighborhood in Washington, D.C. His father had taken an assignment as a consultant to the Agency for International Development, while his mother became a department head at the National Institutes of Health. Preston was admitted to the premed curriculum at George Washington University. With his mother's connections, he was easily admitted to GWU Medical School, and he graduated in the top 10 percent of his class. Having chosen forensic psychiatry as his ultimate specialty, he underwent four years of residency training in psychiatry and then a two-year internship in forensic psychiatry before sitting for his licensing examinations. Throughout his medical education, his ability to speak Mandarin fluently brought additional networking opportunities, as his various schools tapped him to attend seminars, workshops, and other official functions at which visiting Chinese doctors would be present. This in turn attracted the attention of a CIA recruiter, who enticed Allender to join the Agency, which was just then coming to grips with the scope of the People's Republic of China's espionage programs in America.

That pattern continued once he'd been with the Agency's training directorate for a while. He would regularly attend diplomatic functions in Washington that included Chinese officials, because they presented an opportunity to put an intelligence-trained psychiatrist alongside a senior or otherwise interesting Communist Party member. As Allender rose in the Agency's operative-development program, the Chinese Ministry of Security Services became aware of him, which meant that when he did appear at State Department receptions or other top-level functions involving Chinese officials, they had all been briefed to beware of the American doctor with the upper-class Mandarin accent and the unsettling amber eyes. A Russian official who'd been warned about Allender would have limited his conversation to the weather, but Chinese officials seemed to enjoy a little mental sparring: I know who you are, and you know who I am, so let's put that aside for a moment and just see who can mess with whom. The generous spectrum of meanings and maybe-meanings of Mandarin made that game even more interesting, and Allender had a huge advantage over the State Department's Foreign Service Institute–trained American officials of having been speaking Mandarin since he'd learned to talk.

He'd first encountered Chiang at a UN-sponsored antiterrorism conference in New York. The US ambassador to the UN had requested linguistic support and the State Department had requested Allender. Chiang had been just a lieutenant colonel at the time, but Allender had noticed how the other members of the People's Republic delegation were deferring to this intense army officer, so he'd casually closed in and made his acquaintance. Chiang had been astonished to hear an American speaking university-level Mandarin and they'd ended up spending more than a little time conversing on the margins of the conference. Chiang had presented himself as a midlevel police bureaucrat in Beijing, and Allender had adopted the role of an NIH psychiatrist specializing in the modalities of terrorist recruitments. By the third and final night of the conference, they'd reached the *ganbei* stage at a private banquet hosted by the Chinese delegation. Allender, anticipating the inevitable exchange-of-shooters challenges, had taken an Agency compound before the encounter which changed alcohol into sugar. It gave you a bit of a stomachache, but you stayed pretty much sober while your drinking opponent went blotto, which was when Chiang let it slip that he was perhaps more than just a run-of-the-mill policeman.

The next morning Allender debriefed the diplomatic intelligence officials at the US embassy to the UN, where he learned that Chiang was most likely an up-and-comer in the Ministry of State Security, the intelligence and counterintelligence arm of the Central Committee of the Communist Party of the PRC. The officials had told Allender that since the MSS was like an amalgamation of

America's CIA, NSA, and FBI, Chiang was definitely someone to cultivate if the opportunity ever arose. They also warned him that he, Preston Allender, had probably entered the MSS database, if only because of his Mandarin.

"Somebody will be assigned to research you and your family history in Taipei; where you went to school, what your father did, will all be discovered. They'll eventually assume you're with us, so if you do encounter Chiang again, it's going to be a different game."

That prediction had been spot-on, as Allender discovered two years later at a reception held at the PRC embassy in Washington. At the pre-briefing for the reception, the Chinese desk officer had told Allender that Chiang was now a senior officer at the MSS, specializing in the coordination of the dizzying array of Chinese intelligence networks operating in the US, covering academia, the banking system, industrial technology and R&D, military affairs, diplomatic affairs, the national infrastructure, medical science, counterterrorism, the Internet, and, last but not least, the Agency itself.

"Don't kid yourself," he'd been told. "The rise of Chinese intelligence operations in the United States has resulted in the greatest transfer of wealth in the history of the world. Period. Go into any advanced technology laboratory in the country—computer science, astronomy, medical research, energy, and biochemistry—and count the number of Caucasian faces. Then count the Chinese. Three to one, on average. Go to any high school graduation in America where they have a half-decent academic program, and see who the valedictorian is; you'll find the top graduates are either Chinese or Southwest Asian. They own us. The only thing holding them back from world domination is their delusion with Communism."

"What time in the morning, sir?" his driver asked, interrupting his musings. They'd arrived at the Residence.

"Eight will do it."

He went into the Residence and walked up to the desk. "Is the SCIFF available?"

"Yes, sir, it is," the lobby clerk said. "Let me get this hour's key codes."

Once in the secure communications vault, Allender sent a brief e-mail message to Carson McGill, the deputy director for operations. "Sloan will do. Tell the controller to call me."

An hour later, a Mr. Smith was on the secure line seeking instructions.

"Activate the clone" was all Allender said, and hung up.

He went upstairs to his room, which was a small suite in deference to his rank as a member of the senior executive service. He cracked a bottle of Scotch from the minibar and then stood by the window, with its view of nondescript government buildings scattered everywhere.

Ms. Melanie Sloan in full war paint had been quite a sight this evening. He'd had to work hard at not getting a little bit more personal with her at dinner, but he'd learned long ago that every budding romance had ended once the lady got a good look into those dragon eyes of his. Now that he was fifty-five, there didn't seem to be much point in pursuing attractive women, so now he was pretty much accustomed to being a professional odd duck. Being a senior odd duck helped, though.

FOUR

Melanie Sloan sat back at her table in the Residence bar and enjoyed the warm buzz from her first drink since dinner with Allender. She'd spent the last week at the cultural indoctrination school on the Farm, getting acquainted with all things Chinese. She'd made it a rule not to drink during the workweek, which made Friday evening at the Residence bar even more appealing. The bar itself wasn't that large, and it looked like the bar in just about any military officers' club, which it had once been. Subdued lighting, an actual mahogany bar stretching across one entire wall, mementos and military plaques on the walls, with waitresses wearing black slacks and white shirts flitting efficiently among the tables, keeping the all-important booze flowing. The ratio of men to women was about four to one, but she didn't recognize any of the men. She herself was wearing jeans and a lightweight Harvard sweatshirt, and drinking a double Bombay gin over crushed ice with a lime wedge. Mark in Portugal had introduced her to Bombay, telling her it was the perfect antidote to the heat of Portugal's summers, among other things. She'd elicited a gratifying number of interested looks when she'd come into the bar, but after a week of fairly intense schooling, she was mostly just tired. Besides, she was here to meet with Allender.

The week had been interesting. A variety of so-called old China hands had walked her through the bewildering strata of modern Chinese society, pointing out the formidable number of dialects, the cultural norms and taboos, the way that Communism skewed political, personal, and economic perceptions in China, the rigidly bureaucratic government power structure cladding them all in the dialectic of Marxism and Socialism while pretending not to notice how much the entire nation-state resembled the days of the emperors. As in all crash courses on China, even those conducted by genuine experts, the net result was a sense of being totally overwhelmed, a feeling shared apparently by most modern-day Chinese themselves. The sheer size of the Chinese population practically guaranteed that no one individual could grasp the scale of it. The lecturers had emphasized that the sole purpose of the government and all its Communist BS was to control its vast population. Not understand it, not improve it, not educate it, but control it. Any analysis of Chinese government policy had to be viewed through that lens and that lens alone. It became obvious to her after just a week that the Chinese government was, at the most elementary level of political theory, afraid of its vast population.

There'd been only one disturbing element to her first week with the Chinese experts. The course director, a stocky Chinese woman whimsically named Mary Jones, asked Melanie why she was attending the course. Melanie said that Dr. Allender had arranged it. The woman asked if Allender was going to be her controller. Melanie said she didn't know; in fact she didn't know what Allender had planned for her. The woman then asked if Melanie was married or in a relationship. No, again. "Good," the woman said, because if you're getting involved with Allender, it will be intense and, to all intents and purposes, you will disappear until it's over. And maybe even *after* it's over."

The offhand way she'd said that, as if just making an observation about the weather, had unsettled her. That said, she found herself getting a little excited about meeting up with the spooky doctor and his fiery eyes again. Like coming face-to-face with a tiger—a blend of being frozen in fear and an intense desire to look back at him.

She became aware of a change in the room's atmosphere, a sudden dampening of the hum of casual conversation. She looked up to see Preston Allender himself gliding across the room toward her table, those wolf eyes shining in her direction like headlights, while everyone else in the room was pointedly looking somewhere else.

"Ms. Sloan," he said, in his best undertaker's voice. "May I join you?"

"Absolutely," she replied, her voice perhaps a bit louder than normal. Bombay gin, she thought, will do that to you.

He slid into the chair across from hers without appearing to have moved anything, but then again, she was looking at his face and wondering if he was seeing right through her. For a second she longed for those smoky glasses. He was wearing a suit that looked really expensive, which reminded her he was senior executive service and she was just barely past her apprenticeship.

"How was your week?" he asked. "What did you learn?"

The hum of conversation around them had resumed except for the people at the nearest tables, who now seemed to be concentrating on not attracting his attention. A waitress sidled up to the table with a refill for Melanie and a glass of white wine for the doctor.

"China is—complicated?"

He laughed, a surprisingly warm sound. "You think?" he said. "On the other hand, often Chinese are entirely predictable. Your course will get to that aspect, eventually. But in the meantime, I have another course set up for you. You'll do China in the mornings, and in the afternoons, a bit of boudoir France."

"Oka-a-y," she said. "I assume there's no point to questions yet?"

"You assume correctly," he said. "But I've got one: Have you ever heard the term 'black swan'?"

She thought for a moment, but her brain was just a little fuzzy. Should have eaten something, she thought. Damned gin. And those disturbing eyes. It was like sitting at the table with an eagle. A hungry eagle. "Yes," she replied, finally. "Something to do with Wall Street. But I can't remember what."

The waitress arrived at that moment and deposited a plate of fried calamari with some marinara sauce. "You should eat something," he said. "Bombay gin is rather fast-acting sometimes."

She stared at him. He'd done it again—echoed the thoughts in her mind. She grabbed a calamari ring and tried not to look right at him.

"A black swan is an event," he said. "A totally unexpected event, that usually has some kind of dire consequence that seems to be out of all proportion to the actual event. A single, unimportant bank fails, and then everyone discovers that this bank had so many interlocking ties to many other major banks that now they're *all* going to fail, and maybe the entire financial system is going to collapse."

"Two thousand eight," she said. "Suddenly the whole world was scrambling."

"Yes," he said. "Exactly like that. Two more things: It's not a new concept—the Romans used the term. And, second, when a black swan appears, everyone searches frantically for a cause. A reason why this happened. It's human nature; big bad surprises like this can't just—happen."

"Why is that important?" she asked, having some more calamari and not yet touching that second Bombay gin.

"Because if one is in the business of *causing* a black swan, one has to take care not only to make it effective but to then provide a plausible 'cause' when the victims go looking. A cause that doesn't point right back at the person instigating the swan."

"I don't get it," she said.

"Well, suppose I wanted to precipitate a black-swan event in order to do some damage. Wouldn't it make sense to also orchestrate that inevitable desperate search for a cause or reason for it to have happened? If you can implicate yet another target, you can double the damage, yes?"

She quit trying to avoid his eyes. They took possession of hers for a moment and she suddenly couldn't speak. She felt a hot, numbing sensation that blazed from her belly to her brain. Not the gin, she thought. She felt as if she was being probed. She found herself blinking. He did not blink. Then he relaxed and sat back in his chair, casually looking away as he finished his wine. Jesus, she thought. What *was* that?

"China indoctrination in the morning, boudoir France in the afternoon. And do not speak of black swans. To anyone."

"*Boudoir* France?"

"Yes, and here she comes now."

Melanie blinked again, but then realized that a woman was approaching their table. She looked, and then looked again, just as she realized that all the men in the bar were also looking. Staring, even. Allender stood up and made introductions. "Melanie Sloan, I'd like to introduce Minette de LaFontaine, from our psychological analytics division. Minette, this is Melanie Sloan."

The woman who'd materialized at their table was five-six and somewhere between thirty-five and forty-five years old. She was, Melanie thought, absolutely gorgeous, with luminous dark eyes, a perfect complexion, a figure to die for that was accentuated by clothes that seemed to cling to all the important bits while overtly revealing nothing, and a mouth that was both an enticing smile and a direct sexual challenge. Melanie felt that challenge in a way that entirely surprised her, and she realized that, as with Allender, it had nothing to do with Bombay gin.

Minette sat down in the chair that Allender had just vacated and gave Melanie an appraising look. "A pleasure, Ms. Sloan," she said finally, her voice a velvety mix of French accents and the raspy sound of an habitual smoker. Melanie could almost feel the hot stares coming from around the room and then detected a whiff of some expensive scent.

"Well, then," Allender said. "Regrettably, I must go. Ms. Sloan is drinking Bombay gin, Minette. Can I get you something?"

"A Goose martini would be lovely, Doctor," Minette said, shedding the sleeveless silk sweater onto the back of her chair with a fluid shrug that made her exquisite breasts shiver. A young man whose blue-edged badge identified him as a candidate agent was locked on to Minette with a mildly stunned expression on his face. Minette turned in his direction and gave him a smile that probably provoked a near orgasm.

Minette arched her eyebrows at the calamari but apparently decided against it. Melanie was ready to wolf down the whole plate if only to give herself some breathing room from this—she couldn't come up with the word. The waitress brought Minette's martini, which contained a single, large stuffed olive on a toothpick. Minette fished out the olive and delicately licked the gin off its surface, all the time looking directly at the young candidate, who slowly turned bright red before he turned away.

"You must be important," she said, after devouring the olive and letting the suffering candidate off the hook. The word "important" came out in three distinct syllables. "That one is rarely seen in here."

"Beats the shit out of me," Melanie said, eyeing her second gin. Minette gave a tiny smile and then offered to touch glasses in a languid *salud,* forcing Melanie to pick up that second glass. Oh, shit, she thought. She took a sip and quickly had some more calamari.

"That is often the case," Minette said. "It is said that the doctor plays a close game at all times. How did you come to his attention?"

"Again, I don't really know," Melanie said, enjoying the brain-sweetening wave of that first sip. "I get the impression that he's got a mission planned, and that I'm somehow a part of it."

"Lucky you," Minette said.

"Maybe," Melanie said.

"Well, yes," Minette said. "With him, always the 'maybe.' Although he is not operational. It is more likely that the operations directorate needed him for some part of what they are planning. A consulting specialist, if you will. I am also a specialist, and, no, we will not be talking about France. To begin with, we will be talking about lingerie, and how to use it."

"Um—use it?"

Minette rolled her eyes. "I forget," she said. "You are an American."

Melanie bristled. One thing she did *not* like was a European insinuating that because she was an American, she was some kind of hopeless naïf. Minette caught her reaction and raised a hand.

"Please," she said. "Let me explain. Most women get up in the morning and put on their clothes: clean, basic underwear, a brassiere, pantyhose or perhaps stockings, and then a dress, blouse, or slacks and a blouse. Functional clothing, yes? We're going to work. Then we come home and if the day is over, we shed all of that for jeans and a sweatshirt, as you are wearing now. Then later our nightclothes. But: Suppose we have a date? A date with definite possibilities. What then?"

"Okay," Melanie said. "We ditch the workday clothes and then we put the play clothes on. Panties from Vicky's Secret instead of Hanes for Her. Maybe stockings instead of pantyhose, with a belt to hold them up. A lace bra instead of a cotton slingshot. Perfume. I get it—what's your point?"

"The point is that you anticipate your special someone *seeing* what you've got on underneath that pretty evening frock, while in the morning, headed for the office, that thought does not cross your mind."

"Right," Melanie said, impatiently. "And?"

"And, well, 'seeing' is the operative word. No heterosexual man can resist looking at your legs *and* underwear if you happen to expose them to him, whether intentionally or by accident."

"Right, guys will always stare when a woman forgets to keep her knees together, just like our mommies told us. I get all this. It's called teasing."

Minette smiled, ignoring Melanie's obvious impatience. "Yes, indeed, teasing. But here's the thing: Men see with their eyes *and* with their imaginations. That is what you're teasing when you let them get a look—bits of nylon, a flash of lace. Not your actual naked body. His imagination does the rest."

"Again, I understand," Melanie said. "But what does this have to do with operational tradecraft?"

"Permit me to demonstrate," Minette said. "See the young man two tables over who can't keep his eyes off our table?"

"Yes," Melanie said, "but he's looking at you, not our table. And you've been encouraging it."

Minette rolled her eyes. "I'm going to the ladies' room," she said. "When I come back I'm going to sit back down in such a way as to give him an eyeful. You watch what happens next."

"O-k-a-ay," Melanie said, still mystified. The last time she'd talked to another woman about boys' obsession with girls' panties had been in junior high school. But after a few minutes, Minette returned, pulled her chair out, and sat down in a swirl of fabric, only to "discover" that there was something wrong with one of her shoes. As she bent to take care of it, she indeed gave the young man an eyeful, at least if his expression was any clue. Melanie then saw a woman sitting at the table next to the young man get up, extract an overly large, stainless-steel revolver from her purse, walk over behind the young man, and push the barrel into his neck. He practically jumped out of his skin when he felt the cold steel and heard the cylinder rolling. Other people in the lounge who saw the big gun froze in place as the young man now also went rigid. The woman with the gun nodded at Minette, who nodded back as she straightened up and realigned her skirt. The woman put the revolver back in her purse and walked out of the lounge as if nothing had happened. The rest of the people began to relax and look at each other as if to ask, Did you just see what I saw?

Minette turned in her chair to look at Melanie, who was still swallowing her own surprise. "Ordinarily," Minette said, "he would have noticed her standing up, and he *certainly* would have seen her pulling that gun. But he did not, because he was totally focused on looking up my skirt, especially since I made it look like an accident and not a deliberate, I-dare-you-to-look challenge of some kind. The point is that almost every woman has the power to make a man look at her for at least a second or two, and *that* is long enough for her accomplice or teammate to take him out. Just by what you Americans call 'flashing.' Okay?"

"Got it," Melanie said, looking around at the rest of people in the room, who now seemed to have forgotten the little drama they'd just witnessed. It was after all, the Farm, where training vignettes could take place anywhere and at any time. The young man himself had left the room, still blushing like a beet. "It's like they're hardwired to look."

"Yes, they are, especially since they've been told repeatedly, since childhood, even, *not* to look. This is an especially valuable distraction technique, especially if your target happens to harbor a fetish involving women's underwear. According to Doctor Allender, your target does."

"Now how in the world could he know a thing like that?" Melanie asked.

Minette took a thoughtful sip of her martini. "The doctor," she began. "He knows things in the most unusual ways. Some say he reads minds. I hardly credit that, although . . ." She paused, as if searching for words. "My point is he is the most frightening interrogator we've ever had, because he appears to see and hear at some subliminal level the rest of us cannot achieve."

"Yes," Melanie said. "I've actually experienced that, or I think I have. He will say something—a phrase, or a thought—that I was thinking just a little while ago."

Minette gave her a long, almost concerned look. "That is very interesting, Ms. Sloan," she said finally. "He is probably measuring you. Or perhaps probing. He was not wearing the glasses this evening, and that tends to upset people."

Melanie shrugged, trying to be nonchalant. "And now you, too, are going to tell me to be careful around Doctor Allender?" she asked.

Minette gave her an almost affectionate look. "I would say that it's much too late for that, my dear. So: Tomorrow, after Chinese culture, we will go shopping, yes?"

FIVE

"The DDO will see you now, Doctor," the pretty young assistant announced breathlessly, as if just amazed that it was all happening.

"Thank you," he purred, squinting against the afternoon sunlight flooding the DDO's outer office. Allender was there to call upon the deputy director for operations, Carson McGill, the third most senior official at the Agency. He wondered what had happened to Caroline Haversham, an aging career administrator whose encyclopedic knowledge of where the Agency's bones were buried had made her a formidable person within the Agency. As a gatekeeper, she'd had no peer. Probably moved up when Hank Wallace had taken over as deputy director of the entire Agency, he thought. She would have scared the pants off of Carson M. McGill, who'd been DDO for three years now. This bouncy little number would have made Caroline laugh out loud.

J. Leverett Hingham III, director of the CIA, mostly faced outward, engaging daily with the highest levels of executive power in official Washington, including the president himself, as long as that worthy was so inclined. Not all of them were. The Agency's deputy director, now Hank Wallace, ran the Agency administration from within, dealing with budgets, organization, congressional relations, the principal department heads, and internal bureaucratic issues. The deputy director for operations was just what his title implied; he directed the Agency's entire gamut of clandestine operations, both offensive, which was intelligence collection against America's enemies, and defensive, known as counterintelligence, against those same enemies' own intelligence agencies. In effect, he was the spymaster for the entire Agency.

By all outward appearances Carson McGill was an unlikely-looking spymaster. For one thing, he was a natural-born fat boy. There was no other term for it. He was of medium height, balding with a grayish fringe, and evoked the word "round" at first sight. Round face, double chins, a respectable belly inevitably encased in a straining vest, short arms and legs, soft, twitchy hands, and unusually small feet. He had the voice to match: high-pitched, tinny, with what passed for an aristocratic if pedantic New England accent. He was one of those Yale graduates whom you'd expect to actually come out with a Boola-Boola from time to time.

Underneath all that public softness, however, was a totally different animal: cunning, smart, and capable of effortlessly keeping several operational balls in the air at any one time. He was known to hold career grudges and to act upon them when vulnerabilities presented themselves, especially if that would help his own prospects. He was thoroughly disliked in the upper echelons of the Agency and yet universally respected as a player—a dangerous player, but always a player. Allender had often wondered what it was about this man that attracted young women, if the rumors could be believed, but he'd made it a cardinal rule to never underestimate Carson McGill.

Ordinarily, Preston Allender, consulting psychiatrist and Agency interrogation specialist, wouldn't come into contact with the DDO himself. Minette thought that he, Allender, might be running an operation. Nothing could be farther from the truth. He was providing some specialized support to whatever McGill and his people had in mind for General Chiang by choosing the best possible candidate for someone to execute a black swan. As usual, the DDO wasn't sharing details with a consultant, even a quasinotorious one like Allender.

"Preston, my dear fellow, come in, come in," McGill chirped from behind his overlarge desk. "Do sit down. Tell me something interesting—I need an antidote to all this"—he pointed theatrically to the large number of folders and briefing books scattered over his desk—"secret *stuff*."

"I think I've found our swan," Allender said.

"Ooh, goody," McGill said, rubbing his hands together. "What does she look like—is she *deliciously* pretty?"

Allender fished in the leather folder he'd brought along and produced an eight-by-ten black-and-white picture of Melanie Sloan standing in front of his desk. He was amused to see McGill's eyes go wide. "How in the *world* did you get a picture like this?" he exclaimed. "She's—she's, well, stark naked! And, oh my God, is that your office? You *didn't*!"

"It is, and I did," Allender said, extending his hand to retrieve the picture. McGill took one last, longing look and reluctantly handed it back.

"Does she know *that* exists?" McGill asked.

"She was told that there were no cameras in my office. The point of the exercise was to see if she could disassociate her body from a mission. At first she refused outright, but then she came back—on her own volition—and agreed to disrobe. Carol was present if that makes you feel better."

"Good Lord," McGill said. "And she's his type?"

"He's apparently an omnivore when it comes to his sexual pleasure," Allender said. "I arranged for him to get a glimpse of her at a restaurant down in Williamsburg. He was playing tourist with his wife and grown children, but he noticed her, and since she was with me, and the Farm is right there, he's probably made the appropriate association with the home team."

"That's right—I forgot. He would know who you are."

"Which was the point of our 'date.'"

"What's next, then?"

"Training," Allender said. "I have her with Minette de LaFontaine and also the Chinese cultural conditioning people."

"I *so* remember Minette," McGill said, fondly. "If anyone can amp up an operator's sexuality, she can."

"Precisely," Allender said.

"Excellent, indeed," McGill said. "I've decided to direct this one myself. We'll have an ops cell here in town, a senior controller, of course, and the appropriate mechanics, but not for long. I propose two encounters, one to really whet his interest, one to execute the exposure."

"That's rather quick, isn't it?"

"My people tell me he doesn't indulge in long romances. He likes sudden, exciting encounters. Fancies himself a predator: I see it, I want it, I take it. Then on to the next one. I'll give him a few days to vet her between encounters, but he'll have to do that locally. Beijing Center would never allow such a liaison; they're already tired of his philandering, but, as we know, he's too connected for them to recall him."

"Surely he or at least his people will suspect a honey trap," Allender said.

McGill leaned back in his chair. "He has a methodology around that," he said. "His last conquest was the assistant secretary of the air force for gender assimilation or some such bullshit. She was a lawyer, unhappily married, and something of a cougar on the prowl. He encountered her in a hotel exercise room and apparently it was on after about a half hour of strategic bending in the spa. He's just that impulsive, and thereby gets more ass than a toilet seat. But this time I'm going to double down. Sloan's going to *tell* him she works for us. That she's important, some kind of superspy, high up in the Agency, and that it's all very secret what she does."

Allender snorted. "And he will believe such bullshit?"

"Of course not. Universal rule: The more senior you are, the less you ever reveal about yourself. That's why I'm going to give him time to make a quick vetting, but not too much time. His people will verify that she is, indeed, an Agency employee. I'll have her name and picture stashed in a discoverable, low-level clerical research position in S and T, so she'll end up sounding like some ambitious airhead with a great body and hot pants. Just his style."

Allender smiled. He liked it. "When?" he asked.

"First face-to-face contact in three weeks. Second and strike will come three, maybe four days later. Timing is negotiable, of course. They'll first meet at a dinner sponsored by the IMF right here in town. I'll have them placed across the table from one another or something. You'll be there, too, sitting near her and this time, ignoring her utterly. It will buttress the legend. They know you're senior. That should confirm that she is not."

"And the second time?"

"The second time will be at the Wingate during the Global Warming Conference awards banquet. The strike will occur in a suite of rooms we control there, ones that look like something she could afford."

Allender absorbed all that. "You know," he said, "when you first brought me into this operation, I had some doubts, until you called it a black swan. What a wonderful name—and connotation. A Chinese general of intelligence. Family ties to the Central Committee. His own network. Exposed in such a dramatic way. A black swan indeed! Why not a fancy suite?"

"She's a nobody, but she wants him, so she's sprung for a single right there at the Wingate hotel. Even that costs seven hundred dollars a night. He will have had his people check her out. A suite would fairly scream setup. Keeps her in character right up to the last moment."

Allender nodded. Hearing all this made him regret that he hadn't ever gone into operational counterintelligence, especially since the final stroke here, which he'd kept from McGill, had been his idea.

"Have you briefed Himself?" he asked.

McGill made a face. "Why *ever* would I do that, Preston," he said. "The last thing J. Leverett Hingham III, would want to know are the details of what I'm about to do to General Chiang. You know how he feels about China."

Allender did. Everyone in the Agency did. Hingham was purportedly one of the Boston Brahmins whose family had been in New England at least since God had invented rocks, and if you didn't recognize that right away he would be sure to tell you all about it. He had "the" accent, the proper clothes, the obligatory private school and university education, and a studiously haughty demeanor. He was slender and tall enough to pull it off, being able to look down his long, bony nose at all the little people while trying to think of something to say to them that would be sufficiently droll. His appointment to head the Agency had come as a shock to the rank and file at Langley, because he had zero national security experience. For that matter, he had zero governmental experience, being a privately funded academic and homegrown philosopher. His only qualification had apparently been that the sitting president had wanted someone at Langley who shared his own distaste for and distrust of all things concerning national intelligence.

Previous directors of the Agency had all been serious players of one level or another. Hingham, in contrast, was the penultimate gilded figurehead. Whenever senior staff had to meet with him he would inevitably treat them to long-winded discourses on the insurmountable forces of history that inevitably rendered the efforts of mere mortals utterly insignificant. As in, specifically, trying to compete with or control the destiny of the most populous nation-state on earth. The Chinese were an inherently superior race of people, according to him, and their ultimate hegemony was pretty much foreordained. As to the eternal turmoil in the Middle East and the dangers that conflict posed to the United States, Hingham thought that it was just Sturm und Drang, simply further evidence of the friction that necessarily occurred as a result of the tectonic struggles for world domination between America and everyone else, especially China. By all means we need to quash the myriad attempts at terrorism here at home, but only if we recognize that we are all, as a people, and as an agency, sweeping against the Oriental tide.

The thousands of people who staffed the Agency headquarters took one long look at Hingham and then turned to the Agency's deputy director, Henry "Hank" Wallace, to become the default chief executive at Langley. Hank Wallace had been the number two at Langley for almost twelve years. Prior to that he'd been a senior executive overseeing the US Secret Service. He was perfectly suited to running the show while trying his best to cocoon Hingham in his fancy executive suite, known Agency-wide as the Ivory Tower. The fun part was when they sent Hingham to Congress to testify for the Agency's annual appropriations and authorization bills. It was said that only a fire could clear a hearing room faster than J. Leverett once he got going on one of his ether-lipped lectures. The only small comfort that the career spooks at Langley could take was the sure knowledge that the Chinese security services were so paranoid that they would spend years trying to figure out what the Hingham appointment was really all about.

"Okay," Allender said. "That reads. I'll be in touch."

Once finished with McGill he took a motor-pool sedan to the nearest Metro station, and, from there, rode the Metro subway to the Dupont Circle station in lower northwest Washington. If he'd chosen to stay in the sedan it would have taken over an hour in Washington's atrocious commuter traffic; from the Dupont Circle station it was a five-minute walk to his home.

Allender lived in one of the larger town houses on Massachusetts Avenue near Dupont Circle. Three stories high and architecturally a bit pretentious, it was faced with actual brownstone instead of one of those extravagant color schemes decorating its neighbors on either side. Enhancing its desirability was a turreted tower at the right front corner. An uneven brick sidewalk, rumpled by the roots of two large maples, proclaimed its great age. Two tiny patches of struggling ivy flanked the sidewalk inside a wrought-iron fence. Three rounded stone steps led up to an oversized mahogany front door. The gate screeched when he opened it, which Allender thought appropriate, given its age. When he unlocked the door he was greeted by an enormous Maine coon cat named Horrible.

He went through the living room to the tower study, where he dropped his briefcase, kicked off his shoes, liberated two inches of single malt from a decanter, and then sat down in a leather recliner. The study took up the first two floors of the house, with a spiral staircase wrapping around the room up to a landing. From there a doorway gave access to the top, attic floor of the crenellated tower, which he'd had converted to a rooftop atrium. A stack of circular bookshelves lined the two-story wall above the top of the windows; one could stand on the staircase at any level and rotate the nearest shelf to bring the book of choice to hand. He had a large rosewood desk, a computer station equipped with a secure phone, and some unobtrusive file cabinets embedded in the walls. On the floor was a circular Persian Tabriz rug measuring twenty feet in diameter. There was a cat bed under the computer desk for Horrible.

He actually liked living alone. The woman who lived in the town house on one side ran a high-end domestic cleaning service company. She had a crew come in every other week to clean and polish, much to Horrible's vocal annoyance. Two gay decorators owned the house on the other side, which they had restored to a glowing Victorian masterpiece inside. As far as his neighbors knew, Allender was a senior bureaucrat in the HEW Department who had something boring to do with training. He'd learned how to cook while growing up in Taiwan and frequented the two very good Chinese markets that were in walking distance. Otherwise he'd simply go out, having nothing better to do with his salary.

Sipping his Scotch, he thought about Melanie Sloan. He didn't think the op would be too dangerous unless the general himself lost it and pulled a gun. Even then, he had the sense that Melanie would be equal to the occasion anytime someone started some shit. She had a tough streak in her, a willingness to stand her ground that belied her extraordinary good looks, probably because she was older than the conventional newbie in the CS. He found himself interested in her as a woman, a thought which he immediately clamped down on, based on painful past experiences. Not for you, old son, he reminded himself.

After fixing himself a Chinese concoction for dinner, he threw Horrible out for the night, gathered a Borsalino hat and a walking stick from the hall closet, and went out for his evening walk. Living alone meant rather more food and whiskey than was healthy, so on most nights he would go out after dark and walk, sometimes for miles, around the so-called Federal area. It kept him trim and in good cardio health, and he enjoyed watching the city transform once the sun went down.

As a consultant, as opposed to an operator, he was not authorized by the Agency to carry a gun. Walking in Washington, D.C., at night, even in the monuments district, had its risks. Once the thousands of commuters slipped back into their surrounding county suburbs, a different population emerged from the shadows, so Allender had equipped himself with a custom-made Burger walking stick that contained a twenty-inch-long stainless-steel sword. The local Metro police would certainly have considered it an illegal concealed weapon, but his Agency credentials offered considerable protection from intruding civilian police forces.

In all the years he'd been night walking, he'd never once had to bare that blade, but it was still comforting to have it along when the homeless, the drug addicts and their suppliers, small groups of teenagers on the prowl for some "action," or just run-of-the-mill drunks appeared. Ever since 9/11, the Mall and the parks surrounding the

White House had become comprehensive surveillance zones, which had the benefit of deterring the carjack and holdup gangs from the area. The cars one did see still parked along the Mall often had federal police in them, and every major federal building had rooftop surveillance teams or at least extensive camera coverage. He was convinced that all the watchers by now knew who he was, because he'd rarely been stopped by an unmarked patrol car and asked for identification or the purpose of his being out there at night, wearing a suit and a Borsalino and carrying a twelve-hundred-dollar walking stick.

Tonight he walked down Mass Avenue to Connecticut Avenue, thence down Connecticut to the White House tourist plazas, out onto and across the Mall, up the Mall to the Capitol building, and then back to intercept Mass again, and back home. Labor Day had come and gone, and there was a hint of fall in the night air. He'd seen a few sketchy characters along the way, but to them he looked like bait in a Metro street-crime division sting net. The Mall was pretty much empty now that all the hordes of tourists were back in their hotels. The white marble monuments and memorials towering overhead all seemed grateful for the reprieve, and his only company was the grounds crews making a final trash sweep or tending to irrigation systems. An entire herd of tour buses was parked along the Mall perimeter, their windows beginning to fog up as the night air cooled.

It would have been a nice night to have had a lady friend on his arm. Someone like Melanie Sloan, perhaps. He sensed she'd be a handful and a half, but when he'd looked into her eyes down there at the Residence bar, the emotion that he'd detected had been excitement and not the usual sudden apprehension he was used to. She'd left State for the Agency because she'd been bored, and a stint at the embassy in Lisbon probably hadn't provided the kind of nights one might expect in, say, Moscow. Her brief fling with the station chief had ended, at least according to her, with the same equanimity as it had begun. Would she really be interested in him? Or was it the usual case, that his fiery eyes and all the stories about mind-bending interrogations simply intrigued her? Face it, Dragon Eyes, he told himself. These are questions you'll never answer.

SIX

Two weeks later, Melanie Sloan, together with Minette, Twyla, plus one of her costume assistants, arrived at Allender's town house at three in the afternoon. They'd been driven up to Washington in an Agency SUV. Allender welcomed them in and directed them to the main living room while the driver brought in some small luggage, two sets of hanging suit bags, and what looked like some shoe boxes. Twyla's assistant began inventorying what they'd brought up, while Allender disappeared upstairs with Twyla in tow. Melanie relaxed and looked around, curious to see how the mysterious Doctor Allender lived.

The ceilings were at least twelve feet high and the room was tastefully appointed in what looked to her like Victorian furniture, with a large Oriental rug and a fully operational wood fireplace. There was one large bow-front window in the living room, flanked by narrow secondary windows. There was a dining room with French doors at the back that led out to a patio and a small walled garden. There appeared to be a garage at the way back, next to a gate leading to the alley behind. Large mahogany doors led to the tower in the front corner. Must have been some real money somewhere, she mused, for even a senior civil servant to be able to afford one of these grand old mansions. The walls in the living room were paneled in squares of highly colorful wood veneers, many of a kind she'd never seen before.

Melanie's last two weeks had been truly interesting. Mornings at the cultural-indoc center, learning as much about Chinese customs and manners as one could in just ten days from some painfully patient instructors. Her afternoons with Minette had been all about the arts of discreet seduction, from how to sit, smile, laugh, walk, and cross and uncross her legs in a variety of skirts, to makeup, and even voice lessons. Apparently the Chinese had elaborate rules for beginning the dance between a sophisticated gentleman and an upper-class woman, similar to the intricacies of a Spanish lady's deployment of her lace fan. Minette acknowledged those assets, but claimed that the lingerie method was far more effective—and took much less time.

Allender reappeared at the front door to welcome another man, who was literally tall, dark, and handsome. He took one look at Melanie and said, "Wow. You're right, sir. She's gorgeous. This is gonna be a piece of cake."

Minette made an impolite noise. "Wait until she is properly decorated, young man. *Then* you may whimper."

Allender grinned. "Ladies, this is David Smith, who will be the controller for this little escapade."

David Smith was marine-lean, with a shaved head and the physique of a long-distance runner. Melanie speculated that he could be anywhere between twenty-five and thirty-five years old. He had boyish good looks but with a definite edge. "I would have thought you would be the control," she said to Allender, still blushing a little from Smith's outburst. Allender seemed amused.

"Not qualified, I'm afraid," he said. "David is a professional controller. I'm more of a fuse lighter. Let's everyone sit down. I'd like to discuss this evening's adventure. David: Start us off, please."

"Yes, sir," David said, still stealing glances at Melanie, who had just possibly transitioned into one of Minette's poses. For a moment she thought he was about to actually squirm.

"Tonight," David said, "it's a reception at the Hilton Garden Inn for some visiting UN officials. Here's the drill: Ms. Sloan will arrive in company with Doctor Allender. There will be a receiving line, after which they'll migrate to the canapé table. Once General Chiang is in view, they will have a short but intense exchange, and then Doctor Allender will move off, obviously annoyed with her. Chiang either will or will not move in. Ms. Sloan will be indignant, sulk a little, then she'll turn on the charm. She will deploy her legend. Once Chiang signals real interest, Doctor Allender will reappear and whisk her away. She will sneak one back-look, and then she and the doctor will leave the reception."

"That's it?" Melanie said. "So quick?"

"A taste," David said. "Just a taste—and the legend. We need to have him check you out. His people are well used to his sudden infatuations, but he's a general, and a connected general at that. They will scurry to find out more about you, and we have the appropriate baits in place. Your association with Doctor Allender is all part of this. So: Ms. Sloan, are you ready?"

Melanie was taken aback, but quickly nodded. "I think so," she said. "I've learned some lacy moves and a little bit about what might spool up a Chinese general."

"And if he asks about Doctor Allender?"

"He is a senior director. When he asked me to accompany him tonight, I agreed. You know, he's senior, but so am I."

"Right," David said. "That's the correct tack. Your legend—that you're important—has to unravel gracefully. At the professional level, you'll be seen to be reaching. At the sexual level, you're on fire, and anxious to be rid of the much older, senior director."

"Of course," she said, shooting a sly look at Allender.

"Ahem," Allender harrumphed, and everyone laughed. "What's our signal to end the fun?"

"Ms. Sloan will bend over and reveal décolletage. Assuming the general locks on, you will swoop in and signal that the car is waiting."

"He will probably address me in Mandarin."

"Fine. It will signal that we're all adults here, and that whatever he and Ms. Sloan are contemplating, it has nothing to do with business."

"Got it."

David looked at his watch. "Okay, team. Go suit up."

Twyla, her assistant, and Melanie followed Minette upstairs to the guest room. Allender sat down and asked Smith where the possible derailing points were.

"For starters, his minders," Smith said. "They may draw the line at an Agency employee, for the obvious reasons."

"Are they intelligence professionals or simply bodyguards?"

"A bit of both, because of his political connections. Best described as faction guards. At least one political commissar type is always present."

"Will the Chinese ambassador be there tonight?"

"No, sir. He will be at the dinner, and, by the way, he is *not* a fan of General Chiang's amorous escapades. But: It seems our general has *protectzia,* as the Russians call it."

"Any other possible pitfalls?"

"Sloan could blow it," Smith said. "She's pretty green."

"Is Smith your real name?"

Smith grinned. "What do you think, Doctor?"

Allender removed his glasses and studied Smith's face for what was probably an uncomfortable moment. "I think it's Farmer," he said, finally. "Lionel Farmer. Close?"

Smith, obviously surprised, blinked. "Um," he began, but Allender waved him off.

"Don't worry about it," he said. "I may have been briefed. As to Sloan's inexperience, that's a good thing, I think. No inconvenient track record. Lisbon's a backwater posting, and she wasn't actually doing much HUMINT there. She was usually in company with the station chief, so that will bolster the legend."

"And her claiming to be some kind of senior spook?"

"I think that'll work," Allender said. "She's older. His ego, plus his libido, will take that as a challenge. Either way, as long as Sloan establishes that famous short circuit between Chiang's brain and his crank, you're probably in good shape."

Smith grinned. "Well, I have to say . . ."

Allender gave him an arch look. "You ain't seen nothin' yet," he observed. "I need to change. I don't anticipate any rough stuff, but you will have a team in place?"

"Always," Smith said. "If only because you're going to be there."

"I'm flattered," Allender said. "And no one knows about the clone, right?"

"No one."

"Not even McGill?"

"Especially him, as per your directions."

"That's vital," Allender said. "That's the feature that's going to take it from a simple honey trap to a black swan."

An hour and a half later, Allender and Melanie Sloan stood next to one of the buffet tables in the main reception room at the Hilton. There were probably two hundred guests, many in evening dress although there were several people, like Allender, wearing just a dark suit. If you were really important, you came directly from your cabinet office. Lesser mortals had time to go home and change. There was the usual hubbub of voices, clink of glassware, a string quartet trying manfully in one corner, and the occasional peal of feminine laughter. Melanie was positively stunning in her Dior, and a good many men were struggling not to stare at her. At the moment, however, she wore a somewhat annoyed expression, and Allender was playing along, feigning dissatisfaction with something she'd just said. On the other side of the table stood General Chiang, dressed tonight in a civilian suit and looking every inch the urban predator he fancied himself to be. Melanie had exchanged a nod and a smile at a distance already, and now Allender muttered something in a semi-sharp tone of voice and walked away toward the bar, leaving Melanie apparently stranded for just a moment, looking exasperated.

"Permit me to introduce myself," a quiet baritone voice intoned from behind her. "I am General Chiang Liang-fu, from the Chinese embassy. I think I have seen you before, in Williamsburg, perhaps?"

Melanie turned and gave him one of Minette's best sultry looks. "Yes, I believe we have seen each other before," she said. "I'm Melanie. Is your family here tonight?"

He smiled and said no, he was by himself, and did she perhaps need another glass of white wine?

"That would be most kind," she said, handing over her glass and making sure their fingers touched. He was bigger than she'd remembered, but not fat like so many Chinese senior officials. They were of the same height so, she was able to look directly into his sharp, black eyes. He bowed slightly and left for the bar while Melanie found two empty chairs together and sat down in one. As he returned with drinks in hand she arranged her skirt in a seemingly unconscious maneuver designed to reveal just the tops of her pale white stockings. He joined her and then made a *salud* gesture with his drink. She hoped he wouldn't start a *ganbei* round, but knew it wasn't likely with her drinking wine.

"So," he said. "What brings such a beautiful woman to such a boring event?"

She pointed with her chin in the direction of Allender, who was about twenty feet away, deep in what seemed to be a serious conversation with an Indian official. "One of our senior directors," she said.

"Doctor Allender? Ah, yes, I recognize him. Do you also work at Langley?"

She nodded.

"And in what capacity, if I may ask?"

She gave him a look that said, Are you kidding?

He smiled again. "Yes, yes, I know, that was foolish of me. It's just that I think we are in the same business. I am attached to our embassy here in Washington, in a, how shall I say it—related capacity?"

"Really," she said, sipping her wine and pretending not to care, while smoothing her skirt with her other hand, running it down the inside of her thigh. "I thought you said you were a general?"

"I am," he said, sitting up a little straighter while keeping track of her hand. "In our system, which calls itself the Ministry of State Security, there are many military officers."

She nodded. "As in our system, now that I think of it. Sometimes we have senior military officers at the top of our—company."

He laughed quietly at her use of the word "company." "Do you find the work of your—company—interesting?" he asked.

She giggled. "Truthfully?" she said. "Not always. These days it's mostly about data, ones and zeroes, as my people are fond of saying. There are times I wish I was back overseas, but once you reach a certain level, that becomes out of the question, as I'm sure you know. Are those your people watching us?"

Chiang didn't even look. "Well, of course," he said. "And Doctor Allender—is he minding you tonight? I would have thought he was too senior for such duties."

She tossed her hair impatiently. "We are of similar rank," she replied. "Besides, he is not a pleasant man. People in my company are afraid of him, I think."

"I understand he is called Dragon Eyes," Chiang said. "That would have a specific meaning in our language."

"Really," she said. "Now that I think of it, I believe he does speak Mandarin. Your English is impeccable, by the way."

"Thank you," he said. "I have spent years developing my modest understanding of American English, and you are correct, Doctor Allender speaks excellent Mandarin. He grew up in Taipei."

"We have some people in my directorate—not that many—who can speak Mandarin," she said. "But they are unanimous in saying they have a long way to go in getting to true proficiency."

"And yet our two-year-olds manage it in their sleep," he said.

"I wouldn't know anything about that," she said. "Two-year-olds, that is."

"Are you not married?" he asked, seeming surprised.

She realized that he was being forward, indeed, if her instructors at the cultural center had been correct. On the other hand, at her age, it probably would surprise a Chinese man that she was not married. Mission accomplished, she realized, and bent forward to adjust one of the straps of her shoes. Minette had taught her a way of doing that that made for something of a cleavage show, but it was also the signal to Allender that she thought the hook was, if not set, at least being firmly nibbled.

Make contact, he'd instructed. Use body language to indicate interest, then back out. Tantalize, but no more. She straightened up and gave him a look that said she'd seen him looking. Then Allender materialized.

"General Chiang," he said, in Mandarin. "Enjoying the scenery?"

Chiang laughed quietly as he stood up to shake hands. "It is spectacular scenery, Doctor."

Allender made a face that said, I can't argue with that. "However, General, your staff do not look pleased that your are associating with not one but *two* members of the opposition."

"It is just their duty," Chiang acknowledged. Then he switched back to English as he got up. "Melanie, it has been a pleasure. Perhaps we will meet again sometime."

Melanie had been briefed on how to respond: "You must be careful of the company you keep, General. In fact, I am required to report our brief—if pleasant—meeting."

"Yes, of course," he replied. "In any event, have a good evening." He turned to Allender. "You, too," he said in Mandarin, with just a hint of a leer.

Allender brushed it off. "This one plays her own game, General. I am not part of it."

"Oh, of course," Chiang said, bowed slightly, and headed off to the bar.

"Well done, I think," Allender said to Sloan, as they made for the lobby. "He and most every other man in the room couldn't keep his eyes off you. You look extraordinary tonight."

"Well, thank you, kind sir. I had a lot of help from my friends. Are you taking me to dinner again? This secret agent is starving."

"I'm not one to waste a beautiful woman's time on a dinner date unless it's business," he replied. "But there's David Smith."

Smith met them at the main entrance. "David," Allender said. "Ms. Sloan says she's starving. Can you help?"

"*Hell,* yes," Smith said, positively gawking at Melanie. "Assuming the lady's agreeable?"

"Of course I am," Melanie said, shining a brilliant smile at Smith. Allender beamed and off they went; but when Smith got tangled up with someone coming through the lobby's revolving door, Melanie Sloan looked back over her shoulder and gave Allender a look that clearly said that Smith was not who she'd had in mind. Allender bowed slightly and gave her a polite smile, but he couldn't help but look at her as she slipped into the revolving door.

Wow, he thought, not for the first time. What was it the Brits said? Damn my eyes? Then reason returned. Your job is over now that Smith has taken charge. He wondered if she knew what was coming next. He almost wished he could go along and help her.

SEVEN

Deputy Director for Operations McGill was apparently in one of his pacing moods. He walked back and forth in front of the windows in his office, coffee mug in hand, pipe in mouth, as he listened to Allender's report of the reception encounter with Chiang Liang-fu. It was late in the afternoon, and the building was beginning to clear out. When Allender had finished, McGill began shaking his head.

"I don't know," he said. "There's no *way* that his people won't suspect a honey trap." He emphasized his words with the ornate pipe, which Allender had never seen actually lit. "No way in *hell*."

Allender disagreed. "Look," he said. "A honey trap traditionally involves a woman planted by one country's service to snare and then embarrass or even blackmail someone in another country's service. She is always under deep cover—a schoolteacher, a medical person, even a straying wife, but in no way connectable to our business. Sloan was with me. Chiang and I know of each other. She even admitted she worked for the Company. Said she was senior, and complained about how hard it was to find decent Chinese linguists. In other words, I *do* work for your opposition, General, so if we do hook up, it's not going to be about business."

"If one of my senior people brought me that scenario I'd warn him off in the strongest possible terms," McGill said. "So would you, I hope."

"Neither of *us* allows his groin to lead his brain," Allender said. "This one does, and regularly, and his boss is not pleased, apparently. If he weren't some senior party boss's brother or cousin he'd probably be a tour guide on the Great Wall by now."

"Okay, but: When I brought you into this one, I explained that this wasn't about mousetrapping a single spy. It was about breaking their entire organization by doing something extraordinary. So what's this bright idea you've given to David Smith—that's not his name, by the way—that's going to achieve *that* objective?"

"Smith works for you; ask him, why don't you."

"He won't tell me, if you can believe that. Says it won't work if anyone but the controller and a few assistants know what the plan is."

"Well, then, Carson, there you have it."

"Goddammit, Preston—it's your idea. You're the expert manipulator who also knows the damned Chinese. So what are you going to do to him, assuming he can't keep away from the delectable Sloan?"

Allender smiled. "That's a secret for now."

"Fuck that noise, Preston—I'm the DDO."

"That's the difference between creating a black swan and every other op you can think of," Allender said. "That was *your* tasking to me, remember? I'm not an operator, but if you want to cause a black swan within the MSS, then you must leave your controller to it. It will not disappoint. By the way, how high have you briefed this?"

"I'll have to tell our beloved director about this, eventually," McGill said. "By law, actually. But for now, I'm as high as this one goes."

"I think you should at least let me brief Hank."

"Before or after?"

"Before. I agree with you about the director, but Hank's the Company's wise man. If there's a reason *not* to proceed, Hank will see it."

"Perhaps," McGill said. "Let me think about that, but if Hank does get briefed, *I'll* do the briefing, understand? So what's the deal, again?"

Allender smiled. "Nice try."

McGill broke out in expletives. Allender waited patiently.

"This cannot ever be acknowledged as a Company affair, Carson," Allender said. "It goes down and then it goes dark, for ever and ever. No backgrounders for reporters, no leaks to our best friend over there on Capitol Hill, just panic and pandemonium within MSS and its senior leadership and a united 'Who, us?' here at Langley."

McGill groaned at Allender's reference to Congresswoman Martine Greer, chairwoman of the House Permanent Select Committee on Intelligence and the Agency's current nemesis in the House. "The way you've set this up, the Chinese will *know* it was us," he pointed out.

"That's the best part," Allender replied. "You still keep some Scotch in that cubby over there?"

By the time he'd arrived home he was more than a bit pleased at how the mission was shaping up. He had met earlier with David Smith to review some details for the actual strike. Smith had suggested giving Chiang one more taste of the eye candy before they executed the mission.

"Think of it as a photo op," he'd said. "I think we should let him see her one more time, exchange a look, maybe, but not actually talk or interact. This time she'll be with someone under deep cover. An innocent encounter, recognition across the room, a sexy smile from her, then back to paying attention to whomever she's with. No looking back."

"And if he makes a move?" Allender asked.

"We'll have an interceptor in place," Smith said. "Someone who stops his move by recognizing him as a long-lost acquaintance, or a senior Chinese official—whatever, but takes up enough time for Melanie to make her creep."

"'Melanie' is it now," Allender had said.

Smith had the good grace to blush. "She is by *God* the best-looking thing I've ever seen," he said. "And nice, too. Down-to-earth. Real people."

Oh, dear, Allender had thought. Maybe the op needed a new controller. On the other hand, he now knew that Smith would certainly be paying attention, so he'd agreed to the additional "viewing," as Smith had phrased it.

He brought a bottle of chilled white Burgundy and a stemmed glass to the tower office while he decided whether to go out or burn something in the kitchen for dinner. He still hoped that McGill would let him go brief Henry Wallace, *the* deputy director of the Agency. Hank Wallace was something of a legend at Langley, the man career Agency people thought of as the Company's executive flywheel, especially with Hingham in the front office. He was the closest thing in the American government to what the British called a permanent undersecretary. British cabinet officers came and went at the whim of the electorate, but the PUS remained in place so that whatever member of Parliament was given the portfolio, at least someone in the front office knew what time the tea lady came around.

Wallace had seen several directors come and go in the unending whirl of high-level presidential appointees during his twelve years. He was in his early sixties, a bit crusty, a cunning bureaucrat, a keeper of both bones and secrets, but fiercely loyal to the Agency and its people. He kept himself firmly in the background and, as best he could, tried to steer newly appointed directors away from the traditional minefields peculiar to running the CIA in the rough-and-tumble world of Washington factional politics. Some listened, some didn't. The ones who did tended to last longer than the ones who didn't. McGill was, of course, correct in demanding that he, the DDO, brief Wallace, but Allender had made it a condition of his own participation that motormouth McGill was not to be briefed on just exactly what was coming. Allender knew, however, that it would be foolish to keep Hank Wallace in the dark. He was going to have to think of some way to get around McGill's sense of the Agency's pecking order.

One thing he did know: If this thing worked, the damage to the MSS operation here in town was going to be substantial. Chiang was part of an important faction in the Chinese government, which meant that the dozens of Chinese based out of the embassy owed their jobs and careers to him. Hit the warlord, take out the clan.

He thought about the way Sloan's ample front had spilled invitingly out in front of the poor general. Then he chided himself—he was supposed to have been watching Chiang. He smiled and had some more wine.

EIGHT

Melanie stood in the shower at her new apartment with her eyes closed, imagining that she was luxuriating in a large porcelain tub with a magnum of champagne sweating nearby. She and Mark used to do that after an afternoon of lovemaking in one of the villas he liked to rent outside of Lisbon. It had been a tedious couple of days of house hunting, and she was now ready to pretend that she was "home" at last. Being quasi-homeless came with the territory of being a junior operative in the Clandestine Service. You went overseas for two to three years at a pop, came home for training and some time off, and then back out into the wide, wide world of human intelligence work at yet another grubby embassy. Some officers bought homes or condos, rented them out when they were gone, and then did a time-share routine when they came back for a few months, but if one had to bail out of station on short notice, there was always a scramble to find somewhere to live while the lease worked itself out. The Agency had solutions for this at its various installations around Washington, but most operatives wanted some separation from Biggest Brother in their daily lives when not actually on station.

She'd finally found a fully furnished one-bedroom apartment in a tower block near the Ballston Metro station, known to the locals as Randy Towers. It was filled with bachelor diplomatic staff, the occasional spook, contractors on short-term jobs, and even politicians who worked in Washington three days a week and then went home to the district. The absence of wives and families lent credence to the building's nickname. Because she was in between duty stations, Melanie's apartment was paid for by the Agency, and the Metro station two blocks away gave her access to everything official in Washington—except, perversely, the headquarters building at Langley.

As she rinsed the shampoo off her body with a washcloth, she thought again about weekends with Mark. She hadn't been entirely honest with Allender about who'd come on to whom. Once she'd figured out that Mark's marriage was mostly about having a well-trained hostess for all their diplomatic functions, she'd decided to make a run on him. He was handsome and certainly aware of her during the official times they spent together, although there'd been no exploratory asides. All that changed one late Saturday afternoon when she'd had to take an urgent cable from Washington to his residence, an apartment building in downtown Lisbon. He'd opened the door wearing only a towel around his hips. She'd presented the cable in a locked pouch and then casually checked him out while he was reading it. He'd been perspiring heavily, and she spotted a weight set out on the balcony. The veins on his upper body stood out among all the muscles.

"Like what you see?" he'd asked, while still reading the message.

She smiled when she remembered blushing just a little and then saying something truly subtle like she wouldn't kick it out of her bed.

"I'm headed for the hot tub," he'd said, handing her back the message. "It's right through there."

The bathroom had a stand-alone tub that doubled as a Jacuzzi. There was a separate shower, and another enclosure for the toilet. He'd dropped the towel and stepped into the swirling tub. She'd done her best impression of a demure striptease, and then stepped into the shower, where she'd slowly soaped off the day's sweat and urban fug with the shower curtain fully open before getting into the tub with him, kneeling between his legs and then turning around to sit down and press her back against his chest, all with desirable results. Remembering gave her a warm feeling in her belly. She wondered how Dragon Eyes would have reacted to all that. The thought made her giggle, but the thought did not readily disappear.

Once out of the shower she put on jeans and a T-shirt and went out onto the tiny balcony to enjoy the sunset and a glass of wine. The balconies were all separated by concrete-block privacy screens, which suited her just fine. She was on the eleventh floor, with a magnificent view of the backs of two other apartment buildings and their connecting alleys. The rental agent had told her that the people in the apartment next door, a corner unit, were Southwest Asians and in diplomatic status. Based on the familial noise, the unit probably contained five times the number of people registered on the lease, and the eau de turmeric permeated that corner of the building when the breeze was right. On the other side was supposedly a Defense Department contractor whom she'd not actually seen. Just about everybody in the building was a transient, usually with a government stipend for the rent. There was a pool and gym in the basement, and a party venue up on the roof. It was as anonymous as you wanted it to be, and Melanie rather liked it. Genuine solitude was a difficult thing to achieve in the Clandestine Service, where everything you did had a controller's strings on it.

Her dinner with young Mr. Smith had been mostly awkward. He was younger than she was, and after the first half hour of his undisguised adulation, she'd decided she was definitely an older-man kind of girl. Smith was super nice, physically quite attractive, and unabashedly trying to score. Dinner had been fine, but the table conversation had centered on what she termed millennial activities—the urgent pursuit of things to do and places to go on the weekend, almost as if the weekend wouldn't be complete if not spent walking a piece of the Appalachian trail, attending symphony night at Lincoln

Center, or taking a day trip to Antietam, all aimed at casual brag-
ging rights on Monday morning when the coffee-station crowd
inevitably asked, "How was your weekend?" She recognized some
familiar symptoms; she was becoming tired of the daily grind of trying to get ahead in yet another government bureaucracy, interesting
as this one was. And a lot more interesting since she had encountered
Dr. Dragon Eyes, she had to admit.

That said, she knew this Chinese thing was going to be a one-
shot operation, which would either succeed or it wouldn't. She understood that she was mostly a fancy prop, the well-dressed and
well-coiffed bait in some intricate upper echelon game in the—what
was the term that woman had used? Serious-shit arena. Whoopee.
When the op was over, she would still be thirty-three, unmarried
and alone, with no prospective relationships, and, to be honest with
herself, an almost disturbing *dis*interest in establishing a relationship.
As Allender had warned her, she might even have to leave the Agency
and find other employment, especially if this thing "succeeded,"
whatever that meant. The bonus would be cool, of course, but she
had a clear idea of how long even a big lump sum like that would
last her if she did have to leave the intel world, especially when one
was a professional woman who would not be able to describe any aspects of her previous employment with the Agency. "I worked in
government. Period." She knew any sophisticated Washington em-
ployer would know what that meant in a heartbeat, but she wondered
if there was much of a future in the Washington game of what one
of her office friends used to describe as white-collar welfare.

She speculated about the doctor and his upscale town house near
Dupont Circle. That part of town was known as a haven for wealthy
gays who renovated the nineteenth-century mansions along the avenue into truly valuable properties. Except: He didn't strike her as
being that way. More like a confirmed bachelor who wasn't above
taking a look at all the pretty women but not to the extent of lighting the fuse on any kind of relationship. Some of that came with the

job, she supposed. His rep in the Agency was borderline scary. And those eyes: *Jesus.* She wondered if that's what kept him from getting close with a woman. And if he was some kind of mind reader, who would want to go to bed with *that*? A little voice in her head had an answer for that: He'd know exactly what you like. . . . She giggled again.

She heard her cell phone ringing. Somehow she just knew it was young David Smith.

"Call me back with the KY attached," he said.

She hung up, went and found the attachment that turned her cell phone into an encrypted radio, and called him back.

"We're going to do one more encounter with the general," he said. "No actual contact beyond letting him see you and your reaction to seeing him."

"Will I be alone?" she asked.

"No, of course not," he replied. "You'll be escorted by one of our deep-cover operatives. Someone who is not known to the opposition as being one of us."

"What if Chiang makes a move?"

"We have an app for that. Basically, we want him to see you one more time, and we want you to signal your continuing interest—but only for a moment."

"Don't you think he'll realize he's being teased?" she asked. "I mean, he's definitely a player and he sure as hell knows the signs and signals of a willing woman. At some point he's going to review the bidding and then say—WTF."

"We don't think so," David said. "He's impetuous. He likes the sudden collision of desire, situations where an adult woman telegraphs that she'd like to bed him, and he jumps at it. And then he's gone. Tigers mating in the night and then withdrawing to a respectful distance."

"Interesting analogy, Mister David Smith," she said.

He cleared his throat. "Too many books, I guess," he said. "But that's what we need. Ten seconds of eye-to-eye acknowledgment that you and he are going to have a go. He'll go away wondering how and when, and we'll go away to rehearse exactly how."

"Rehearse?"

"Oh, yes," he said. "We've built a mock-up of the rooms involved, and we're going to rehearse each move, from the point where you two decide to find someplace and get it on to the final exposure. That's how it's done, Melanie."

"Wow," she said. "When I go to the hotel, how many people are going to be involved in this thing?"

"On whose side?" he asked, and then hung up.

She detached the KY device and wondered if she was imagining that David Smith was no longer sounding like a horny young millennial and a whole lot more like a controller. Had she missed something at dinner?

The next morning she took a taxi out to the headquarters building and was escorted to a section of the building she'd never seen before. Being escorted felt strange; she was a bona fide member of the Clandestine Service with a chainful of badges to prove it, and yet Smith had instructed her to call him when she got there so that he could send an escort. The low building behind the main headquarters structure looked like it had been a basketball gym at one time, which, she later found out, it had. On the floor was a freestanding maze of rooms, hallways, doors, and stair entrances—all walls with no ceilings.

"This is a pretty close mock-up of the fifth floor in the Wingate hotel," Smith began, after introducing Melanie to a group of ten men and women dressed casually. Melanie was wearing a suit and heels, as previously instructed by Smith. "Especially the heels," he'd said; "we need to see how fast you can move in those things."

"The Wingate is probably Washington's second-most-prestigious hotel," he said now. "You can book the Jefferson Suite for five thousand dollars a night if you feel really important. Your room costs us seven hundred dollars a night, which will dovetail with your puffed-up legend. You're there for one night so you can attend the awards function, drink, and not have to drive to your apartment over there in Ballston."

"I wonder if I should even mention my apartment over in Ballston," she said. "To the general, I mean."

"Absolutely not," Smith said. "If he asks, you say that your domestic arrangements are necessarily private. Remember, he's supposed to think you are a department head or better. But: By this time, if they have access, and we think they do, they'll know that you're a low-level worker bee in S and T. Now, here's the script. I'd like you to read through it, and then you and all these folks are going to rehearse each page of it. They, by the way, will be your security and support team, and you may or may not even see some of them when it goes down. The first time we'll walk it in slo-mo as we all absorb the details. After that, we'll try to get to real time by the end of the day. Can I get you some coffee?"

She felt a little bit like the star in a soap opera when he handed her the thick folder. The group ended up sitting on what had been the stands while everybody looked over his or her copy of the script. For her, it was indeed a script: start positions, end positions, dialogue, movements, place marks, timing marks. She didn't know what the others were reading. She skimmed through the entire thing while sipping some coffee, and then announced that she had a question. David Smith raised his eyebrows.

"This is amazingly detailed," she said. "But—if I understand the game, we're going to bump into one another, talk, get all hot and bothered, and then agree to meet somewhere where we can satisfy our mutual desires. How can that be scripted?"

"Your 'bumping into' one another is going to be scripted, based on where you are in the room and where he is at the appropriate time. Two of the folks here will ensure that you do in fact get physically in range. What happens after that will depend on your powers of seduction and his horns, right?"

"Okay."

"What happens just before the earth moves also has to be scripted, too, because we have to ensure you end up in your room and not his, for instance. Or a third room set up by *his* people. Remember, we have to assume his security team will think this is a honey trap, no matter what the general's little head is telling his big head. Thus the scripting."

Melanie sighed. "Look, I'm having some doubts about all this, okay? I know we're going to do one more show-the-bait session, but after that we're moving to the execution phase, without the general and I ever having had more than a few minutes together. Does that read? Seriously? What important, experienced, senior intelligence officer isn't going to realize that all this is Kabuki? He'll *have* to know that I'm bait of some kind. His people will have been shouting that fact at him. Is he really this stupid?"

"Apparently so," Smith replied. "Or perhaps 'impetuous' would be a better word. He's done dumber things than what we're setting up. He obviously gets off on the risk. He always has some cleanup crew with him when he goes into the bushes, and that's ended badly a couple of times—for the woman involved. This will be no different, except *we're* going to have some people in the building who can and will deal with any rough stuff."

"But a script?" she asked. "Boy meets girl, they lock horns, and the only word that comes to mind is—'urgency.' "

"Precisely, and that's why we're scripting this, Melanie. From the moment that you light his fire, urgency is everything. One long, deep, meaningful look into each other's eyes and then you move—but you move the way we *tell* you to move. Did I mention I will be directing you through the whole thing?"

She stared at him. Directing? A magic earring, perhaps?

He stood directly in front of her now, while the others seemed to shuffle or otherwise move out of earshot. The expression on his face was no longer that of lust-smitten David Smith, almost panting with barely disguised desire at her very presence. "I am the controller in this op," he said, in a voice she hadn't heard before. "You will do exactly what I tell you to do if you want to live through this op. You don't—and can't—know everything about what's going to happen, but it is imperative that you do exactly as you are told. That's the real reason for the script. We know it won't play out precisely that way, but we also know that if you—we, the team—have practiced it, whatever departures from the plan we might *have* to make will be easier."

He leaned down to stare directly into her eyes, and she realized that she no longer recognized this man. "Got it?" he asked softly. "This is how it's done, especially when the boss has declared that you are *not* expendable. It's when they *don't* say those words that *you* get a vote. So: Please read the fucking script, absorb what you can, so we can all get to work."

"Okay" was all she could manage. The menace in Smith's voice had been palpable. One of the other women in the "cast" gave her a welcome-to-our-world smile over Smith's shoulder. She couldn't believe that she'd thought this guy was just another late-twenty-something lightweight. Then she realized that her dinner "date" had probably not been the spur-of-the-moment encounter she'd assumed it was.

Allender, the puppet master. She groaned, mentally. She should have known.

They worked for the rest of the day, starting with a general walk-through of each phase, followed by a scene-by-scene practice. Smith was the director, and there was even a cameraman, because Smith wanted to watch each scene later so he could make improvements. At the end of the day, Melanie was tired but a lot more confident in the plan. The following day she found out that her confidence had been misplaced, as Smith began to throw some shit into the game and everyone, including her, fumbled badly. By the end of day two, Smith was speaking in monosyllables and the members of the cast weren't looking at each other if they could help it.

It went like that for the eight days leading up to the awards dinner, but by then the team had clicked into place and were able to deal with contingencies with a minimum of disruption. The intervening visual opportunity had been a nonevent, except for the way General Chiang had stared at her when she glanced at him over someone's shoulder, saw him looking, and wet her lips for just a fraction of a second before turning away. She'd been wearing a clingy, white skirt that draped over her curves like lingerie, and she'd followed up the lip-tease with a casual fake wedgie adjustment with her left hand when she had her back turned toward him. Smith had later shown her a picture of the expression on the general's face, and it was not the face of a man who was disinterested.

Smith was now satisfied with both her performance and the general's obvious desire. They had three days to go to showtime. He told her to take two days off, go see the sights in Washington, and then return to Langley the day before the Wingate gala for final preps. He, in the meantime, needed to spend some time at the hotel getting his people in place and integrated into the hotel's operations.

"How do you do that?" she'd asked.

"We have an arrangement" was all he would say.

She did exactly what Smith had recommended for the next two days. She toured the monuments district of Washington: the Mall, the Lincoln, the Jefferson, three of the Smithsonian museums, and the Hirshhorn modern art gallery. She even took a bus out to Dulles to see the big-boy toys at the Air and Space Museum annex. On the second day, she rested her aching feet until the evening, when she took a Potomac River scenic dinner cruise that launched out of the Maine Avenue wharf. The boat docked at just after nine. Having had a bit too much to drink and eat, she decided to walk straight up Twelfth Street back to the Mall before finding a Metro and calling it a day.

The evening was cool and clear. She wore comfortable walking shoes, jeans, and a light sweater, and carried a nine-millimeter in her handbag in case some night people decided to make a move on her. As it was, there was absolutely zero drama. Typical of many people who actually worked in Washington, she'd never "done" the sights, and she resolved to do this again. There was far too much to see in just two days. The dinner cruise had been relaxing, except for having to fend off a couple of middle-aged Lotharios. They had produced some Bombay gin, which was the reason she now needed to walk. There weren't many people about, but it was clear that the closer she got to the White House, the more security there was on the streets.

She turned left and walked down the Mall to the World War II Memorial, with its plashing fountains and Stonehenge-like circle of columns whose names revealed the scope of that tragic conflict. She sat down by the main pool to rest her feet and just chill out. Two Park Police on foot patrol were sitting across the pool, having a cigarette. They'd given her the once-over but then ignored her. She thought they'd probably decided that she was too old to be a prostitute. That thought resurrected the op, which she'd been putting out of her mind these past two days. There was still the question of what Allender and Smith had planned and whether or not it involved actually doing it with Chiang. She knew she could if she had to, especially given the bonus. Maybe she was a prossie after all. Then she saw Allender approaching from the direction of the Lincoln.

It has to be him, she thought. Nobody walks like that. All he needed was a deerstalker hat and a cape to complete the picture. She saw the two cops watching him as he came up the gravel path that ran alongside the reflecting pool and stepped up the marble stairs to the memorial fountain area. She saw them both straighten up when he walked under one of the faux gas lamps, which made his amber eyes flash for the briefest second under that antique hat. He walked around the fountain and then joined her on the bench. He didn't say anything, just sat down and stretched his legs out in front of him, the stick resting across his lap. She was about to greet him when the two cops materialized beside them. Allender showed them his credentials and they backed off, trying not to stare at his face.

"Cold feet?" he asked once they'd walked away.

"Hot feet," she said. "I just walked up from the riverfront."

"I know," he said.

She turned to look at him. "Eyes on *me*?"

"So close to your command performance? You bet."

"Chinese eyes, too?" she asked. She looked out into the semidarkness, but didn't see any obvious watchers. She remembered he'd told her that he liked to walk the Mall at night to keep fit. A small breeze blew a mist of spray from the fountains over them.

"It's possible," he said. "But that wouldn't hurt the legend. In fact, Chiang might like the idea of poaching my woman." He spoke the words "my woman" in a faked deep voice.

Melanie snorted. "So I'm *your* woman now?"

He smiled, and she was surprised to see the light in his eyes become subdued. "I suppose it would be possible. In another life. But back to my question: You still okay with this op? We're asking a lot."

"A little hesitation," she said. "I was just thinking of that old joke about the guy propositioning a woman at a party."

"The one where he offers a million dollars?"

"Yeah, that one."

He was silent for a moment. "I feel your pain," he declared, finally, with a completely straight face.

She turned to stare at him and then saw his shoulders shaking. OMG, she thought. Dragon Eyes is *laughing*! She elbowed him in the ribs but then smiled herself.

"C'mon," he said, getting up. "I'll walk you to Smithsonian Station. It's the least I can do."

As they walked up the Mall, she put her arm in his. She could feel the tension in his arm, but after a while she felt him relax a little.

Better. Much better.

NINE

Melanie and her escort joined the throng of people heading into the main ballroom of the hotel. There were thirty round tables set for dinner, and her escort knew right where to take her, even though he was assigned to an adjacent table. He checked to see that the general's name was on the place card to her immediate right, and then seated her as the table's other guests found their places. The ballroom was spacious and well appointed, with a stage at one end and a wall of double doors to admit the attendees at the other. Melanie spotted Smith, dressed in a stylish tux, sitting down two tables over. She smiled when she saw him switch two place cards so that he would have a better view of Melanie's table.

"Ah, we meet again, Miss Sloan," General Chiang announced as an aide pulled back his chair so that he could sit down. "What a pleasant surprise."

She turned to smile at him. "An amazing coincidence," she murmured, and he grinned. The aide bowed and withdrew.

The general turned to his right to greet the rather large lady who'd sat down next to him, and then turned back to Melanie. A rather serious-looking Chinese man was the last to take his place at their table. He sat down directly across from Chiang and stared intently at Melanie. She was worth the look: She was wearing a Dior ensemble with spaghetti straps and a cleverly designed lace bodice. Her skirt was calf-length and fashionably slit on one side, but not so high that anyone would remark on it. She leaned in toward the general. "Your minder?" she asked softly.

He smiled again and pretended to be interested in the menu card at the center of the table. "For as long as I allow it," he replied. "In our government, everybody watches everybody."

She sighed. "Kinky," she said. He snorted quietly.

The dinner service began with wine stewards pouring out reds and whites. Melanie recognized the young man who came to their table as one of the cast members from the practice sessions. As he went around the table, Melanie indicated she wanted both a white and a red. Chiang did the same. The large lady to Chiang's right asked him a question. Once he was turned away from her, Melanie rotated the hem of the skirt so that the slit was now front and center, and then hiked it up to just the right elevation to make things interesting. She was wearing nude-colored nylon stockings that had a black lace band at the top. Then she spread her linen napkin demurely across her lap. Minette had warned her to not indulge in any casual knee-bumping contact under the table. Keep it all visual. Let him see, but not touch. Touch was for later.

Dinner proceeded uneventfully with the typical casual conversation until the dessert course was served, at which point Melanie picked up her napkin and wiped her lips. She could almost feel the general's hot stare before she folded the napkin in half and put it back in her lap. But it was half a napkin now, and her thighs and lace-topped stockings were still just visible. She finally looked directly at him.

"Are you staying for the awards presentation?" she asked.

"Of course—our ambassador is receiving an award. Are you not?"

She shook her head, aware now that the minder across the table was trying desperately to hear what they were talking about. "I feel like drinking tonight, so I got a room. I'm going to 'withdraw' to the lounge."

He looked positively crestfallen until he realized that she'd just told him she had a room, right here in the hotel. "Well, then," he said, much more quietly than he'd been speaking before. "Perhaps I will see you there. Protocol demands, you understand."

"Of course I understand, General," she said, teasing him with a mildly flirtatious smile. "I'll be sorry to miss all the speeches."

It became clear that dinner was over. People were starting to move around, visiting other tables or heading outside for a quick cigarette. Melanie gathered herself to push back from the table. The general beat her to it, rising and sliding her chair back to one side as she got up. For an instant their faces were inches apart. The sexual tension between them flared, minder or no minder, as the general remained well within her personal space. "Hurry," she breathed.

She visited the ladies' room, where there were two attendants dressed in the hotel's livery. One was tending to a woman whose dress had begun to disintegrate and who was well versed in drama. The other attendant was one of the cast. Melanie tended to business and then stood before one of the mirrors to brush her hair and touch up her makeup. She reached behind her as if to adjust the back of her dress, and the attendant came over, offering to help.

"Hook set?" she asked quietly while pretending to fiddle with the dress.

"Yes, indeed," Melanie replied. Then she tipped the attendant and left for the lounge.

General Chiang showed up forty-five minutes later, saw her sitting alone in a corner, and joined her. The minder was ninety seconds behind him, and then there were two thirty-something Chinese "businessmen" two minutes behind the minder. The three Chinese spread out in the lounge, one to a table. The lounge hadn't filled up yet. The noise level was low, disturbed only by a large-screen television flickering above the bar.

"You brought a crowd," she said.

"I think the ambassador saw me leave right after his award."

"And he knows you, doesn't he," she teased.

He shrugged. "He's old and married to a niece of the president. She is something of a dragon, I am told." He saw a waitress approaching. "What are you drinking?"

"Bombay gin and tonic," she said. The bar had a new assistant bartender tonight. He'd fixed Melanie's first "drink," which had been plain tonic water with a wedge of lime. The second one, the one the general was going to order for her, would have mostly tonic water but with a dollop of the gin poured gently on top in case he checked.

He sat back in his chair and gave her an admiring look. "You are quite beautiful tonight," he said. "But I must tell you, my minders are quite worried."

"Let me guess," she said. "I work for the Company and have ensnared you with my womanly wiles. Soon I'll ask you up to my room, for some—cognac, perhaps, and then, once we have become um—involved, spring some kind of a trap, and then demand that you tell me everything you know or I'll go to the press with the embarrassing videos captured by all the secret cameras in my hotel room. Close?"

He laughed out loud. "Very," he said. Then he leaned in to her as if about to propose some even more complex plot. "So the trick is: Get involved, as you put it, quickly."

She stared directly into his hot eyes. "Go fast, you mean," she whispered. "Hard and fast."

"Yes, go fast. That is what I like."

She leaned back and scanned the room, as if to see who might be watching besides the now worried-looking Chinese guards. She squared her shoulders and then smiled when the minders stopped looking at Chiang for a moment. "That is what I like, too," she said. "And besides, here's what *I* think. Your wife might be offended if someone produced a video of us in bed, but every man in China would probably be saying: *hell,* yes, as our cowboys say. In America, too."

He laughed again. "You are quite direct," he said.

"And fast," she said. "Don't forget fast. Hard and fast. And you must of course promise to respect me in the morning."

This time he positively shook laughing, but stopped when she turned in her chair, crossed her shiny legs, the slit skirt showing him the rest of what was on offer. A waiter brought the drinks and they paused to enjoy them. The minders all pretended to do the same. More people were coming into the lounge by now, including one couple who were also members of the cast. Pretty soon, she thought, there'll be as many of my minders in here as his.

"How shall we work this?" she asked finally.

He finished his drink, took a deep breath, and asked for her room number. She told him.

"Go there now," he said. "I will come after an appropriate interval."

"Yes, you certainly will," she said, not smiling this time. She watched him blink and swallow hard. She gathered herself to get up from the table but with enough body language to make even the minders look. She could hear Minette: *Reach for your purse. Knock it off the table and into a chair. Bend to retrieve it. Stretch that amazing material across your bottom. Take one second longer than necessary. Hear them all inhale.*

She stepped into the elevator and punched the number five. The doors closed, but only went up one floor before stopping. Three Chinese men got in, all wearing plain gray suits. One, who was older and had the look of authority about him, was carrying a metal attaché case. They were not the same men who'd been in the lounge and they had a hard look about them that fairly shouted security. One reached for the control panel, saw button 5 lit, and lowered his hand.

Oh, boy, Melanie thought, but then saw the tiny camera mounted in the elevator's ceiling. *Some*one would be watching.

When the door opened at the fifth floor, the older man indicated that she should go first. She did and the three of them got out and then followed her down the hallway at a discreet distance. When she stopped to fish out her key card, they also stopped. She looked back at them, and all three of them did their best to smile.

"Can I help you guys with something?" she asked, sliding the card into the door slot. The moment the light turned green, the older one stepped forward. She instinctively turned the door handle but he was there in a heartbeat. The next thing she knew she was being gently pushed through the door and into her room. One man had taken possession of her elbows, while another held his hand over her mouth—firmly but not painfully. For an instant no one moved, and then the older man put his finger to his lips to indicate silence. He raised his eyebrows as if to ask, You going to scream? She took a deep breath, shook her head, and then relaxed. When he saw that, he signaled the man holding her mouth to release her. The elbow man did not move.

"Excuse," the older man said. "We must search this room, and your person, before your 'guest' arrives. We will not hurt you, but we must be sure this room is—safe."

"May I please sit down?" she asked. "And, yes, I understand what you need to do."

His face brightened. "Good," he said. "Yes, you may sit down. Please keep hands in sight."

Once she was seated, hands primly on her knees, the older man opened the attaché case, punched some buttons on the console inside, and proceeded to do an electronic sweep of the room. The second man meticulously searched every part of the room—fixtures, furniture, receptacle covers, lights, the television, and even the coffee maker—for hidden cameras. The third man went to work on the interconnecting door locks between her room and the rooms on either side. He nodded to the older man when he had the locks compromised, which had taken all of thirty seconds.

Melanie knew there were cameras, but not exactly where except for one. She did know that they were so miniaturized she was pretty sure they'd never find them. The plan had taken into account the fact that wireless cameras had to transmit their images, which meant that a competent sweep kit could detect RF energy. So tonight her controllers were depending on a passive sound-source alone, with two hardwired microphones outside the sliding glass door, posing as one of those decals that keeps one from walking into the door. The actual transmitter was two floors above. Their receivers were two blocks away. The cameras would be switched to the RF mode only after the minders were satisfied that the room was "cold."

Once they were satisfied, they proceeded into the hotel room on one side, which, from what Melanie could see, seemed to be unoccupied. The one on the opposite side was occupied, based on clothes and luggage, but apparently not a threat. The man who'd done the locks relocked them and then placed a silvery strip of metal like a Band-Aid across each door. The older man concluded his sweep and said something in Chinese to the other two. They nodded, and then went back out into the hallway, leaving the door partially open.

"And now," the older man said. "Your person, please?"

"Please, what?" she asked indignantly, knowing full well what he wanted. Both the other men had positioned themselves in the corridor so they could see into the room while also watching the hallway.

He cocked his head to one side. "Please?" he asked again, as in, Stop wasting our time. And the general's time.

"Oh," she said, pretending surprise. "You want to know if *I'm* wired."

"Yes. Please?"

"Okay," she said, standing up. She peeled the straps of her gown off her shoulders and let the fabric drop to her waist. The dress was the only topside support she'd worn, so there she was. Wireless but sufficiently distracting, she hoped. The older man stared appreciatively, and then looked lower. Melanie frowned, put her top back together, and then, crossing her arms, raised the hem of her skirt as high as it would go. Then she turned around, slowly, trying not to be seductive about it, until she faced him again. He, and his minions kept staring until she slid the skirt back down and went back to the chair. Then she looked pointedly at her watch.

"The general?" she asked. "Do you *like* to keep him waiting?"

The older man composed his face, nodded, and then they all left. As soon as the door closed, she got up and went to the bathroom. She turned on the overhead fan, which was the signal to the controller that she was alone again. They would have the corridor on cameras, but they needed to know when to turn on the room cameras and take them online. It was now time to change. She took off all her clothes and put on a filmy, white, full-length nylon slip. Then she went back to the chair and sat down.

After five minutes she wished she'd had more than a few drops of Bombay. Her script called for her to wait in the chair until the general came to her room—or didn't, if his security team called it off. The local control room was two floors directly above, and the room's sprinkler-system fixture had been replaced with a wide-angle camera, presumably, she figured, to capture the action on the bed. Any time now, she thought.

She had steeled herself to go through with what would probably resemble a rape. All that talk about hard and fast had been aimed at fanning the general's fervid expectations, but she hoped it wouldn't turn into some painful back-alley assault. That said, it had been something of a long dry spell.

There was a click from the unoccupied room's interconnecting door, and then it swung open. The metal Band-Aid broke, but then she saw that an even longer strip had been stuck to the other side of the door, allowing it to open without disrupting the alarm circuit. Two men who had been part of the "cast," but whose roles hadn't been clear, beckoned her to the doorway. A voice in her right earring told her to go with them. They then hustled her out of the room into the unoccupied room, and from there through a doorway into the *next* room, where she saw something that totally floored her.

Standing in the room was her doppelgänger, also sporting a full-length white slip, but wearing panties. Her face, her body, her hair—everything the same. Her almost identical twin. As she gaped in surprise, her clone got up, smiled at her, said, "Good job, Melanie," and then went through the door with one of the other agents. The room crew closed the door, and one of them handed her a bathrobe. She put it on, almost unaware of what she was doing.

"Good job, Melanie," he'd said.

He?

Then she grinned. The other guys saw her get it and they also grinned.

"Gonna be a good one," one of them said. "Wanna watch?"

"*Hell,* yes," she said. "Oh. My. God."

TEN

Preston Allender sat in an armchair watching two screens. One gave a wide-angle view of Melanie's room, where special operative Torrance LaPlante, Melanie Sloan's double, lounged languidly in an armchair, his lithe body stretched in such a way as to disguise his big surprise. He'd gone into the bathroom and wet the front top half of the slip, which accentuated his perfect, if plastic, breasts. There was only one bedside table light on in the room and the covers had been turned down on the bed. He'd put on enough perfume to infuse the room and tousled his hair to make it look like the lady was already agitated. The door was unlocked and actually just barely ajar.

"The general's going to react badly," Allender observed, recognizing the face in the picture he'd had in his desk drawer when he'd first interviewed Sloan. *Damn,* he thought.

"Four guys, two in each of the adjacent rooms," Smith said. "See those shiny strips on the doors?"

"Yes?"

"Chiang's security people put them on the doors to alarm should either one open. Our guys have paralleled them to get Sloan out, but they'll break them both at the right time."

"Which will bring his minders in on the run at a really inopportune time?"

"Exactly. They're waiting down the hall in the vending alcove, and there are two more in the nearest linen closet. If anybody makes a move on Torrance, an entire bank of white lights is going to flash on in Chiang's face. They're mounted in the valence above the window's privacy curtain. Our guys will get Torrance out of there, and, well, the cameras should do the rest."

"There's the ambassador," Allender said, looking at the other screen, which was covering the lounge with a wide-angle lens. "Are those different minders?"

"Yes, they are. Some are probably embassy aides, but, yes; they've probably got twenty people here tonight."

"Crowds are not a problem for China, are they," Allender observed.

"The unit of issue is a horde," Smith said.

"Where's Melanie now?"

"In the video control room, two over from her starting point. She's safe now."

"I wasn't sure that one guy doing the sweep was going to leave," Allender said.

"Can you blame him?" Smith said.

No I can't, Allender thought, but he was glad she was clear now. There was nothing to say Chiang wouldn't pull a weapon when he realized what had been done to him.

"Target's in the elevator with a team of three," one of the cameramen announced.

"Showtime," Smith muttered into a tiny microphone.

Allender saw Torrance become more alert and then rearrange his face. It was hard not to stare at him. From the waist up he was a female. Melanie Sloan, in the flesh. Soft features, sophisticated makeup, full lips, parted now in naked anticipation. Even the way he looked at the door was female: longing, desire, impatience, one slim hand running through his hair. Her hair. A woman's forearms, delicate hands, nails painted in something not too over the top, but definitely painted. Even from the waist down, there was no sign of what was about to be revealed. His shapely legs were shaved and polished.

"Approaching the room."

The light in the room changed as the door swung open and hallway light spilled in. Chiang stopped and stared. Then he stepped through, pushed the door shut, and took two steps into the room.

"Did it lock?" Allender asked.

"Supposed to, but, no, it did not."

"I want to *see* you," Torrance said, in a voice that was a dead match for Melanie's. Then he put his hands behind his head, thrust his fake breasts up in a deliberate challenge, and wet his lips—her lips—in an equally challenging manner. Allender thought he heard Chiang swear softly, but with admiration, and then the general began taking his clothes off.

"Prep the feed," one of the technicians said. They had their own bank of screens, and there was some quick switch-work going on.

Then Chiang was naked, his muscular body gathering in anticipation of his go-fast encounter. Torrance smiled seductively, rubbed his hands over his breasts, and then beckoned him. Chiang was entirely ready.

"Open the feed," one of the technicians ordered.

Allender turned to the lounge screen and watched that big-screen television picture suddenly flutter with a few white frames, and then there was Chiang, in all his rampant glory, advancing on Torrance. One of the techs opened the sound channel from the lounge, and Allender heard the sudden gasps and "whoa"s from the people in the lounge. Then Torrance stood up, reached down to rearrange himself, and revealed an equally impressive erection underneath all that nylon. Allender concentrated on watching the ambassador, whose expression changed from consternation to red-faced fury as he saw what was unfolding on that big screen. It was almost as dramatic as Chiang's expression when he saw that his supposed temptress was a man, and not just a man, but a really *interested* man. Chiang's roar of angry surprise was audible over all the "oh my God"s erupting in the lounge. Torrance lifted the nylon and then pursed his lips in an obscene kissing gesture and began moving toward Chiang. The room's door burst open just as a bright white light infused the screen and then the picture faded to black.

"Torrance is clear," Smith announced, a moment later. "Barriers in place. Okay, guys, electronics down. Take it all apart and let's blow this pop stand." He turned to Allender, unable to tamp down a triumphant grin. "Well, Doctor," he said. "This being all your idea, what do you think?"

Even with the old hotel's thick floors and walls, Allender imagined he could hear Chiang howling in fury two floors below, while his minders were probably staring at him in stunned surprise.

"I think," Allender said, nodding in satisfaction, "that General Chiang is in for some interesting times, in the traditional Chinese sense of that expression."

Allender met with McGill the following morning in his office at Langley. The DDO was almost beside himself, having seen the videos. He was pacing again, but this time with his hands wringing in undisguised delight.

"*Gawd,*" he exclaimed. "They're gonna crucify him. He'll be wrangling night soil in outer fucking Mongolia by tomorrow night. Fucking beautiful, sir, fucking beautiful!"

"I'm told that the ambassador had been waiting a long time to get something on his bad-boy general," Allender said, getting himself a cup of coffee from the sideboard. "And the ambassador is the younger brother of a Central Committee member."

McGill went back to his desk. "Will some of this incident blow back on him, do you think?" he asked.

"Possibly," Allender replied. "Loss of face, as in: 'He worked for you so why didn't you *do* something a long time ago' kind of thing.

On the other hand, Chiang had his own power base in Beijing. Not quite a private intel network, but close to it. You have to understand—all Chinese bureaucracies are made up of factions, most based on clan or family. The MSS will recover, but there will be turmoil."

"Will it really disrupt things that badly?"

"Absolutely," Allender said. "Within Chinese top-level bureaucracies, the factions are always infighting. Chiang's clan stood astride a real plum here in Washington. When he goes down, his people go down with him. Then there'll be a fight to see who replaces him—and maybe all his people, too. Chaos, for a while, anyway."

"How long before they realize *we* did this?"

"Chiang's certainly figured it out," Allender said. "He's been close enough to Sloan's sexuality to know that she was no she-male. On the other hand, what's he going to say? I didn't know she was an 'it'? Or, I *did* know, and that's my scene?"

"Beautiful," McGill crowed again. "Where is the magnificent Sloan, by the way?"

"Took a red-eye out to the West Coast last night to see some preeminent plastic surgeons in Hollywood."

"I'm not sure I'd change a thing with that package."

"We have to, I think," Allender said. "David Smith agrees. In fact, I'd told her that she might have to exit the intel world entirely, depending on how the MSS reacts. Hate to lose her, though. She was brilliant."

"A swan indeed," McGill said, reaching for his obnoxious pipe. Like reaching for his worry beads, Allender thought. "We need to do this again."

Allender raised a hand. "No, we do not," he said. "Word of this *will* eventually get out—too many people in that lounge saw what happened. There's something else."

"Yes? What?"

"The Chinese will not forget this. They won't write this embarrassment off as just a learning experience. I grew up in Taiwan, and

I know something about Chinese culture. The Mandarins at the imperial court did this kind of thing to one another for fun, but if *they* got caught short in a power play, they died in truly interesting ways."

"But won't the ambassador feel we've solved a problem for them? The influential general with the dangerously loose zipper?"

"Perhaps," Allender said. "But I believe they'll analyze it, stew about it, punish someone, and then set about planning appropriate revenge."

"*Revenge?*" McGill squeaked. "Really? How unprofessional. It's the intelligence racket. You win some, you lose some. That's why it's called the Great *Game.* Even Kipling knew that."

"Yes, that's exactly what I'm saying, which is a good reason not to try this gambit again. What we do now is keep a straight face, admit nothing, especially within the Company. That was why you had *me* conjure this thing up, remember? Nobody associates me with operations, *and* you can maintain your deniability."

McGill considered that last point. "Yes, you're right. But you might want to think about dabbling in operations, Preston. This was brilliant."

Allender dismissed that notion with a wave of his hand. "Bury this episode, Carson. No gloating or wink-wink asides and grins over Scotch at your club. It's important."

"Yes, yes, keep it all exquisitely professional, I know, I know," McGill said dismissively. "I totally agree. But what if we did it to someone who's theoretically on our side?"

"Meaning?"

"A certain congressperson comes to mind."

Allender groaned. "No, no, and *hell* no. Much as you despise that woman, taking down a House committee chairman would produce some serious blowback."

"In your humble opinion?"

"In *anyone's* opinion, Carson. Give it the *Washington Post* test, for God's sake."

McGill appeared to visualize the headlines and then waved the whole idea away. "By the way," he said. "The director wanted to know what that commotion in the lounge was all about. Some eager beaver put a clip of it in his morning brief."

"What'd you tell him?" Allender asked, sharply.

"That we're looking into it, of course, but that it appears to be a Chinese embassy personnel problem. Some general indulging odd tastes. Reminded him that the Chinese embassy is a tough nut—you know, all those inscrutable Orientals. Pivoted to a more urgent problem in Africa that we simply *had* to deal with, and off we went on that little firefly. I even avoided The Lecture."

"Lucky you," Allender said. "So: David Smith assures me that Sloan's being taken care of. The team's been dispersed and reassigned to other duties. The hotel's been cleared and paid. General Chiang's undoubtedly on his way back to China, possibly in a shipping container, and the MSS operation here in Washington has been neutralized—for the moment, anyway. I guess I'll go back to my day job."

"*Capital* idea, my dear fellow." McGill beamed. "Commendations to follow, of course. A nice year-end executive bonus, too, if I'm not mistaken. Very, *very* well done. Tell me: Do you still do that dragon-eyes routine when you're doing one of your notorious—'interviews'?"

Allender finished his coffee and stood up. He walked over to McGill's desk and leaned down to look at him. Then he took off his glasses and gave McGill a good look at those golden eyes and their shape-shifting black irises. McGill, despite himself, recoiled.

"Yes, I do," Allender said softly. "And you need to forget all about running a swan on Congresswoman Greer, Carson. I guarantee you: That would end badly."

ELEVEN

At home that night, Allender put a call in to Langley telecommunications on his secure phone, asking them to find Sloan and have her call him on a secure channel. She called back thirty minutes later, her voice chirping a little owing to the encryption card.

"Doctor Allender," she said. "How nice to hear from you."

"Hello, Melanie Sloan," he replied. "How are they treating you?"

"With twelve operations, now that we've settled on the new face."

"Twelve," he said. "That's a lot."

"These docs seem pretty blasé about the whole thing," she said. "Of course, they're at the blunt end of the scalpel, aren't they. They said breaking my nose, eye sockets, and cheekbones would be the most painful part, but after that it'll be all lift, suck, and tuck. Their words."

"Lovely," Allender said. "Who are you going to look like?"

"Variation eighty-seven," she said. "Facial only, they said the rest of me didn't need changing."

"I would have to agree," he said, almost without thinking. Then he did think. Oops.

"I forgot," she said, with a barely suppressed giggle.

"I apologize," he said. "That was unprofessional of me."

"But nice, none the less. So: Do I get to stay in the business?"

He shifted uncomfortably in his chair. "That will depend on whether or not the operations people think they can protect you. If the surgery is sufficiently extensive, then probably yes, although they'd keep you in-house for a while. No foreign postings."

"How long?" she asked, her tone of voice making it clear that a few years of cubicle work was not appealing.

"A year? Maybe two? Until they figure out what the MSS has decided to do about getting taken for a ride. If we determine that they want your bones in the embassy chipper, then they'll hide you for real."

"Anyone going to keep an eye on *your* safety?"

"Me? I wouldn't think so. The Chinese know who I am and what I do, and especially that I'm not operational. I'm just an Agency shrink who happens to speak Mandarin. In fact, I'm scheduled to attend a dinner at State next week precisely because I can speak Mandarin."

"Don't you think General Chiang may make the association?"

"Who's General Chiang?" Allender said.

"Will it be that bad, for him?"

"The Chinese hate to lose face, possibly even more than the Japanese. I have to tell you: He may not even be alive anymore. Just remember, if they do decide to get revenge, you might be in considerable personal danger. I think that was part of your brief, yes?"

"Yes, Carol did say that," Sloan said. "But then she brought up the bonus."

"Which *will* be forthcoming. Minus the cost of the cosmetic surgery of course."

"*What?*"

"Just kidding, Melanie Sloan," he said, laughing quietly.

There was a pause on the line. Then she was back. "You called me Melanie," she said.

"I did."

"Well, if you're going to call me Melanie, what am I supposed to call you?"

"Sir?"

She giggled again. "Okay, I walked into that one. But here's the thing: I'd like to see you again, when this nose-breaking, sinus-grinding, and lift-suck-tuck holiday is over."

"You're saying you want an interview with Dragon Eyes?'

"Something like that. Or am I out of line here?"

"About an inch," he said. "Maybe a bit more." He paused. "But that's probably not a good idea, Melanie. For a variety of reasons, chief among them that you and I were seen together by the MSS on two occasions. They are going to be looking for links."

"So they *would* they come after you?"

Damned right they would, he thought. "More a case of their coming after *us*," he said, trying to muddy his answer.

"I thought that's what you'd say," she said, sounding a bit wistful.

"Not because I wanted to," he said. "How long will all this surgery take?"

"A year, at least. They do it in increments, and then they give everything time to heal. Maybe I'll just surprise you one day. See if you recognize me."

"After a year of work, I'd better *not* recognize you."

"Probably not," she said. "Unless of course I'm standing in front of your desk, and you say—"

He laughed out loud. "You did brilliantly," he said, finally. "Now we just have to play it professionally safe. Okay?"

"Right."

He didn't want to break this off, but he knew he must. "Keep me informed on how you're doing," he said. "And especially if your Spidey sense activates. You know what I mean?"

"Yes, I do," she said.

"Well," he said. "Until then."

"Until then," she said, and then the line dissolved into a series of beeps.

He had another Scotch, and called the director's office social coordinator, asked for a table for one at Charlie Palmer Steak for eight o'clock and a driver for the evening. Then he went upstairs for a shower.

An hour later he was ensconced at a private corner table and finishing off a bottle of Orin Swift's The Prisoner after a perfect filet. The restaurant was beginning to fill up, but no one was rushing him. He'd kept the smoky glasses on throughout dinner; no reason to frighten the waitstaff unless they overfired his steak, which they almost never did, and besides, people for whom the director's office made a reservation were never rushed. There were the usual visual power sweeps going on across the dining room—the men checking to see if anyone really important was there; the women sizing up the men. A few of the shinier women had given Allender an appraising look, but something in the way that the waitstaff was acting around the tall, thin man wearing those strange glasses had warned them off. The maître d' approached.

"My apologies, Doctor. There is a gentleman in one of the private dining rooms who wishes to approach your table," he said quietly. "A Chinese gentleman."

Allender raised an eyebrow. "Does this Chinese gentlemen have minders outside the room?"

"Yes, sir, he does. And out front, and in the valet parking area. I believe he is the Chinese ambassador, Dr. Allender. He was extremely polite and told me only to inquire and not to insist, so—"

"No, of course I will see him," Allender said. "What is he drinking?"

"He barely drinks, sir, but I've been told he's fond of strong Tennessee whiskey. In small, diplomatic quantities, of course."

"Could you please prepare a dram of Booker Noe's small-batch bourbon in an appropriate glass, and then tell him I will be honored to make his acquaintance."

"Right away, sir. With a splash? That's a hundred and thirty proof."

"A shot glass of water on the side."

"Very good, sir."

He smiled as the maître d' moved away gracefully through the tables, issuing barely detectable visual signals to waitstaff where he saw something needing attention. Leave it to the maître d' to know what the Chinese ambassador liked for an after-dinner digestive, he thought, and then gathered himself for what was certain to be a fairly oblique but angry conversation. But inevitable, he thought, glumly. He was glad Sloan was in California. They might think twice about coming after him, but a woman?

A few minutes later he caught a fleeting glance of two minders giving him the once-over from the dining room's main entrance. They appeared to be older and more experienced men than General Chiang's crew. Different clan, no doubt, he thought. Then the ambassador himself appeared, materializing from the private dining room area like an Imperial Mandarin from behind one of the jade screens at the imperial court. The ambassador looked every inch the dignified and highly polished diplomat that he was, crossing the room with a bearing that was almost regal and fixing Allender with an imperious stare as he approached the table. People definitely noticed. Allender was tempted to remove his glasses.

He remained seated until the last possible moment without giving offense, and then he pushed back, stood up, and made a formal deep bow. The maître d' was ready to pull back the ambassador's chair, and then they were seated.

"That was elegant," the ambassador said in a level of Mandarin that Allender hadn't heard since being summoned to the headmaster's office in the American School.

Allender acknowledged the compliment. "If you're going to bow, always bow low," he replied, citing the old Chinese proverb. The ambassador nodded in agreement. "We can speak in English if you'd like," he said.

"I need the practice, if you don't mind," Allender said.

"Not much, Doctor. Your Mandarin lives up to your reputation."

"Or at least to your briefing."

A hint of a smile crossed the ambassador's face. "Just so, Doctor." His voice was smooth as silk, as was his tightly controlled face. Allender couldn't tell how old he was, but this man personified the word "gravitas," by his calm voice, exquisite diction, and regal bearing.

The maître d' himself brought the ambassador a crystal snifter with the whiskey and a touch of water on the side. The ambassador was surprised when he sampled the vapors. He did not touch the water. "You, too, are well briefed, Doctor. Thank you for this. It's just right."

"Thank the maître d', Your Excellency. He's the one who knew. I do not receive briefings in my line of work."

"Really."

"Yes, really," Allender said, sipping some wine. He was glad it wasn't the 130-proof whiskey the ambassador was dealing with; an entire bottle of The Prisoner was formidable enough. "I work in the training directorate. I evaluate our staff's ability to perform their duties, and the candidates' prospects for becoming—useful."

"That is important, of course," the ambassador observed. "You are a psychiatrist, I am told."

"That is correct. Technically, I am a consultant."

"Which means you are a proper medical doctor: premedical university, medical school, postgraduate training in psychiatry, boards, and then a lifetime of regular psychoanalysis thereafter?"

"Correct, except for the last part. Ordinarily, yes, if I were practicing in the civilian world. As I am not . . ."

"Yes, of course, I understand," the ambassador said. "Thank you for not being coy with me, Doctor. With your acquiescence, I will now be frank with you."

"Yes, Mister Ambassador?"

"The matter of General Chiang's recent—indiscretion."

Allender took a sip of his wine and waited for the ambassador to proceed to the matter at hand.

"You are aware, I assume," the ambassador began, "that our chief of station recently embarrassed himself rather egregiously here in the capital. Quite dramatically, in fact. I personally witnessed it, at the Climate Change dinner reception and awards dinner."

Allender nodded but didn't say anything.

"The general has long had a reputation for indulging his particular appetites, impulsively and, unfortunately, without much regard to possible consequences."

"Some generals are like that, I'm told," Allender replied. "I would assume he is quite well connected back in Beijing?"

"Not quite well-connected enough after this latest indiscretion. To be blunt, the general is no longer with us."

"At the embassy, you mean?"

"No, Doctor. He caused serious embarrassment to the Party and to the government. That can have only one result."

"Oh, dear," Allender murmured. "Consequences, indeed."

The ambassador shrugged. "Here's the question," he said. "Some officials back in Beijing are wondering if the general's downfall was because of his usual heedless behavior, or the result of an elegant trap at the hands of someone else. Someone like *your* employers."

It was Allender's turn to shrug. "That would be an operational matter, Your Excellency," he said. "And while I am an assistant director, my work is in training and evaluation. As I'm sure you can appreciate, the ones who train the operators are *never* the ones who oversee actual operations. The trainers must have experience, of course, but as a matter of policy those are two rigidly separated compartments. I would wager it is the same in the MSS."

"And yet, *you* were seen in the company of the woman who was at the center of—what transpired. Twice, in fact. Was this coincidence?"

"I am often in the company of both men and women who are part of our organization. If I remember the incident with General Chiang, he was in pursuit of a man disguised as a woman, was he not?"

The ambassador gave him a long, level stare. Allender was again tempted to remove his glasses and give him one back.

"I came to tell you that I have made representations at the highest levels of your government," the ambassador said, finally. "This is a serious matter."

"I don't doubt that for a minute," Allender acknowledged. "Especially for General Chiang."

"And for me," the ambassador said.

"Ah," Allender said. "You will carry the black bowl?"

"Yes; someone must, as I'm sure you know."

Allender did know. To carry the black bowl was a Chinese expression describing being a fall guy. "But you are China's preeminent diplomat," he said. "You will be all right, I think."

"Perhaps," the ambassador said, finishing his whiskey. "But if we find out that someone did engineer this little disaster, and specifically which official, that person will *not* be all right."

"Quite understandable," Allender purred. He indicated the ambassador's empty glass. "Another, Excellency?"

The ambassador leaned forward. "Have you been listening to me, Mister Assistant Director?" he hissed.

This time Allender did take off the glasses. A woman at one of the adjacent tables who'd been trying to eavesdrop started, spilling her wine. Allender put some fire into his stare. The ambassador blinked despite himself, but, to his credit, did not look away.

"*Listen,* Mister Ambassador?" Allender said, softly. "I am a psychiatrist. I am a professional listener. Do you wish to unburden yourself? Do you have terrors that visit you in the night? I ask, because for a high-ranking diplomat, you do seem to talk a great deal."

The ambassador's eyed flared in anger, but he pretended to ignore the insult. Words formed at the edge of Allender's mind. "Yes, yes, I know," he said. "I am being extremely insolent."

This time it was the ambassador who started, hearing the words he had been about to speak. He leaned back in his chair, took a deep breath, and composed himself, but Allender saw that his right hand was trembling ever so slightly. Seeing the ambassador's frightened face, two of his minders had actually stepped into the dining room, discarding any attempt to look inconspicuous now.

"I thank you for this opportunity to speak to you," the ambassador intoned, formally. "Perhaps we will meet again."

"I look forward to that honor," Allender said, putting his glasses back on, aware now that there were others who had been staring at his face. As the ambassador made his exit, Allender realized that he had been well and truly warned. He swore under his breath; he would have to file a report about this encounter. And then it occurred to him: How had the ambassador known he was here? Did they have eyes on him? Already?

That's what you get for playing spook, he reminded himself. On the other hand, the real spooks seemed to be pleased as punch. What could go wrong?

TWELVE

Everything, as it turned out. Allender got to his office at Langley at eight thirty to find one of McGill's aides waiting for him. The young man seemed agitated as he told Allender that the DDO wanted to see him as soon as he came in. Allender told him he'd be right along but first he needed a coffee.

"Um, sir, the DDO said—" the aide protested.

"As soon as I get a coffee, young man. I said I'll be right up, and I will. Is there anything else?"

The aide made a pained face, shook his head, and left. Allender got some coffee and then took the elevator up to McGill's office. Mc-Gill's secretary stood up to greet him with a sober face, ushered him right into McGill's office, and then firmly closed the door. Allender was surprised by McGill's appearance. The man looked as if he'd just come from a severe ass-chewing, and a messy one at that.

"Preston, my *dear* fellow," McGill began. "It appears we have a problem. A really serious problem, unfortunately."

"May I sit down?" Allender asked, and then sat down and had a sip of coffee.

McGill did not sit down. He stood looking out the window, his back to Allender, as if he was searching for the right words. Finally he turned around, and began pacing. "The director called this morning," he said. "Apparently the president, himself, called him and asked why the Agency had chosen this precise moment, just when some extremely delicate negotiations were ongoing between the US and China, to blow up the Chinese MSS station chief."

"I wonder why," Allender said. "Surely the director had briefed the president after the op went down."

"You don't understand, do you. I never briefed the director, so, no, the director did not brief the president, because the director didn't fucking *know* about it!"

"Oh, Carson," Allender asked, with as straight a face as he could muster. "Was that wise?"

McGill exploded. "Wise? *Wise?* It's been standard procedure, for Chrissakes, ever since Hingham took over. He is not an ops man. You know that. He's a political creature, and not a competent one at that. I never tell him about the serious stuff until *way* after the fact, and I saw no reason to do so with this op."

"So what's the problem?"

"Apparently the Chinese ambassador made a formal representation to the president, and then threatened to break off the talks. Now the president wants someone's head."

"Someone's getting ahead of himself," Allender said. "Who said *we* had anything to do with what happened to Chiang?"

McGill frowned and stopped pacing for a moment. "I might have admitted as much. The director back-footed me, calling direct like that. Normally he would have gone through Hank. As you know, Hank's much better at dealing with angry directors than I am."

"Why didn't he go through Hank?"

"Um, apparently he did. Unfortunately, Hank was also in the dark."

"You kept *Hank* in the dark, too? Good God, Carson, what were you thinking?"

"I was thinking that if this scheme of yours actually worked, Hank and the director would be so pleased that they'd forget about the fact that I hadn't pre-briefed them. As it is . . ."

Whoops, Allender thought. He suddenly thought he knew where this was heading, especially with McGill under the gun. He put down his coffee cup.

"Let me speculate on the resulting narrative," he said, barely controlling his anger. "The director told the president he didn't know anything about any of this. Then Hank Wallace tells the director *he* didn't know anything about this. Next outraged call came down to the DDO—that would be you—and you told the director you didn't know anything about this, either, other than that Chiang had shown his ass in a hotel here in town. You promised to get to the bottom of this ASAP and hold whomever was behind the Chiang debacle personally and professionally responsible. Am I close, Carson?"

McGill had the decency to blush. He turned back to the view out the windows, apparently unwilling, or unable, to face Allender. He cleared his throat. "I fessed up to Hank, and then Hank and I went to the director's office. It was not a pleasant session, as you could imagine. I was then dismissed. Hank remained behind."

"When are you leaving us?" Allender asked.

"*I'm* not," McGill said, and suddenly the "my dear fellow" tone of voice wasn't there anymore. "You are."

"You pinned this on me?"

"Well, no, not exactly. I told them I'd called you in because of your Oriental background and that you had agreed to concoct something truly destructive. I told them about our conversation in re my briefing Hank on what was coming. That you wouldn't tell me exactly what was coming, and that, for my sins, I let it run. All my fault for not keeping them properly informed. Your fault for not telling me exactly what you had planned. And to be candid, the new intelligence organization in our government is also a factor—if the director of the Agency were still the director of central intelligence, he would have known about the secret talks with China, and therefore *I* would have known about the secret talks. As it was, I didn't."

The ambassador isn't going to be the only one carrying a black bowl, Allender realized. "So the president wants a head, and you three have decided it will be mine?"

"Hank and I have consulted at length with the director," McGill said. "We feel that, in the best interests of the Agency, we must be able to tell the president that this was an *un*coordinated, and *un*authorized operation, conducted by someone spontaneously who saw an opportunity to damage the Chinese intel structure here in America, but who was outside of the operations world and therefore didn't know the rules about keeping the head-shed in the loop. And, that that person is no longer with us."

"Spontaneously," Allender said, not giving him an inch. "Nice touch, Carson."

McGill finally returned to his desk and sat down. "Since you are SES, you will be not be fired, per se. You'll be given the opportunity to seek early retirement."

"And if I don't?"

"Please, Preston, don't even go there."

"Funny, in a way," Allender said. "My meeting with the Chinese ambassador last night."

"You did *what*?!"

"It wasn't planned," Allender said. "More of a *spontaneous* opportunity. We happened to be in the same restaurant, and he wanted to practice his Mandarin, I suppose."

McGill was aghast and not pleased with Allender's sarcasm. "Good God, Preston. Do you know what this will look like to the White House?"

"Then it won't be early retirement, Carson," Allender said. "It will be a thirty years, time in service maxed out at my current grade of SES-2, retirement. You can hold off on the bonus until the end of the year, but it *will* be forthcoming. Plus, one more thing."

"This isn't supposed to be a negotiation, Preston. You're the one in trouble here."

"*We're* the ones in trouble here, Carson, or have you forgotten? I know the White House operator's number. Want some more excitement in your life?"

McGill blinked at talk of the White House operator's number. "What's the one more thing?" he asked petulantly.

"Sloan is to be protected. She gets her new face, *and* her bonus, *and* keeps her job with us unless someone can identify a clear and present danger to her as a result of her part in this clusterfuck."

McGill pretended to think about it. "You will not be able to keep your clearances," he said, finally. "That means you are finished with this business of ours. No consulting. No contracting. No think tanks."

"Oh, *no,* Br'er Fox," Allender said in mock dismay. "Not the briar patch. *Anything* but the briar patch."

McGill leaned back in his chair. "All right. Sloan will be protected."

"And rewarded," Allender said. "She did a superb job. It was management that screwed the thing up."

"All right, I agree."

"Then, you know what?" Allender said. "I'm good with it. For the record, I think your actions are craven in the extreme. I actually don't want to work here anymore."

"You can just leave it? Just like that? Walk away as if you'd never been here? Dragon Eyes? The scariest interrogator in the Company?"

Allender took off his glasses, rubbed his eyes for a moment, and then focused on McGill's uneasy face. "At some point, Carson, we all have to leave, and we all have to die, for that matter. Since we live and work in the dark, we'll all probably leave and die in the dark. But understand something: I can, from time to time, look into the minds of men and see or hear things. As you've acknowledged, it's what I'm famous for. If I detect the faintest hint of my name migrating onto *any*body's loose-end file, I will bring Armageddon. Are we clear, Carson?"

"See here, Allender," McGill protested. "I don't much like being threatened." He was trying for a brave face now, but not quite succeeding. No more "my dear Preston," either.

Allender leaned forward and intensified his stare. "Tell me, Carson," he said, softly. "Does your pancreas ever bother you?"

Almost despite himself, McGill touched his abdomen. He tried to speak, but it appeared that his throat suddenly had gone dry. His expression was one of incipient pain. Allender watched McGill make the inevitable association that most people make when they hear the word "pancreas," as in, pancreatic.

"Are we clear, Carson?" Allender asked again.

"Crystal," McGill squeaked.

"I'm going back down to my office," Allender said, putting his glasses back on. "You write me a memo, informing me that I'm being offered retirement under the terms we just discussed. *All* the terms. Put an acceptance signature line at the bottom. I want the director to sign it, and I want Hank Wallace to witness it. Then have it sent down to me."

He got up. "Oh, by the way," he added. "Make sure it tells me to whom I'm to turn over the records of my office. You know, the ones just chock-full of fascinating personnel insights on anyone of importance here at Langley? I'm sure you have someone in mind to replace me, yes?"

"Um," McGill began, but then stopped. Allender grunted. The DDO obviously hadn't thought that far ahead, but he, Preston Allender, had. If anyone made trouble for him down the pike, he could make Edward Snowden look like Snow White.

"Well, then," Allender said. "Color me gone. It was fun while it lasted."

The office door opened and McGill's secretary stepped in. "Doctor Allender," she announced. "If you're finished here, the director wants a word."

Allender looked back at McGill, who simply shrugged his shoulders and put a "beats me" expression on his face.

One of the director's admin aides was waiting for him in the anteroom. Allender followed him down the hall and into the director's outer office. He got to cool his heels for ten minutes before being summoned before the throne. J. Leverett Hingham was sitting with a large book in his hands at his enormous desk. He did not appear to be in a good mood. He didn't offer a chair, but rather launched right into an erudite tirade about just how much damage he, Preston Allender, had done to the heretofore developing détente between the United States and the People's Republic. That years of careful diplomacy had been undone in a single stroke by the debacle at the Wingate hotel. That the president himself was furious beyond words. Allender waited for him to take a breath before speaking.

"Mister Hingham, I did not launch this operation. I did not control it. The nucleus of the idea was mine, but I was principally—"

"I do not *care*," Hingham interrupted. "I have, no doubt, other people with whom I will be further sharing my thinking this morning. But *you*—of all people—you who were raised in China, speaks their language, understands their cultural foibles—you should have known better. Much better. You have done some real damage here, Doctor Allender. You're lucky we're just going to dismiss you. How *could* you?"

Allender had had enough. "It was actually pretty easy," he said. "We had the head of the Chinese security services here in Washington willing to put his head on a plate, all for the sake of a one-night stand. We have wrecked their espionage apparatus here in town, at least for a while. As far as I'm concerned, it was a brilliant piece of counterespionage. *That's* how I could do it. It's supposedly what we're here for, Mister Hingham. To protect our democracy against the likes of the Chinese Communist Party."

"You do display an amazing ignorance of the bigger picture, Doctor," Hingham hissed. "You're just another one of those 'old hand' troglodytes who are determined to continue this endless spy-versus-counterspy-versus-double-agent-or-maybe-even-a-triple-agent badminton game, all of this tit-for-tat while the currents of history and international power flow past your tinted windows. How can you people be so oblivious?"

Allender started to speak, but Hingham slammed that book down on his desk with an explosive report. "You speak of a democracy? Don't you know the inevitable fate of all democracies? They decline in eight steps: from bondage to spiritual faith; from spiritual faith to great courage; from courage to liberty; from liberty to abundance; from abundance to complacency; from complacence to apathy; from apathy to dependence; and from dependence back into bondage. And that was written in 1787. Every democracy in history has trudged through those eight steps, and America will be no exception, Doctor Allender. You think you won a victory. Your 'victory' is of no account whatsoever. Now get out of my office, my building, and my Agency."

As Allender made his way to the elevators, Hank Wallace's secretary, Caroline Haversham, intercepted him and asked if he had a moment to speak to the deputy. Allender wondered, What's one more? After his séance with Hingham, he was not in the mood for any more ass-chewing or grand lectures, but then he decided he should probably hear what Wallace had to say, if only because Hank Wallace was, by intellectual default, the senior spook in the game. Caroline gave him a sympathetic look, knowing he'd been in to see the director. She was more of an executive assistant than just a secretary, and Allender had known her for years and had always nurtured the relationship. Caroline knew many things and even more people.

When he entered Wallace's office, he was struck by the deputy's appearance: He looked much older than the last time he'd seen him. His eyes had a slightly hunted look to them.

"Doctor Allender," Wallace said, getting up to shake his hand. "What you did to that snake was positively brilliant."

"The Company has a funny way of showing its appreciation," Allender said. "And my lord Hingham was definitely not pleased."

Wallace asked him to take a seat. "You wouldn't be the first to fall victim to our DDO's Machiavellian sense of right and wrong. You could have avoided this by telling me about it."

"I realize that now, but McGill wouldn't let me talk to you, and I didn't trust him to not fuck the thing up, so I stuck with it."

"Good instincts," Wallace said. "But you've been here awhile, Doctor, and you should have known that he folded you into this scheme in order to protect himself should things go—how shall I put it—awry?"

"That thought crossed my mind, of course," Allender said. "But I actually believed he wanted me to gin up something really egregious because *his* people can rarely think out of the box. And, I believe I did."

"You surely did. And now this 'interesting' president of ours wants a head."

"The master of accountability and executive transparency himself?" Allender laughed. "How droll."

Wallace smiled. "Tell me," he said, "are you in a position to protect yourself should there be thoughts of eventual retaliation?"

"I've told Carson my terms, and that I want both your and the director's signature on the piece of paper that sends me out into the cold, cruel night. He seemed amenable to making those arrangements conform to my expectations. I just hope Hingham doesn't resist."

"Not to worry. He'll sign, but he'll never learn the terms, trust me. And he won't ask McGill because it was McGill who advised him to throw you under the bus; the least I can do is to give you a chance to avoid the rear wheels."

"And you?" Allender asked.

"I've been here a long time, Doctor. I'll do whatever it takes to ensure my position and the health of the Agency. If I can help you while maintaining that endeavor, I will."

Allender nodded. "The truth, for once," he said.

"The roof will probably fall right in," Wallace said. "But: I mean that. You're getting a bum deal, but I hope you'll look at this as taking one for the team. I appreciate that, and I absolutely applaud what you did to the general."

"Then I have a favor to ask," Allender said.

"What is that?"

"That you warn me if someone here in the building does decide to tie off any potential loose ends."

Wallace's eyebrows went up. "Honestly, Doctor, this isn't Moscow Center. We would *never* do such a thing. Mostly, because we're not that organized."

"Right," Allender said. "You'd contract it out. So will you warn me?"

"I will do that, Doctor, if only to prevent whatever insurance measures you've undoubtedly put in place from causing another firestorm right here in River City."

Allender smiled. "*I'm* not that organized, Mister Wallace, but given time, that might change, especially since I'm leaving here thinking that I didn't do anything wrong."

"And *we* did," Wallace said. "Unfortunately, your public dismissal is how we smooth the waters. And I have to tell you, directors come and go, just like administrations come and go. You might actually be back one day."

"Nevermore," Allender said.

"Never say never, Doctor," Wallace said. "Do you remember what the soothsayer told Caesar to beware of?"

"Yes, I do," Allender said.

"Good," he said, and then stood up. "Remember that phrase. And now, a grateful nation thanks you for your service to your country, and we sincerely regret the circumstances of your early retirement."

Allender was tempted to say, "Sure you do," but decided that would be pushing it. They were giving him everything he'd demanded. This was not the time to snatch defeat from the jaws of victory just for the pleasure of being a smartass.

THIRTEEN

Three hours later, Preston Allender walked out through the gleaming marble lobby of the headquarters building, escorted by no fewer than four security guards and one of McGill's aides. It was all acceptably dignified, and not some kind of perp walk. He'd turned over his pack of building passes, and, even more important, his Langley headquarters parking permit. Someone from the security division would come by later that afternoon to retrieve the secure telephony equipment from his house. HR owed him a packet of paperwork that would finalize his retirement from the federal senior executive service. He was amused to watch the reaction of people coming and going in the lobby. Word traveled fast in the headquarters building. "Dragon Eyes is out." He could almost hear the collective sighs of relief in certain offices.

He resisted the temptation to pat the memorandum folded into his coat pocket. He knew that, in reality, the Agency could always renege and then deny they'd ever agreed to anything. On the other hand, he wasn't too worried about that. The letter spoke mostly about retirement pay and benefits, a coded promise to protect Sloan, and his own acquiescence to taking early retirement in the "best interests of the Agency." There was no mention of black swans or Allender's part in creating one for the Chinese Ministry of State Security.

As he drove his elderly Mercedes out through the heavily defended gate complex, he resisted the temptation to lower his window and shout free at last! at the gate guards. He hadn't realized how tired he'd become of all this BS, aggravated by the growing certainty that, for the past several years, the Agency had been sweeping against an implacably hostile and rising tide and doing so in the interests of a government and people who didn't really care, unless it was in aid of preventing another demented religious nut from getting one through security.

He'd e-mailed Carol Mann, his own EA down at the Farm, with the news. She'd already heard, which for some reason made him laugh out loud, startling the office staff. Interestingly, she'd predicted that he'd be back, and sooner than he might realize, especially with a presidential election looming next year. Given the current administration and the prospects for any major changes, he told her his ever coming back was highly unlikely. She loyally bet him five bucks, and then informed him she was going to retire as well.

Once home he reached for the Scotch before he remembered that it was still early afternoon. And your problem is? his whiskey devil wanted to know. That was when it hit him: He was fifty-five years old, home from work and out of a job at two in the afternoon, and there wasn't a single soul he could talk to about it. Admittedly, it wasn't as if he'd soon be homeless—one of the advantages of staying a bachelor all those years was that there was no clutch of horrified dependents sitting in front of him this afternoon wondering what was going to become of them. The only times he'd even thought about money had been when the bank called to tell him that his direct-deposit checking account had reached its FDIC insurance limit. Again. But, still.

He stood by the front windows in his study, staring idly out at the people walking by on the sidewalk and the seemingly endless stream of traffic all going urgently somewhere and nowhere at the same time. Had he screwed up with his decision to remain an outlier all these

years? On balance, he didn't think so. In the course of vetting just
about everyone of consequence in Agency management over the past
twenty-five years, he'd seen just about everything that could possibly
go wrong in a person's career: the most unlikely people conducting
stupidly illicit affairs or living secret sex lives; middle-grade officials
struggling with huge money problems caused by gambling debts or a
prescription-medicine problem; the effect on an officer's performance
of a surprise divorce or a gravely ill spouse; the usual alcohol addic-
tions, or just the overwhelming financial burdens of having children
in an age where four years at even a public university left parents,
graduates, or both drowning in debt. His own career had given him
some deep insights into the expression that family is everything.

He'd felt he had much more in common with the Clandestine
Service operatives who had to come see him every time they rotated
back through Washington from an overseas assignment. Many of
them had given up on trying to maintain a marriage or even a special friend, given that their service required them to disappear for
months on end, often under deep cover, where homecoming meant
dropping your bags in a temporary rental or an Agency apartment
with all the hearth-and-home attributes of an empty double-wide.
Some of them did manage the double life, a spouse and maybe even
kids who became very independent people. Many these days didn't
even try, because anyone with half a brain knew that, to create a
middle-class family success story in contemporary America, it took
two full-time parents with really good jobs or careers for them to
even have a chance.

No, all things considered, he was right where he needed to be at
this juncture in his life. He could now literally do anything he wanted
to and not have to think about how that decision might impact anyone
else. He would have preferred to have gone out on his own initiative and not be forced to leave because of bungling at the top level
of the Company, but: What was the saying? No good deed goes un-
punished?

He'd had to leave because his op had succeeded beyond expectations. He'd hit one of the Agency's most dangerous enemies hard and where it counted. In these times of nonconfrontational, apologetic crypto-isolationism and multilateral diplomacy über alles, a sudden strike at one of the nation's most formidable enemies was apparently a major faux pas, so much so that he would not have been too surprised if the Chinese didn't approach him one day with an offer to join *them*. They were clever that way, the bastards. Plus they were always willing to indulge in something few Americans had ever mastered except possibly the Founding Fathers: They were willing to take a long, patient view.

Hell's bells, he thought. I think I will have that Scotch. It's not like anyone's going to call with an urgent problem.

Attaboy, his devil whispered approvingly. Why not two?

A little after nine, Melanie Sloan called from the West Coast. The tech division had retrieved their special phones and the Agency's computer terminal, so he had to remind her they were on an open line.

"I just heard," she said. "WTF, over?"

"How goes the nipping and snipping?" he asked, ignoring her question. "Like your new looks?"

"Right now I look like a raccoon accidentally mated with a woodchuck and then got run over," she said. "An ugly woodchuck, who's toying with an addiction to Blessed Mother hydrocodone. They asked if I wanted to become a black woman. Can you believe that?"

"Now there's a trick question if I ever heard one," he said. "On the other hand, the Chinese would never look twice at you—they're the original racists. Can they really do that?"

"Apparently someone in the Company developed an injection that can change the pigments in the body's largest organ."

"Hunh?"

"The skin," she said, triumphantly.

"Ri-i-ght," he said. "I knew that. A thousand years ago in med school. Can they reverse it?"

"Now who's asking trick questions?"

He laughed.

"What will you do now?"

"Still thinking and drinking," he said. "Early days."

"I've met some people who say they're important in the Hollywood scene," she said. "I'll bet they could find a use for those eyes of yours. You'd make a phenomenal vampire."

He laughed again. "I'm sure I would," he said. "But I've had a lifelong fascination with trees, or rather, the woods and veneers they produce. Some of them are so rare that I have the only specimens in this country."

"Cool," she said. "So—import-export? Artwork? Museums?"

"Try Washington decorators," he said, and this time she laughed.

"Oh, that's perfect," she said. "And lucrative, too. Would you travel?"

"Yes," he said. "I know a lot of people who spend time in faraway places. I can call in some favors, I think."

"I'll just bet you can," she said. "Need an assistant, Doctor?"

"I think they have plans for you, my dear," he said. Shit, he thought. My dear. I'm starting to sound like McGill.

"What kind of plans?"

"Discreet plans."

"Oh, right. Well, eventually I hope to be back in the land of guns and posers. Perhaps you can show me your etchings one evening."

"Veneers," he said, but smiled to himself. Etchings, indeed.

"What I said," she replied. "Keep well, Doctor. You never know when opportunity might knock. So to speak."

"I will do that, Melanie Sloan. But keep your eyes peeled, okay?"

"They've been peeled by professionals," she said. "Right now they're swollen shut, but I'll try. Who or what should I be watching for?"

"One of us, maybe?"

She had no answer for that, so he wished her well and said good-bye.

He felt a smidgen of regret, which surprised him. Listen to you, he said to himself. She's in her thirties. You're in your fifties. She's been trained in how to lay waste to an entire room full of unwitting men. You've been trained to scare people. How's that for a match?

II

THE RED SWAN

FOURTEEN

Melanie Sloan relaxed on the protected balcony of her new Washington condo with a glass of wine and a view of Rock Creek shimmering through the trees in the gorge behind the building. It was early evening. An amazing number of cars were running the Rock Creek Parkway five floors below. She'd invested every cent of her generous bonus, after taxes, of course, in buying the condo, which had two bedrooms, two full baths, a living room–dining room combination, a kitchen with a breakfast counter, and this delightful balcony. Twice a day it was filled with the hum of Washington's commuter frenzy down below, but the rest of the time it was as quiet as a tomb. Her neighbors were mostly retirees living on their government pensions. By nine thirty at night hers were probably the only windows still lit. She thought it was perfect. There were upscale markets only a few blocks away, underground parking, card security at the front doors and on the elevators, and even a twenty-four-hour concierge service that she couldn't afford.

The condo was a big step up from the Randy Towers and a far cry from the faceless Los Angeles suburb where she'd spent just over a year creating the new and improved Melanie Sloan. Having been whisked out of Washington literally on the night of Chiang's Big Surprise a year ago, she'd been dropped into the hands of the Agency's discreet plastic-surgeon group, kept on retainer for those occasions which demanded the complete reconstruction of someone's face either because of injury or, as in Melanie's case, a need for someone to morph facially into a brand-new person. The practice occupied a large, six-story medical-arts building at the edge of one of the movie-star neighborhoods north of the city. Various other medical practices operated out of the first two floors. The middle two floors consisted of one-bedroom apartments where patients who were in for a major siege of cosmetic surgery could stay until their faces healed sufficiently as to no longer frighten people. The surgical suites occupied the final two floors. It had been a long and surprisingly painful year, the first part of which had been a blur of time, powerful painkillers, and lots of tubes and lines.

She was only now able to say that she had just about managed to expunge the more uncomfortable parts from her memory. She'd been surprised to find that real cosmetic surgery was rarely done in one fell swoop but rather in a series of operations, some of which had to be done to recover from a previous surgery that had had an undesired effect. But they'd been good, really good, Hollywood good, as she reminded herself every time she looked in a mirror these days. She now looked enough like a young Grace Kelly that some older people at LAX had done double takes as she went through security.

The best news was that she'd kept her job at the Agency, especially after someone senior had seen her "graduation" pictures. What that job entailed she would find out tomorrow morning, but apparently it was going to be something based right here in Washington, just as Allender had predicted. She wondered if they'd send her to a reception at the Chinese embassy just to test the new face. She was confident she'd pass that test, but secretly wanted to go find Dragon Eyes and see if *he* recognized her. She still remembered those times when he'd verbalized the thought that she'd been about to speak, but she'd resisted the temptation to call him until she found out what

Langley wanted of her in her next posting. They'd forced him out, and she knew enough to realize that consorting with one of the Agency's more prominent exiles was not the way to begin a new assignment at headquarters. Still, she smiled to herself; she'd kept his home number.

Her first day back on the job found her sitting outside the office of the DDO himself at ten in the morning. She'd been assigned to the Office of the Director for administrative purposes and then told to call on the DDO at ten. She'd turned down an offer of coffee and was reading *The Washington Post* on her phone when the DDO's secretary called for her to go in. The inner office was expansive and decorated in a faintly British style with incandescent lighting only, rich rugs on the floor, and lots of brass accouterments. The chubby little man sitting behind the desk was apparently trying for the same effect, dressed as he was in light gray wool trousers, a tweed jacket, and a bow tie, and, inevitably, she thought, fooling with an ornate pipe.

"My good gracious," he exclaimed as Melanie entered. "That's phenomenal. How in the world do they do that?"

"With knives?" she said, stepping forward to shake hands. "I'm Melanie Sloan."

"You are when you're here within the fold," he said. "On the assignment we have waiting for you your name will be—" He checked a three-by-five card on his desk. "—Virginia Singer." He sat back down at his desk and indicated a chair for her. "I'd say you're absolutely safe from recognition."

"I don't recall meeting you before, Mister McGill."

"Oh, we haven't met, but Preston Allender showed me your picture. You were striking then and more so now, which is perfect for your next assignment."

"How is the good doctor?" she asked as innocently as she could. "Still scaring people with those vampire eyes?"

"I don't actually know, my dear," McGill said. "He retired after the black swan. I'm told he's doing something in the export-import world, of all things. Exotic wood veneers from equally exotic places. Childhood hobby he learned while growing up in Taiwan. Are you comfortably situated here in D.C.?"

"Yes, sir, I am, thank you, courtesy of that generous bonus."

"Oh, good," he said. "Smart way to invest it, too. So: Here's the program. I'm going to send you down to the Farm for some special training, something vaguely similar to what you did for the black swan. Once we see how that goes, I'll reveal your target and put you together with young Mister Smith again."

"Mister Smith," she said. "I remember him."

"Thought you might. Has anyone told you how much you look like Grace Kelly in her movie days?"

"One or two," she replied. "I had several choices of faces, but that one jumped out at me, I have to admit. I never saw her in person, of course. Long before my time."

"Mine too, unfortunately, but I have seen her movies. The good news is that no one could mistake you for Melanie Sloan. The bad news is that no one will forget your face once they've seen it."

"Then this will be a one-time deal?"

"Clever girl," he said, silently clapping his hands. "*Very* clever girl. That's *just* what I meant."

He must have pushed a button under the desk somewhere, because the office door opened and the secretary called her name. Melanie told McGill it had been a pleasure and then left the office. McGill's secretary sent her down to the travel office to set up her stint at the Farm. On the way down she realized that McGill might be contemplating yet another black swan. Except: That program had supposedly been extinguished after what they'd done to General Chiang. She knew she'd have to be careful here; what had happened to Allender could well happen to her. Then she realized that the likelihood of losing everything increased as a function of how well the upcoming op went. Wasn't that just perverse! Welcome back.

Two days later she went in for her first day of mission training at the Farm. She'd been told to report to Gabrielle Farrell in a branch euphemistically called Applied Physiology. Farrell turned out to be a hard-bitten-looking woman in her early fifties who was dressed in a severe gray pantsuit and wearing shoes that looked a lot like men's brogues. Her hair was cropped short and she wore no jewelry of any kind. She had slightly protruding eyes that made it look like she was glaring and a surprisingly deep voice. She took Melanie to her private office and closed the door.

"Did they tell you anything about the mission?" she asked as she sat down behind her desk and pointed Melanie into a chair.

"Nope," Melanie said. "The DDO told me to come down here for training, and that's about it."

"Carson McGill, himself, told you that?" the woman asked in a challenging tone.

"Yes," Melanie said.

"What division do you work out of at Langley?"

"The director's office," Melanie said, wondering now why this woman seemed to be angry with her.

"Oh, great," Farrell snorted. "Another goddamn prima donna from Hingham's 'special branch.' Funny how all the really pretty girls end up in the director's office."

Melanie rolled her eyes and got up to leave but Farrell just laughed. "Hold your horses, sweet cheeks," she sneered. "If this mission folder is accurate, you better get some thicker skin than that. Sit down."

Melanie thought about it for a moment. She wasn't going to put up with some kind of plebe-year indoc bullshit from this dyke or anyone else.

"Please?" Farrell said in a grating voice. "We haven't even started yet and right now you're wasting my time."

"I think we're even, then," Melanie said.

This time Farrell really did glare. "Repeat after me, Virginia Singer or Melanie Sloan or whatever the fuck your name is: I am a lesbian."

Melanie was taken aback. "I am *not* a lesbian," she replied.

"Got shit in your ears, baby-cakes? Repeat after me: I am a lesbian."

"I am most definitely *not* a lesbian."

"But you're gonna be," Farrell said, softly. "If you're gonna do *this* mission. That's why you're here, and that's why *I* will be your training supervisor, because I most definitely do play for the other side."

Melanie was surprised. This was as bad as Dragon Eyes casually telling her to disrobe. A *lesbian,* for God's sake? Farrell watched her absorb the news.

"You don't have to look so disgusted," Farrell said. "Lesbians have to get their licks in, too, sometimes."

After three seconds, Melanie burst out laughing despite herself and then saw Farrell grinning back at her.

"Let's start over, shall we?" Farrell said. "Welcome to the Farm's hall of mirrors. When we're done with you you're going to be just as good an actress as the one you look like. Call me Gabby."

Melanie's introduction to the curriculum of the Applied Physiology Department came thirty minutes later when she accompanied Gabby to a lecture in the department's small auditorium. There were six attendees, five men and herself. She deduced that the lecturer was an Englishman as soon as he began speaking. He was also the poster child for the effete world of Old Boy public school graduates, tall and willowy, complete with supremely languid gestures, a broad Oxbridge accent, just a little too much hair, and a three-piece suit that fairly shouted bespoke. His subject was the television miniseries *Brideshead Revisited,* and in particular, the character portrayed by the actor Nickolas Grace, called Anthony Blanche in the show. He showed a few scenes from the series, where Blanche manages to outrage just about everyone within visual range with his bombastic homosexual antics.

"There's 'out-there,' and then there's '*out* there,'" the lecturer drawled. "No one encountering *An*tony, as he pronounced the name, would have any doubt whatsoever that *here* was most definitely a *queer*. And yet, many at Oxford back in the twenties and thirties would have simply smiled and said, So what? Remember, the author of the book was Evelyn Waugh, himself a homosexual when even *being* a homosexual was a crime in England. Anthony Blanche outed in a pub in the East End of London would have been found headless in the Thames by morning. At Oxford, he was just another self-promoting eccentric and his homosexuality was of *zero* consequence.

"So: How does Anthony Blanche bear on what you will learn here in the Department of Applied Physiology? I've been told that you are operatives who are going to have to adopt a homosexual cover in order to meet your objectives. One would think that the easiest way to do such a thing is to employ actual homosexuals, but apparently, that's not an option. Here's the thing. Most people who are gay are pretty much indistinguishable from people who are not gay. Except, some of the time other homosexuals can sense that another person is gay. The term of art is 'gaydar,' a semimythical sixth sense that allows a gay person to detect, as it were, that another person is one of 'them.' It is hardly infallible, but an awful lot of gay people believe in it. So, if you are *not* gay, and are going to pose as someone who *is* gay, then you will need to explore the phenomenon of gaydar, and we will show you how.

"Now if one ran into Anthony Blanche, as amazingly depicted by the openly gay actor, Nickolas Grace, one would not need gaydar, would one. But recall the scenes I showed you: Charles Ryder encountering Anthony Blanche. Was Charles gay? Waugh hints at it in one of the chapters, where he has Sebastian Flyte comment that 'we sunbathed naked on the rooftops of the estate, and we were at times, wicked, very wicked, indeed,' or words to that effect. Recall that Charles Ryder and Sebastian were close friends, but it was more of a case of the young and relatively impoverished Ryder being swept into the decadent orbit of the obscenely rich Lord Sebastian Flyte, whose house measured thirty-two thousand square feet, not counting the wings, situated on three thousand acres of lawns and gardens. And yet their friendship, patron to hanger-on, was not really depicted as a gay situation, nor would Ryder's classmates have assumed that. It was more a whiff of something going on behind closed doors than overt sexual display. That's what you're going to be exposed to.

"The second thing you will learn here is how to avoid the inevitable 'proof of purchase.' If you've been masquerading as a gay person and your target calls the question, as it were, what do *you* do? We will teach you what to do, what to say, and how to get out of actually consummating a homosexual relationship, unless of course you want to, although I would assume the Agency has its own version of gaydar, what?"

There were some uncomfortable sniggers in the tiny audience.

"Now: I work for British counterintelligence. We have had some sad experiences with gay people in our organization. Historically, to be outed, found out, or compromised as a homosexual in the intelligence business led to blackmail or worse. Nowadays, the more enlightened elements of the Great Game would say: Not so much. Or, as the privileged boys at Oxford would have said: Who cares? That said, in certain parts of the world being *accused* of homosexuality gets you thrown from the roof of a six-story building. Don't let so-called modern and enlightened views of gender equality—the end of the he-she-it labels—lull you into a complacent view of the danger associated with this particular label. Let's watch some more movies."

At the end of the lecture, Melanie accompanied Gabby back to her office.

"What'd you think of that?" Gabby asked as she handed Melanie a bottle of water. "And, by the way, I'm going to call you Virginia because that's going to be your name in this op."

"No fucking way, is my first reaction," Melanie said. "My first op of this sort they wanted me to vamp a Chinese general. I give good vamp. But the physical realities of a lesbian relationship just leaves me cold. No offense, Gabby—this isn't some religious bias."

"None taken, Virginia," Gabby said. "What sort of men do you prefer? I know that's personal but I need to know."

"Older men. Sophisticated, interesting men, men who're amusing, like to have fun, and who are not on the hunt for a wife and kids."

"Is there anyone now we have to think about?"

Melanie smiled. "There's one but he's well out of reach, I think. I may make a play one day, but . . ."

"Somebody in the Company, perhaps?"

"Not anymore," Melanie said.

"Okay, then here's what we need to do with you. You've had a facial remake and it's drop-dead gorgeous. In the pantheon of sexual objects, unattainability can be a serious amplifier of desire, as in the millions of young men who fell in love with Grace Kelly—fancy that!—after seeing a couple of her movies. She seems to be the perfect woman, thanks to the gallons of illusion they pour over the silver screen. In our world, *my* world, however, that phenomenon is just a bit different. The most exciting game of all is when we meet another woman who *doesn't* know she harbors latent homosexual desires. She's beautiful, sweet, nice, friendly, soft, a little demure, possibly a bit fragile, and not the least bit gay. But like those Grace Kelly fans, *we* can imagine the possibility of softly enveloping the dear little thing and introducing her to her *real* role in life."

"Okay, I get that," Melanie said.

"Good, because that's what we're going to teach you how to be, with perhaps just a fillip of discreet tease included."

"And also that bit about how to avoid the inevitable 'proof of purchase,' right?"

"Of course, my dear. Of course."

FIFTEEN

Preston Allender, sole proprietor of the Birnam Woods Import Company, escorted a breezy young decorator to the front door of the house.

"It's for Corinda Wadley," the young man gushed. "So, of course, it has to be special *and* unique."

"Of course," Allender said, fighting an urge to roll his eyes. He had no idea who Corinda Whazzit was, but obviously she was an architectural trend-setting goddess of some kind, one of many in this town of superheated egos. "I can guarantee the 'unique' part; the trees that produce that wood grow on the quiet side of a single volcano on Java. An entire wall paneled in that will absolutely be one of a kind. Think amber room."

"*Per*fect," the decorator said. "Michaela Valentine told me to contact you; she said if anybody could come up with a one-of-a-kind it would be you."

"Let me know the precise square footage plus your craftsman's wastage estimate and I'll put things in motion," Allender said, as they shook hands and the decorator left.

Allender went through to his tower study and made some notes on what he needed to acquire. It had been over a year since he'd left the Agency, and he'd found the perfect endeavor to pursue. His father, who'd hailed originally from Northern California, had long been a woodworking enthusiast. Living in Taipei, he'd discovered the amazing world of Asiatic trees and their exotic woods. Allender could still remember sitting in his father's woodworking shop in the back of the family compound, with the scent of perfumed veneers taken from trees in Java, Burma, Japan, and Malaysia permeating the air, while his father turned sheets of gleaming wood from skinned tree branches.

His father would take him along on his expeditions out into Asia's jungles in search of exotic trees. He would also collect rough-cut gemstones, such as unpolished rubies in Burma and blocks of jadeite along the coastal villages of Indochina. From Japan he accumulated a netsuke menagerie crafted from Borneo rosewood and ivory, and from Hong Kong a Qing dynasty chess set made entirely of exquisite white jade. His parents slowly sold off the jewelry collection to fund their own retirement years; the exotic-wood specimen collection, however, was never sold, and Preston still had the bulk of it stored in his town house basement. With his parents now gone, he still liked to take a Scotch downstairs and ruminate through the drawers of gorgeous veneers stored between sheets of rice paper. The most expensive and rare woods were kept in a walk-in vault, built during the Second World War by a previous owner. The vault was twelve square feet, with concrete walls two feet thick and containing six large safes.

With literally nothing to do after being forced out at the Agency and the usual postgovernment jobs proscribed to him he'd decided to resume his passion for acquiring beautiful veneers from faraway places. He traveled mostly into Asia, where his Mandarin gained him admittance to the more selective markets. The idea to turn his hobby into a business had come when he'd had some of the rooms in his own town house refurbished. He'd wanted to panel one of them in a spiral-grained walnut, but couldn't find anyone who could actually supply the veneers in a size suitable for paneling. He'd asked his neighbors on one side, both decorators, and one of them observed that someone could make a fortune in Washington if he could provide veneers like that. Birnam Woods was born a month after.

Finding the wood wasn't that difficult. Getting through all the import restrictions brought on by environmentalist groups was. Allender knew ways and means of getting exceptions from the ever-expanding regulations and special licenses by enlisting the aid of people he knew on the Hill. At the supply end in Asia, of course, all it took was money for the product and the occasional well-directed bribe.

The phone rang as he was enjoying a Scotch while perusing his order book. It turned out to be a staffer in Carson McGill's office. Could Doctor Allender come out to a meeting at Langley first thing in the morning? He asked the caller why. That briefly stumped the staffer, who could only come up with a rather lame "Because he told me he wanted to see you first thing in the morning? Sir?"

He told the flustered young man to inform Mr. McGill that he was busy tomorrow morning, and then hung up. McGill himself called back five minutes later.

"My dear Preston," he said, in an exasperated voice. "Don't be an ass."

"I have things to do tomorrow morning, Carson, and Agency business is no longer my concern, remember?"

"Yes, yes, I know that. I still need to talk to you, and I need to do so in a secure environment. I'm the acting deputy director, now, by the way."

"Well, *good* for you," Allender said.

"How's your little ex-im scheme working for you these days, Preston? No problem getting federal licenses or anything like that? No EPA queries on whether those precious veneers of yours are sustainably farmed?"

"Fuck off and die, Carson," Allender said, mildly, and then put the phone down. Officious little prick, he thought. Come see me or

I'll call Commerce and get them to claw back your licenses? He snorted in disgust. His first response had been the correct response.

The next morning when Allender came down for coffee, however, he groaned when he spied a black Suburban with tinted windows sitting out in front of his house. Another one was parked across the avenue. He shook his head, went to the kitchen, fired up the coffeemaker, and made two cups of coffee, which he took to his study. He then went to the front door and opened it. A minute later Carson McGill was sitting uncomfortably in an antique Victorian wing chair as if he had a broomstick up his grommet.

"Okay," Allender said. "Since you went to all this trouble, why are you here?"

"I'll get right to it," McGill said. "Hank Wallace is dead."

Allender blinked as he absorbed this news. "What happened?"

"We have no goddamned idea, is the short answer," McGill said. "He didn't come in to work, so his EA went out to the house in McLean and found him sitting in his study, in a recliner, wearing PJs, bathrobe, and slippers, eyes wide open and deader'n a doornail."

"Who'd the EA call?"

"Me, of course," McGill replied.

"Oh, right," Allender said.

"Yes," McGill sighed, ignoring the sarcasm. "Naturally. The cause of death is officially 'undetermined.' Autopsy revealed *no* causative mechanisms. No trauma, no toxicology vectors, organic disease. There were no signs of forced entry. No evidence that anyone else had been in the room. Nothing moving on the security cameras. No houseguests. According to the housekeeper, nothing out of place."

"When did this happen?" Allender asked. "I've seen nothing in the news."

"Two weeks ago," McGill said. "We've kept it clamped down. That's why I'm now the acting deputy director, by the way."

"Who else?" Allender said.

"In any event, the Agency decided to keep it close-hold until we could determine what happened. Or at least that's what I tried to do."

"Meaning?"

"Meaning that *the* director, in his unending quest for bureaucratic transparency and fair play, told our best friend in Congress, Congresswoman Martine Greer, who immediately asked the *Bureau* to conduct an investigation."

Allender grunted. The Bureau. The enduring enmity between the FBI and the Agency was legendary throughout the Washington bureaucracy, a fact of which the chairwoman of the House Permanent Select Committee on Intelligence was undoubtedly, and happily, quite aware.

"They getting anywhere?"

"They are not," McGill said, giving Allender a meaningful look. "In fact they've asked for some help. From us. Actually . . ."

"No, thank you," Allender said quickly. "I'm retired, remember? I distinctly remember doing that. Retiring. In your office. Harsh words and everything, yes? And all at *your* initiative."

McGill raised his hands to forestall any further protests. "The Bureau has formally requested that the Agency assign a senior liaison officer to their investigation team. I want you to do it."

"Good grief, Carson. Don't you think they want someone who's still in service and not some guy who was forced out and doesn't even have his clearances anymore?"

"Actually," Carson said. "they will recognize that this is a great idea. An active-duty Agency officer would always have *two* masters—his boss back at the Agency, and the Bureau's team leader. A retired officer, on the other hand, could work exclusively for her."

"Her?"

"Yes, her name is Rebecca Lansing."

"If she believes that, she must be pretty new in town," Allender observed.

McGill laughed. "Indeed," he said. "She's actually one of Hingham's pets, seconded a year ago to the Bureau headquarters. Basically, I suspect that the older hands at the Hoover Building fell all over themselves ducking this tasking. She apparently zigged when she should have zagged. If it's any help, she's quite attractive."

"Wait a minute," Allender protested. "If she's an Agency cross-deck, then what the hell do they need a another liaison officer for? Isn't that why she's there in the first place?"

"Why she's there is known only to J. Everett," McGill said. "I don't know her background, other than that she'd recently completed three years as the Company officer on a joint antiterror task force out in LA at the FBI field office. She's probably one of Hingham's famous 'dark' sources. Is that coffee for me?"

Allender handed over the second coffee. McGill took a sip and then his face brightened. "Excellent," he said. "To be candid, we're not exactly enthusiastic about having Buroids under our feet. I think they want a second liaison officer so that they can spread the blame when they come up empty-handed."

"Exactly what I would think, too," Allender said. "So, are we done here?"

"Well," McGill said, ignoring him again. "I talked to His Lordship, himself, just this morning. Told him I wanted to bring *you* back in for this one."

Allender grunted. "I'll bet he just broke wind with joy at that proposition," he said.

McGill smiled. "You're half right," he said. "Between you, me, and the gatepost, I think he agreed in order to give you the opportunity to step in something so that he could fire you all over again."

"Sounds about right," Allender said. "So tell me: Why would *you* want *me* to get into this mess?"

"Because we think Hank Wallace was running a swan," McGill said.

Allender stared at him for a moment. "You've *got* to be shitting me."

"Not one pound, unfortunately," McGill replied.

"But I would have assumed that that program's long dead."

"And that's what I thought, too."

Allender thought for a moment. "Okay," he said. "Let's review the bidding: Since that program was supposedly terminated when *I* left, it seems to me that you've got two problems. First, what happened to Hank, and, second, how did a cauterized program come back to life without *your* knowledge, O Great DDO?"

McGill sighed as he leaned back in his chair. He took off his glasses and began to rub his eyes. Allender remembered this routine, too, and could almost predict the speech that McGill was about to crank up. Sometimes in the course of human events . . .

"Spare me," he said, before McGill could get up a head of steam. "I'll reluctantly lend a hand, but I'll want a signed contract. From the director. Clearances as necessary, and, of course I *must* know the identity of the swan."

"I can get you all the paper cover you need," McGill said. "Clearances, access, pay, and allowances, but not the operative who was going to initiate the swan."

"Carson," Allender began, but McGill raised his hand.

"We don't know who he or she is," he said, quietly.

Allender stared. "Wow," he said, finally.

"Yeah," McGill said. "Wow."

"How is this possible?" Allender asked. "You were still DDO when Hank cranked this up, correct?"

McGill flushed. "Yes, I was. Still am, actually. Double-hatted."

"Because when you and I ran a swan, I had a boatload of support from your ops people. Controller Smith, central-casting prop managers, a top-tier team, and even a pet hotel. You're telling me Hank got all that without your hearing about it?"

"Don't rub it in, Preston," McGill said. "But, apparently, yes to all of the above."

"Damn!" Allender said. For a moment he even sympathized with the portly DDO. Then reason returned. "Well," he said. "That means someone in your organization went around you. *Way* around you. That's where you need to start, not with the Bureau. And not with me, either."

"Trust me, Preston, I'm well ahead of you there."

"Then what the hell do you want *me* to do?"

"Frustrate the goddamned FBI, of course. Lead them on every kind of wild-goose chase you can imagine. You're a shrink—you can do that. Baffle them with bullshit. Lay down hints of dark deeds and sinister plots, and then seduce them into chasing down every fucking one of them. They're a bunch of robots, for Chrissakes. Give 'em the dragon-eyes treatment. Do whatever it takes to give *us* time to figure out what the *fuck* Hank Wallace was up to."

Allender didn't know what to say that could get him out of this one. McGill's vulgar language indicated how upset he was. "And you have *no* ideas?" he asked.

"One," McGill admitted. "And, truth in lending, it's not my idea. It's the director's."

"I'm all ears," Allender said.

"It's something to do with Martine Greer."

Allender closed his eyes. Holy shit, he thought. We talked about this a long time ago. Carson, you idiot. Run, he thought. Run. Now.

McGill read his thoughts. "Full active-duty pay," he said. "The Bureau will treat you as an SES-2; you know how rank-conscious they are. You will report to me and me alone. I'll assign a security detail and a car."

"No."

"Please, Preston. I know we can't really make you do this, but you offer some special—skills that I think this problem will need. And besides, I think somebody killed Hank. We have to know who that somebody was, but we have to find out *our* way."

Allender took off his glasses and treated McGill to as cold a look as he could manage. McGill was clearly uncomfortable with that look, but this morning he was being terribly brave. "That somebody probably speaks Mandarin," Allender said.

"Yes," McGill said. "And so do you. Please?"

Allender felt a black weight descending onto his shoulders. "Carson," he said. "They're not dopes over there in the Hoover Building. They'll recognize a stall when they see one."

"Our feeling is that they'll be so busy trying to figure you out that they won't recognize a stall."

"Who's working it for the Agency?"

"If you don't know, you can't tell," McGill said. "It's not that we don't trust you—just standard compartmentalization. The important thing is that our people will know who you are and why you're working with the Bureau."

"Is there an autopsy report?"

"Yes, and the Bureau has a copy."

"Who did the autopsy?"

"The Borgias," McGill replied, obviously getting tired of answering questions. Allender wondered when McGill would recognize that *he* was being stalled.

"The Bureau's lab is the best there is, when they're not cooking the books. Why the Borgias?"

"The Borgias" was the in-house nickname for the Agency's poison laboratory, which was part of the Chemical, Biological, and Radiological Weapons Department. "Because the autopsy revealed no apparent cause of death," McGill said.

"Couldn't he have just—died? He's what—sixty-something? Smokes? Drank like a fish, from what I was told."

"All of those vices—booze, tobacco, old age, sexual perversion— leave traces. A heart attack leaves traces. A stroke leaves traces. What the hell, Preston: You're a doctor—there were no fucking traces!"

"You still have the remains?"

"No," McGill said. "He was a lifetime bachelor, like you, no surviving relatives, so we had the remains cremated after the examination.

We did save tissue samples, of course, in case someone comes up with a viable theory."

"What if the Bureau comes up with a viable theory?"

"Report it."

"What if *I* come up with a viable theory?"

"Report it, but only to me. But theories aren't your brief, Preston. The big stall. That's your brief."

"This is beginning to sound as if you *know* someone in the Agency had a hand in this little whodunit."

McGill got up, his coffee unfinished. "Now you're catching on, Preston." He looked at his watch. "I must go," he said. "Logistics to follow. I've told the Hooverites to expect you tomorrow at ten o'clock."

"Everyone in the Hoover Building is at his desk and urgently leaning forward by seven thirty in the morning," Allender said.

"Set the precedent on the first day, Preston," McGill advised. "You're a senior liaison officer from another agency, not a Buroid temp. If they're all in at seven thirty, then they should be well prepared to brief you by the time you arrive. At ten. It's kinda like what old wives tell new wives: Don't do anything in the first week of marriage that you don't want to do for the rest of your married life."

The next morning, Allender surveyed his new office and wondered who'd been kicked out of it on short notice. He'd been delivered to the Hoover Building in an Agency car and met at the main entrance by an athletic-looking young man with a shaved head and a friendly greeting. His building passes were ready except for a picture. The ID tech asked him to remove his glasses, and Allender obliged. After a moment the tech said he could go ahead and put them back on. Then he took the picture. Once they were on the third floor, the agent had shown him where the bathrooms and the elevators were and warned him that the elevators were unreliable and the bathrooms something of an embarrassment. He then told him that Supervisory Special

Agent Rebecca Lansing would be down shortly to meet him and give him an in-brief.

There was neither a computer nor a secure telephone in the office, but McGill had promised him both would be supplied from the Agency, the Bureau's comms equipment being notoriously antiquated. The office was spacious enough but shabby. In fact the whole building was shabby, victim of ten years of budgetary neglect while the General Services Administration tried to decide where to build a new headquarters. The GSA had been getting lots of help and advice from the competing congressional delegations of Maryland and Virginia, who were desperate to acquire the eleven thousand federal taxpayers who staffed Bureau headquarters.

"Doctor Allender?" a voice said from behind him. He turned to find an attractive if somewhat stern-looking woman standing in the office doorway. She was in her late thirties, with black hair, an enticing figure modestly dressed in a dark pantsuit, and lovely blue-green eyes. "I'm Rebecca Lansing. I'm running the Wallace case."

She offered a handshake and he took it, which was not his usual custom at all. She indicated that he should sit at the desk and then she took one of the two armchairs parked in front of the desk. She pulled out a gold-plated NRA bullet pen and a notebook.

"Before I start filling you in, can you tell me what your area was at the Agency?"

He nodded. "I was in the training business," he replied. "I trained our interrogators and what you would call our profilers. I also conducted annual interviews with management staff to assess their emotional and intellectual capacity to continue in their present positions."

"May I ask what qualified you to do those things?" For a brief moment he started to take offense to that question, but then realized she hadn't asked it in any sort of "what makes you so special" manner.

"I'm a psychiatrist, for one," he replied. "I also have some small ability to seize control of or manipulate an individual's emotions once I have him or her under suitable duress."

"Are you a mind reader, then?" she asked with a completely straight face, as if mind readers were a common occurrence.

"Most of the time I am not," he said.

"Most of the time."

He smiled but did not reply.

"Oka-a-y," she said. "Did Mister McGill tell you what's happened?"

"Only that someone found the Agency's deputy director, Hank Wallace, dead in his study, and that there's been no apparent cause of death or manner of death determination, either by the Agency or by the Bureau's review of the autopsy. That's about it."

"Are you familiar with homicide investigations?"

"No," he said. "Nor was I aware that the Bureau did homicide investigations."

She nodded. "Normally we don't. We assist local police authorities, when asked, or if we think the incident bears on something bigger. And I guess that's my next question for you: Is there something bigger going on here? Something that would provoke the chairwoman of the House Permanent Select Committee on Intelligence to inject the Bureau into what looks an awful lot like an Agency goat-grab?"

He smiled. "It's possible, Special Agent—is that the proper form of address, by the way?"

"Langley told us that they brought you back on active service as an SES-2. That means I may call you 'sir,' and you can call me anything you'd like. Rebecca, if you wish, Supervisory Special Agent Lansing if you must."

"Okay, Rebecca," he said. "I've been retired for just over a year. Once someone like me leaves the Great Game we just go, and that's that, as it should be. So I'm not sure what's behind Martine Greer's request, either from an operational or a bureaucratic perspective. It could just be devilment. According to McGill, *I'm* here because *you* asked for a senior liaison officer."

At that moment a young man arrived with Allender's completed building pass and a set of FBI credentials, minus the golden badge.

"It's just that we didn't expect a senior executive service officer," she said, once the young man left. "I was thinking more like assistant division head. Someone who knows who's who in the zoo, but not a boss."

He studied her for a moment. "Did *you* volunteer," he asked, "to head up this task force, assuming that's what it's called?"

"No," she said. "I was assigned by the FBI director's office to run it."

"And could that possibly have been because every other senior agent within shouting distance had already made it to high cover?"

She smiled. "It's possible," she replied, echoing his own answer.

"May have been a similar situation over at Langley," he said. "So, when everybody else has managed to slip the trap, Langley resorted to getting a retiree, a senior one. He's got nothing to lose, careerwise. Even better, he'll be your asset and not the Agency's because no one over there in Langley wants to touch this one."

She nodded but didn't say anything.

"Why'd you want another liaison officer, anyway?" he asked. "There's already a liaison office here for that, isn't there?"

"Actually," she said. "Truth-in-lending time. I'm really with the Agency."

"Sure you are."

"Yes, I am. I'm a special projects officer in Director Hingham's office. I am the unlisted, if you will, Agency liaison officer at the Bureau headquarters. There's another person in the Hoover Building who is the 'public' CIA liaison officer, but I work out of the FBI deputy director's office, where I do compartmented tasking, like this little cluster. Before that I was out in LA, doing pretty much the same thing with the LA field office, except there I was out in the open.

The Bureau has these intel fusion centers in their bigger field offices. I led a team of three operators on their antiterror task force."

"My, my," Allender said. "And before that?"

"One low-level posting overseas in the CS."

"And then, *two* exchange assignments with the Bureau?"

"The Agency sometimes doesn't know what to do with their female officers, especially one tied to Hingham. I think there's a bit of old-guard mistrust involved. You know, spies are supposed to be men, not women."

"As everyone well knows," he said.

She smiled. "Yeah, but. It suits me, though. Working at Langley was getting boring. Everybody my age was much more focused on getting ahead than getting the bad guys. I like working with the G-men—and women. They're serious about the job at hand. Anyway, Director Hingham wanted this one compartmentalized from regular channels, so I was directed to 'volunteer,' to the sound of much applause over here, I must admit. Besides, if Wallace's death was a hit, that would be a really big deal and the Bureau would have an interest."

"Yes, it would," Allender said, remembering McGill's use of that same term. "So: What do you want from me?"

"Senior-level access. I can do the worker-bee-level stuff. Keep us from spinning our wheels."

"I can certainly do that," he said. "But you do realize the Agency's got a team working this incident, too, right? Who would probably be delighted if you spun your J. Edgar wheels right off?"

She cocked her head to one side and just looked at him for a moment. "So," she said, but then apparently changed her mind about what she'd been about to say. She asked a question instead: "Is it true you were called Dragon Eyes when you were still serving?"

"Never to my face, Rebecca," he replied, softly. "So when do I get to meet the rest of the team?"

SIXTEEN

At the end of his first day among the First Team, Allender went out the front entrance to find a black Expedition waiting for him. He got into the backseat only to discover that Carson McGill was sitting in the right front seat.

"Honey, I'm home," Allender announced, and McGill snorted. He told the driver to drive down to the Mall. When they neared the World War II memorial, the car stopped. They got out and went for a walk.

"What do they know?" he asked.

"Not much," Allender said. "They never saw the scene, the body, or a CSI report, and if I'm not mistaken, they don't have a clue as to what to do next."

"Good," McGill said. "I was hoping that's what you'd find."

"There is the slightest possibility that they know they're being fucked with."

"Of course they do," McGill said. "That's why I'm going to provide you with a list of names. These are supposedly people who've gotten across the breakers with Wallace over the years. Some people he fired, some others who wanted his job but were outmaneuvered, two women who accused him of sexual harassment, and a guy who claimed Wallace was working for another intelligence service. Some are still active, some retired. The guy who accused him of being a spy is 'missing.'"

"Any merit to any of those accusations?"

"The women, possibly. Hank was a hands-on kinda guy when it came to pretty women. Grew out of it once he became Deppity Dawg, or so I was told."

"And you want me to hand this list over to the Bureau team?"

"Yup," McGill said. "Give them some bones to gnash. They're good at investigating people, and it fits: who else would have a motive, *if* it was a homicide."

"You think it was a homicide?"

McGill shrugged. "Our lab people say that the absence of *any* evidence of what might have killed him suggests that something seriously occult did the deed. They're talking to the NIH as we speak."

"The Bureau team really wishes you hadn't cremated the remains."

"We kept tissue samples, as I told you. We'll share if they wish."

"I think they do wish, but they've not been able to find out how to get some samples."

"Tell them to talk to their CIA liaison officer," McGill said, as the driver, responding to some signal Allender hadn't seen, drew alongside the curb. "Metro's right up there," McGill said, as he got back into the Expedition. "Your comms gear will be in place at home and in your FBI office by midnight."

As the big black vehicle pulled out into traffic, Allender realized McGill hadn't given him any list. The nearest Metro station was Smithsonian, about a half mile away. He started walking, oblivious to the thinning crowds of tourists admiring all the monuments, but then he found himself having to step aside for an organized tour group of chattering Chinese tourists, who were dutifully following their tour leader down toward the Lincoln Memorial. The tour leader had a bright red flag raised over her head to ensure that none of her charges went astray. They were mostly middle-aged men and women and not the usual giggling crowd of uniformed foreign students one encountered on the Mall.

Then Allender caught sight of one older man, clacking along as fast as he could go, his walking stick swinging awkwardly as he brought up the rear some fifty feet behind the group. He was white-haired, with a heavily seamed, hatchet-shaped face and veined hands. He was wearing a padded jacket straight out of the Cultural Revolution days over baggy black pants and elaborately strapped sandals. There were even some red flag pins on the lapels of his coat to complete the picture of absolute Party loyalty.

As he came abreast of Allender he stopped in midstride, exhaled a loud breath, and then fixed Allender with a beady eye. "Walk with me, Dragon Eyes," he said in high-class Mandarin. "If you please."

The old man turned off onto one of the Mall's many cross paths and Allender, intrigued, obligingly followed him while looking discreetly for minders. They were right below the Washington Monument, which loomed some 550 feet above them. The old man found a bench he liked, sat down, and patted the spot next to him. Allender joined him, having already spotted three likely minders wandering aimlessly out on the grassy expanse of the Mall, but all within pistol range.

"As I'm sure you have surmised, I am not a tourist," the old man said, looking thoughtfully across the grass at the distant White House.

"Your Mandarin gives you away, I'm afraid," Allender said.

"And someone has stripped the *zhuyin* from yours," the old man said admiringly. Allender was well aware that mainland Chinese thought the Taiwanese version of standard Mandarin was, at best, amusing. He'd just been complimented. The banal chitchat went on for a few minutes. In the meantime Allender had spotted more minders. Six in all, so this old man was definitely somebody. Allender waited patiently, knowing that sooner or later he would get to the point. Eventually he did.

"Do you know the fable about marking the boat for the sword?" he asked.

Allender knew better than to say yes, even though, yes, he did. When he'd been a student of Mandarin and Chinese ways in Taiwan, Chinese fables were often used to illustrate a point, but never directly. Keeping the explanation murky imputed superior knowledge to the one telling the fable. Educated Chinese kids figured that out at about age fourteen and learned to just shut up and listen, which in itself was a useful lesson.

"Well," the old man began. "A man from the state of Chu was crossing a river. Suddenly, his sword fell into the water while he was sitting in the boat. He immediately made a mark on the side of the boat. 'This is where my sword fell off,' he announced. When the boat finally stopped moving, he went into the water to look for his sword at the place where he had marked the boat. But, of course the boat had moved, not the sword. The moral being that that was a foolish way to look for something."

"I would have to agree," Allender said. "And what does that story have to do with me?"

The old man turned to face him. His right eye stared right at him; the left eye seemed to be slightly out of alignment. "You are looking for something," the old man said. "In a foolish way."

Allender considered the message. "May I know who you are?" he asked, finally.

"I am Yang Yi. I am visiting your lovely city from Beijing, where I am the deputy minister for state security in the current government of Xi Jinping."

Allender turned to study this man. Up close, he wasn't as old as he'd looked coming up the sidewalk. Maybe early seventies, with a very stern face, whose skin stretched across his cheekbones like a mosaic. If he was who he was claiming to be, he was a powerful official indeed. In China, the Ministry of State Security combined the functions of the American CIA, FBI, and Department of Homeland

Security. What in the world was someone that high up in the Chinese government doing walking around the Mall and wanting to speak to him, he wondered.

"Do not be alarmed, Dragon Eyes," the old man said. "Those people out there are here to protect me, not harm you."

"I understand that, Minister," Allender said. "But why do you call me that?"

"Because that is your file name, Doctor Allender. We are interested in you, even though you are supposed to be retired."

"I *am* retired. For just over a year now."

"And yet you rode off to the headquarters of your Federal Bureau of Investigation just this morning."

"You have *me* under surveillance?" Allender protested. "What on earth for?"

"As you were undoubtedly taught in your fancy American school in Taipei, we Chinese operate on a different time scale than you Americans do. Americans want everything now. We are willing to be patient, to wait and watch, sometimes for years, in order to reach our objectives, even when exercising such patience creates temporary loss."

Allender made a sound of exasperation. "I am not the Orphan of Zhao, Minister."

"Quite so," Yang said, recognizing yet another ancient tale. "But perhaps *I* am. The disappearance of *your* deputy minister is not what you think. Probe your shoulders. See if there are not some invisible strings there." He stood up with a small groan. "It has been a pleasure to meet you. Hopefully not for the last time."

A nondescript sedan had appeared on the access road nearest their bench. Yang Yi clacked his way to the car, where three serious-looking individuals in loose suit coats opened the door, handed him in, and then got in themselves before speeding away into Washington's evening traffic.

Allender sighed, got up, and started walking up the Mall to the

Metro station to begin the trip back to Dupont Circle. This "chance" encounter on the Mall with a very senior MSS official was disturbing to say the least. Allender's reference to *The Orphan of Zhao,* about a wronged son's long wait for revenge, had been deliberate. He'd used that story to probe whether or not this encounter had anything to do with the black swan. Apparently, it did.

Back at his town house he changed into his usual evening wear of slacks and a smoking jacket and went to the tower study for his Scotch. Now he had a problem. Two, actually. Tell McGill about his encounter or not? Normally he would have been on the phone already, but that one comment, elliptical as it had been, was stopping him. "You are looking for something in a foolish way." Throughout his upbringing in Taipei, he had been exposed to the art of the indirect message. Rarely did educated Chinese come right out and say something, especially if it involved criticism. They would reminisce about something that had happened in the past, or, like Yang Yi, resort to fables. You were supposed to pay attention and, sometimes, only later, get the point. That way no one lost face if you didn't understand it right away.

What was it he was looking for? In theory, he was helping the Bureau team look for the answer to Hank's mysterious death. In practice, he'd been directed by McGill to stall the Bureau's efforts, while the *Agency* looked for the answers to Hank's mysterious death. That way, if something embarrassing emerged, the Agency could presumably bury it and generate a story that would satisfy everyone and no one. Basically, it was yet another way to save face.

His second problem was that the Chinese intelligence apparatus here in Washington, or what was left of it after the Chiang affair, was keeping eyes on him. If that was true, for the past year they must have spent a fortune in travel funds, as he'd gone far and wide around the world in his newly reenergized hobby/enterprise. The always slightly paranoid Chinese would certainly have interpreted his ex-im business as a cover for something covert, and yet, if they'd pulled their sources in faraway places such as Indonesia, Malaysia, the Philippines, Brazil, and even southern Africa, there would have been nothing to find. Yes, he would check in with the station chief in each embassy, explain why he was there, and then check out just before he left. The various officers were always polite but distant, having heard that this man, who'd scared the bejesus out of so many people, had been forced out. Their relief when he'd announce that he was leaving had been almost comical. The Chinese weren't the only ones who were a bit paranoid when it came to Preston Allender.

So why the hell would the Chinese security services care about him, unless someone was assembling some payback for the Chiang debacle? Perhaps that's what the little lecture on time scales had been about. We know that was your idea, and one fine day you will pay for it, but at a time and place that *we* will choose, and, as you know, we Chinese take our time, don't we.

What was it McGill had said? Hank Wallace might have been running something against Martine Greer? Then he remembered that McGill himself had mused about doing the same thing. He also remembered discouraging that idea in the strongest terms. Maybe the thing to do was to pulse the putative target, Martine Greer. If Hank had indeed been cranking up some kind of out-there scheme to embarrass or destroy the chairwoman, maybe she could, wittingly or not, shed some light. Whether or not she would tell him was a different question, but if he phrased the question in terms of something being rotten in Langley, she just might.

He stared out the window into the twilight as he finished his Scotch. He was sitting in an armchair that gave him a view up the avenue through the venetian blinds. Traffic was lightening up as the rush hour subsided. Then he saw something that got his attention. Parked about twelve cars up on his side of the avenue and facing in his direction was an older-model sedan with two white faces visible through the windshield.

Well, now, he thought. Maybe he'd better make that phone call after all. Those weren't Chinese. Those just about had to be McGill's people, or possibly even Bureau people. If they were up on his house, then they'd been out there on the Mall, too. He got up and went to the secure telephone console.

McGill called him back in fifteen minutes, and Allender told him what had transpired out on the Mall. He did not mention the car parked up the avenue near his house.

"Well, that's interesting," McGill said. "I need to see if *we* knew that Yang Yi, himself, was in town. We'd better have."

"I'm a wee bit concerned here, Carson," Allender said. "The MSS is keeping book on *me*? And eyes? Only one reason for that."

"Yeah, yeah. I know," McGill said. "Goddamn Chiang. Tell me exactly what Yang said, again."

Allender did.

"Jesus, I wish they would just come out and say what they mean instead of talking in freaking riddles like damned diplomats."

"America's two hundred fifty years old," Allender said. "The Chinese have been practicing the diplomatic and intelligence arts for five *thousand* years. Maybe they know something we don't."

"I forget, don't I," McGill said. "You were brought up in China."

"In Taiwan," Allender said. "Big difference."

McGill sniffed but did not reply. "You want eyes on you?" he asked finally.

Allender realized he had to be careful here. Not asking for protective surveillance might tell McGill that he already knew there *was* surveillance. What he didn't know was whether or not those two guys in that car were protective surveillance—or simply surveillance. There shouldn't be a distinction, but after Yang Yi, he was beginning to wonder. "No," he said. "I'm not doing anything that bears reporting. Let them watch. By the way, where's that list of names?"

"On your new computer, Preston. Time to open it and read your e-mail."

Allender groaned. "Best thing about retirement, Carson," he said. "You don't *have* to read your e-mail."

"Now you do," McGill said. "Frequently. We'll look into the Chinese watcher thing. Maybe roust a couple. Although, upon reflection, maybe not. What could it matter? As you say, you're not doing anything but going to work each day. You just keep going through the motions over there in the Hoover Building. Confusion to the Bureau, right?"

"Absolutely," Allender said, and then the line broke synch.

Upon reflection? Allender thought. Not much of it. He did, however, agree. Let them watch. He had to have been the most boring surveillance subject they'd ever handled.

The following morning he made a call to the congressional liaison office at the Agency and asked them to get him an appointment with Martine Greer. They asked for a topic for the office call. He told them Henry Wallace. Half an hour later they called back and told him that Greer's AA, a Mr. Wyancowski, could see him at eleven thirty. Then he called Rebecca Lansing at Bureau headquarters and told her he was going up to the Hill to see someone and thus would not be in until later. She asked who he was seeing. He told her he'd fill her in if it turned out to be a productive meeting. She started to say something but then just said okay. He needed to keep reminding her that he didn't work for her *or* the Bureau.

Wyancowski turned out to be a sixtyish man who looked as if he'd been on the Hill for his entire life, which was just about true. Allender was relieved. Longtime Capitol Hill staffers were adept at getting to the heart of the matter, which saved a lot of time. The title Administrative Assistant fooled the uninitiated. The AA was the senior staffer on a congressman's Capitol Hill staff and basically the second-in-command in a congressman's office. Looking at Wyancowski, Allender remembered the line from Shakespeare about Cassius' lean and hungry look.

"Doctor Allender," the AA began after they were seated in his office. Wyancowski kept a large, black chess clock that ticked backward from five minutes to zero perched upright on his desk and facing whomever was sitting in one of the chairs. "What can I do for you?" he said, as he started the clock.

"I'm here on the matter of Hank Wallace's unexplained death." Allender said. "I've been retired from the Agency for over a year. They've recalled me to work with the Bureau as a liaison officer to Langley on this matter."

"I've been briefed on who you are, Doctor. Or 'were,' perhaps, is more accurate." He glanced at the clock. "So why are you here, please?"

"I'm curious why Congresswoman Greer asked the Bureau to get into this investigation."

"Surely you jest, Doctor Allender," the AA said. "Given the chairwoman's long and affectionate relationship with Langley, nest of snakes that it is, she probably saw it as a wonderful opportunity to poke someone in the eye with a sharp stick. I don't know this, of course, as she doesn't always explain why she does things. Is this news, Doctor Allender?"

"Under ordinary circumstances, no, Mister Wyancowski," Allender replied. "Her long-standing antipathy is neither helpful nor news. But right now the feeling at Langley and the Bureau is that Hank Wallace may have been murdered, possibly even by a foreign intelligence service. If that's true, this is not the time for bureaucratic bullshit."

The AA sat back in his chair. "I wouldn't advise using that particular term with the chairwoman. Hank Wallace was an institution at Langley. If someone *did* take him out, then the Agency's counterintelligence directorate has a lot to answer for. I suspect she wanted to have some outside eyes looking into this matter so that Langley couldn't cover up their own incompetence. Again. No offense—that's just my opinion."

There was an old-fashioned intercom console sitting on Wyancowski's desk. Allender had noted that one of the little red lights was on. "Congresswoman Greer," he said in a loud voice. "Care to comment?"

There was a strained moment of silence as the AA tried not to glance over at that little red light. Then a door disguised as part of the paneling at the back of the AA's office opened, revealing the chairwoman of the House Permanent Select Committee on Intelligence. She was a large woman, with a round, double-chinned face, short gray hair, and somewhat beady eyes. She had fatty biceps the size of small hams and wore a set of eyeglasses connected to a lanyard around her neck. Lovely you are not, Allender thought.

"I'll take it from here, Tommy," she announced, and then gestured with her head for Allender to follow her into her private office. Once there she pointed at a chair, sat down behind her desk, and flipped her own intercom button to the off position.

"Okay, Doctor, what's this all about, comma, no shit?"

"I would like to know if you felt that Hank Wallace was cooking up some kind of plot or scheme to embarrass you, personally."

Her face settled into a blank mask. Allender wondered if she played poker; she'd be damn good at it with that face. "What a question," she said, finally. "Refresh my memory: What was your role at the Agency, Doctor?"

"I'm a psychiatrist. I was in the training directorate. I trained our senior interrogators in advanced psychological modalities. Sometimes I even did interrogations, myself. I also conducted annual interviews with senior training and operational staff to make sure they were still emotionally and psychologically fit to do their jobs. I was not operational in the Agency sense."

"Ah, yes," she said, nodding to herself. "I have heard of you. You're the one they called Dragon Eyes, aren't you."

"Mostly, they called me Doctor Allender," he replied, quietly.

"To your face, no doubt," she said. "Why'd you retire—you seem a little young to be retired, especially from the SES."

"I was forced out," he said. "An operation that I consulted on succeeded too well and caused the White House some problems. Someone had to walk the plank, and it wasn't going to be Carson McGill, Hank Wallace, or the director."

"The black swan," she said, admiringly. "That was you?"

"It was my idea, and I selected the woman who actually did it. The target was taken back to Beijing and executed, or so I was told."

"So you were told?"

"I was in the training department, Madam Chairwoman. The Clandestine Service handled the operational details and all subsequent reporting. We live in boxes over there in Langley, and one box is discouraged from talking to other boxes. I assume that it's true, however."

"I received a briefing about that caper," she said. "My source told me that the PRC intel infrastructure here in D.C. was decimated. General Chiang took a whole lot of people down with him. Why would that be?"

"Chiang staffed his operation here in town with members of his own faction, possibly even his own family. Competing factions back in Beijing probably saw an opportunity to wreck his whole crew."

She nodded. "One more question, Doctor, and then I'll answer yours. When they recalled you to active duty, did they tell you to help the Bureau or to lead them on a series of wild-goose chases while Langley tries to figure out—and deal with, in-house—what really happened?"

Allender recognized the crucial question. He had never met this woman before, but she had a reputation at the Agency of being hostile to how Langley performed its mission and was always ready to cause trouble for the Agency management. Having finally met her, however, Allender had the sense that to lie to her would get him nowhere, and, after meeting Yang Yi, he was beginning to feel like maybe, just maybe, Carson McGill hadn't told him quite everything. "The latter," he admitted.

"*Thank* you," she said, emphatically. "Thank you for being straight with me. Now I'll be straight with you. Hank Wallace and I have been at each other's throats for years now. I think he played fast and loose with the millions we threw at the Agency, all in the name of national security, and I also think that if he could have found a way to knock me off my perch he'd have done it in a heartbeat."

"So you're devastated that he's dead," Allender said.

"Totally," she said with a cold grin. "But here's the thing: I'm up for reelection, along with everyone else here. It's a year away, of course, but some rumors have surfaced back in my district that I am a closeted homosexual. Now, my district is correctly characterized as a churchgoing, Christian-family-values, Bible-thumping, gun-loving, and hugely conservative bunch."

"How deplorable," Allender mused.

She snorted. "I am, by the way, *not* a homosexual, so this is malicious. It might be coming from the guy who's running against me, but I kinda don't think so. It's just not his style."

"Maybe someone on his campaign staff?"

"No—his family is his campaign staff. It just doesn't add up."

"Someone here, then?"

"Interesting you should say that," she said. "We've had a staff slot here in the committee staff office, as opposed to my district staff office, that's held open for a liaison officer from the Agency. It's not a big deal—he's supposed to interface with middle management over there in Langley and facilitate my committee staff's questions, from both sides of the aisle. Working-stiff level. That being said, I fired the last guy they sent over because he was patently nothing more than a spy for Henry Wallace."

"How'd we react?"

"Langley sulked a little and then gapped the billet for a while. But just lately, they sent a replacement, a drop-dead-gorgeous blonde who has, according to Tommy, rebuffed the best efforts of every one of my male staffers to get a date. In the meantime she's been sidling up to me, personally, with what I would call unearned social intimacy."

"As in, I play for the other side; how about you?"

"Yes, exactly that."

"If you're not gay, what's it matter?" Allender asked. "Calibrate her. Call her in, explain that you're the boss and she is one of the working stiffs, as you call them, and tell her to knock it off."

"Did that," she said. "Since then I've been getting the wounded-doe act."

Allender thought about it. He could sort of see it: Get a photo of the chairman with the thirty-something hottie, preferably something that at least looked intimate, and then get that back to the district to bolster the rumors. On the other hand, that kind of crap would hardly constitute a black swan—that was just standard election dirty tricks, and besides, outing a gay congresswoman was hardly the cataclysm it used to be.

"I don't know this guy who's taken Hank's place, this Carson McGill," she continued. "I've met him, of course, but he's been the DDO so he's not exactly a public figure and Hank made sure I dealt only through him. But, as I said, McGill's the one who called me about the situation with Wallace. I felt something wasn't kosher, so that's why I grabbed the Bureau by the scruff of its righteous neck and threw it at Langley. Kicking and screaming, I might add."

"But the Bureau works for Main Justice," Allender pointed out.

"One of the Bureau's most important missions is counterintelligence, which gives the intelligence oversight committee, namely me, the power to do that. Basically, I'm trying to keep Langley honest."

"Well, for what it's worth, I don't see anything over there resembling progress. They haven't really asked me for anything at all except some potential evidence saved from the autopsy."

"Isn't that kinda strange?" she asked. "You're making it sound like they're just sitting on their hands. Like they don't take this situation seriously."

Allender threw up his hands. "Beats me," he said. "The woman leading the Bureau team is a loaner from Director Hingham's stable."

The congresswoman shook her head in bewilderment. Time to end this, Allender thought. She knows less than I do. He smiled at her. "Thank you for your time and for being straight with *me,*" he said. "I've obviously got a lot more homework to do. May I please contact you again if I think I'm getting somewhere?"

"You betchum, Red Ryder," she said. "Here's something you may not know. Being the chairman of the House Permanent Select Committee on Intelligence I just might—*might,* mind you,—have access to some useful assets of my own. My AA out there will give you a number to call if you ever get into real trouble, okay?"

"Thank you," he said, although he could not imagine what "assets" a House committee chairman could have. Besides, if he needed that kind of help, he'd call the Agency op center, not some congresswoman's AA.

"One more thing," she said.

"Yes, Madam Chairwoman?" he said.

"Can I see . . . ?"

He thought about it for a few seconds. "Remember," he said, as he got up and approached her desk. "You did ask." He bent forward and took the glasses off.

"Holy. Shit," she whispered.

"Just so," he said. He stared down into her eyes until he saw the first nervous tic in hers. Then he put the glasses back on, thanked her again, and left. In the small mirror by the door he could see her sitting at her desk with one hand over her mouth.

He went down to the security office, showed them his newly minted Agency credentials and FBI building pass, and asked for a discreet way out of the building so that he could avoid prying eyes. A sergeant was detailed to take him to the tunnel connecting the Cannon House Office Building to the actual Capitol building. There he went down the white marble steps and then walked the four blocks over to Union Station. If there had been watchers outside the Cannon, of either persuasion, he should be clear of them.

He sincerely hoped.

Metro's Red Line would take him directly back to Dupont Circle, where he would then have to decide whether or not to go into the Bureau. On balance, he thought he needed time to think, so probably not. If they needed him, they'd call.

SEVENTEEN

The following morning Allender had his driver take him to Langley to meet the woman who coordinated forensic investigations within the Agency. Appropriately, she was a pathologist who'd been enticed away from the Bureau's lab ten years ago. They met in her office and Allender asked why there was a problem getting tissue samples in the Wallace investigation over to the Bureau.

"What tissue samples?" she asked. Her name was Dr. Willis Cooper. She was in her fifties, with prematurely gray hair and a heavily lined, no-nonsense face. "And what Wallace investigation?"

"Let me back up," Allender said. He told her what Carson McGill had told him about the death of Henry Wallace and the ensuing autopsy. She shook her head.

"All news to me," she said. "Admittedly, I don't play at those levels. I did see an Agency-wide notice that Deputy Director Wallace would be away for medical reasons for the next sixty days or so, but *dead*? No. And I can assure you that none of my labs, in-house or contract, have done an autopsy on the deputy director of this agency."

Whoops, he thought. He realized that he might just have screwed up. McGill had told him that Wallace's death had been kept close-hold. But he'd also said that the Borgias had handled the remains and the autopsy. If that was true, this woman would know about it.

"Doctor Allender?" she prompted.

"Sorry," he said. "I was thinking. Let me ask you this: If the DDO wanted an autopsy done, and done without anyone *in* the Agency knowing about it, how would he proceed?"

It was her turn to think. "Most forensic pathologists work for hospitals or law-enforcement agencies," she said. "If the DDO has a captive lab, say, at a university med school, or maybe even out at the NMMC Bethesda or the Defense Department med school there, then he could get it done and I'd be in the dark. Still, you're saying Hank Wallace is dead?"

"So I've been told," Allender said.

"Except you have a problem, don't you—you don't habeas a corpus, and that notice was bogus."

"They told me that someone in your office told them the samples would be forthcoming," he pointed out. "Any idea of who that might be?"

She shook her head. "Nobody who works for me, Doctor. You have a name?"

He held up a finger and got on his phone to Lansing. Rebecca put him on hold and then came back with a name. Allender thanked her and gave Cooper the name. Melissa Wheatley. Cooper drew a blank.

"Got a headquarters directory?" he asked. She did and she looked. No Melissa Wheatley in the Langley HQ directory.

Allender sighed. He took off his glasses and rubbed his eyes. When he opened them he saw Cooper's reaction. He put the glasses back on and apologized.

"Holy shit, it's true," Cooper said. "That Dragon Eyes stuff. God-*damn*! And you did interrogations?"

"Among other things," he said. "But now it seems as if I've been drawn into something a little more complex."

"By no less than Carson McGill," she said.

"Yes."

"Well, sir, my advice is to watch your ass. There are rumors upon rumors that he's on the make for the top slot. And while none of us are all that impressed with the current director, most of us cube slaves would be less than thrilled with someone like McGill at the helm."

"Fancy that," Allender said. "So: Do I have to tell you to not speculate out loud about Henry Wallace?"

"No, you do *not*," Cooper said. "I've got four years until I get my retirement."

"It can come sooner than that, if certain people feel so inclined." She grinned at him. "You being a classic example, or so I've heard."

"Just so," he said. "Thank you."

"I've got a suggestion, though," she said. "Go out to Bethesda. It's actually called the Walter Reed National Military Medical Center now, but everyone in town still calls it Bethesda. I'll give you the name of a senior pathologist there. See if his people did the autopsy, assuming what you're saying is even true."

"Would you call him, tell him I'm coming to see him?"

"Want me to say why?"

"You don't know, but I'm some high muckety-muck in the Agency, and I'm also a doctor."

"Can do easy, boss."

His driver took him out Wisconsin Avenue to what had been the navy's national medical headquarters complex and was now the National Military Medical Center. The gate guards directed them to building 9, which contained the Department of Pathology and Laboratory Services. Upon checking in, he was met by a navy commander named Bill Waring, who wore the insignia of the navy's medical corps on his shoulder boards. They sat down in Waring's office. Allender introduced himself and then asked if their department had performed an autopsy on one Henry Wallace of the CIA.

"When would that have been?" Waring asked.

Allender realized he didn't know, but said it would have been within the past thirty days. Waring consulted his computer, which apparently had decided to slow down to a turtle's pace that morning.

"Who was he?" Waring asked as he waited for the machine to find the name.

"A senior officer at the CIA," Allender replied.

"CIA?" Waring said. "You guys have your own labs, don't you? I mean, when Willis called, she didn't say this involved an autopsy . . . ?"

"She didn't know that's what I wanted to talk to you about," Allender said. "I've been detailed to the FBI to help with a tangential investigation. They were told that tissue samples had been retained prior to Wallace's cremation. That's what I'm really trying to find out: where are they, and if they're here, can you get them to the FBI lab."

Waring was still looking at his computer with an expression that said he wanted to give it a glass of water. "Tissue samples?" he said. "We don't normally do that, unless we're talking a homicide or something like that."

Allender said nothing.

"Oh," the doctor said. "Okay, if this damned—wait. Last name Wallace, first name Henry?"

"Yup."

"No record," Waring announced. "Who would have sent the remains here?"

"The Agency."

Waring looked at him as if to ask, The whole Agency, or someone in particular? Allender still did not elaborate.

"Okay," Waring said. "I get it—this is spook shit. But: Whoever did send remains to us would have had to specifically ask for bodily fluids, tissue samples and specifically *which* tissue: organs, brain, extremities, et cetera. Otherwise, we report cause of death and then request instructions for disposition of remains. Okay?"

"And there is no record of a Henry Wallace being here?"

"There's no record of a Henry Wallace being *here*," Waring said. "In *our* clammy little hands. Want me to check the big base?"

"The 'big base'?"

"The whole medical facility, Doctor Allender. This is the *National Military Medical Center*. We have thousands of people come through Bethesda—excuse me, the Walter Reed NMMC. Inpatients, outpatients, vets, civilians, even presidents, occasionally."

"Of course you do, and yes, please, let's query the big base. And I apologize for playing sphinx with you. It's just the nature of our work."

Waring ran the keys and then sat back. "What's your specialty, if I may ask?"

"I'm a shrink. Specialty is interrogation training. I'm actually retired but I've been recalled to help with the Wallace—problem. I was an assistant director in our training department for clandestine services."

"Wow—they do that? Recall people? Don't they have people?"

Allender smiled. "Sure they do," he said. "None of whom wanted to touch this case with a ten-foot pole. So: Get a retiree. No career implications. Once it's done, he goes back to pasture."

Waring grinned. "Now, that I understand. You guys have no exclusive lock on bureaucratic bullshit, believe me. This place—"

The computer finally responded. "Well, now," Waring said.

Allender raised his eyebrows.

"Igor here says that the name, Henry Wallace, is in a restricted part of the database, and that access is denied to us mere quacks by no less than the US Secret Service."

"What the fuck," Allender said. "Secret Service? That's the White House."

"We-ell, yes," Waring said. "But if the president of the United

States has a medical emergency, like, he gets shot here in town, or needs a physical, *this* is where he comes. There are two floors in that big white tower where no one is allowed in, even when His Majesty is not in residence. If access to one Henry Wallace's records is being denied by the Secret Service, then he could well be on one of those floors of the tower building, and probably, he's *not* dead. I didn't tell you that, but . . ."

Allender just stared at him. *Not* dead? This was getting murkier and murkier, he thought. Carson McGill, what the hell are you up to? He decided he'd better go ask McGill himself that question. He thanked the commander, asked him not to speak about his visit, and left.

EIGHTEEN

At the Langley headquarters main entrance he stepped through the security procedures and then was asked to wait. Three minutes later he was met by two men who asked him to come with them to see the DDO. Allender complied and soon found himself cooling his heels in McGill's outer office. After a fifteen-minute wait, five senior-looking men came out of McGill's office, ignoring him entirely, and then the secretary invited him into the inner sanctum.

"Preston, dear fellow," McGill chirped as he came in. "They told me you were in the building."

"And I presume that's because Security had standing orders to notify you if I ever came into the building," Allender said. He needed a coffee, so he went to the side table and helped himself.

"So what's so urgent that you're here, unbidden and unannounced? I'm wearing two hats these days, so please keep it short."

"Hank Wallace isn't dead, is he?" Allender asked. "That short enough for you?"

McGill put down the memo he'd been reading and stared at Allender. "Whatever are you talking about, Preston?" he asked, his face a professional blank now.

"You tell me, Carson," Allender replied. "And for the record, I don't like playing charades. If you're not willing to explain, then I'm out of here."

"Hang on, now, Preston, hang on. Surely you'll understand if I tell you that there are layers to this matter. Boxes within boxes. The right hand doesn't always know what the left hand knows, and that's how we keep secrets, remember. How'd you find out, by the way?"

"A left hand told me," Allender said.

Carson gave a brief laugh, but there wasn't much humor in it. Allender was getting some fright vibes from the DDO. "Okay, he's at Bethesda. He did have a massive stroke. He's in an induced coma. The prognosis is—poor. That much I can tell you."

"So you don't need me playing any more silly games with the Bureau, then, right?"

"Actually, I do. You'll remember that I thought Wallace had been ramping up a swan, and that the director thought it was against Martine Greer."

"Yes."

"I still think so, but the problem is that none of my CS people know anything about it. I need breathing room to figure that one out, preferably without the interference of the fucking FBI."

"Maybe he wasn't doing any such thing, which is *why* you can't figure that one out."

McGill paused for a moment. "Let's just say I have some direct evidence that he was, which I can't reveal at the moment. What I need you to do is go back to the Hoover Building, focus them on that list of names, and start baffling them with bullshit."

"I can do that, but then there's still the problem of the tissue samples."

"I'll have them there by close of business tomorrow."

"How? If he's not dead."

"We'll simply take some," McGill said. "It's not like he's gonna feel it, is he."

While Allender absorbed that little tidbit, McGill got up and helped himself to a coffee from the side table. He then walked over to the window wall and stared out for a moment. "Tell me," he said. "Have you been in touch with Martine Greer?"

Allender laughed. "You know I have," he said. "I think both you and the Chinese embassy have had eyes on me since I came back to 'active duty.'"

"You give me too much credit, Preston," McGill said, sitting back down behind his desk. "I asked if you wanted eyes, remember? You said no. Why'd you go see her?"

"Because none of this was making sense, and I was beginning to suspect Hank wasn't dead. She apparently wasn't comfortable with your story, either, which is why she sicced the Bureau on it."

"But you confirmed to her that your role in this was to help the Bureau find out how he died and by whose hand, right?"

"Yes." Not actually, he remembered.

"Good, then we're still on track," he said with audible relief. "Do *not* tell the Bureau what you now know. I promise not to lead you down any more garden paths. And no more sleuthing on your part, okay? Let the Buroids do that. You just be 'helpful.' When you get home tonight, think about other things. Better for everyone if that's how you play it. Okay?"

"Okay," Allender echoed, suddenly tired of hearing that word. McGill had picked up the memo again. Realizing that that was the DDO's signal that the office call was over, he left the office, thinking he ought to go get the word "pawn" tattooed on his forehead. He decided he'd had enough "fun" for one day. Time to go home.

Then he had another thought as he headed for the elevators. McGill wasn't the only Agency actor in this little charade. Maybe he could get Rebecca Lansing to come out to his house for a drink and, just possibly, find out how much she really knew.

Rebecca arrived by taxi at 6:00 P.M. Allender had called her at the office and asked her to come by for a drink if she was free. She wore dark slacks, an emerald-green silk blouse that complemented her eyes, and the expression of someone who's anxious to end the working day. He took her into the tower study, where she admired the spectacular display of exotic veneers. She said yes to a Scotch, on the rocks with no additional water. He was still in his business suit, minus the jacket.

"So this is what you've been doing since leaving the Agency," she said. "They're gorgeous. I had no idea there were so many different kinds of wood."

"It's been a lifelong interest," he replied. "My father got me hooked when we lived in Taiwan. We spent twelve years there, which is where I semi-mastered Mandarin. Would you mind if I took these glasses off? They're heavyish, and I usually don't wear them at home."

"By all means," she said, but she still blinked when he did it. "I'll try not to stare, but that's just—wow."

He smiled, which he hoped would dim the amber just a little bit. "I researched this phenomenon while in med school," he said. "No one could explain it, but amber eyes, although rare, do exist. It's caused by heavy melanin in the front of the iris and pheomelanin in the back. Mine, however, are apparently somewhat unique."

"I'll say," she said. "Yours appear to be backlighted. Was your mother Asian?"

"Chinese, yes."

"Because that was my first impression—an Asian wolf. But still . . ."

"Have you been to China?"

"I went there once on a tour. There's a zoo in Beijing, which is where I saw a maned wolf with the yellow eyes. Scary monster, that one. Have you been to Beijing?"

They talked about China and the director's obsession with the inevitable victory of China over the West for a few minutes. Then she asked how his visit to Capitol Hill had gone.

He started to tell her but then decided against it. *I* need to know more, he thought. A lot more. Besides, my remit is to keep the Bureau going in circles.

"Not useful, I'm afraid," he said. "But I did get some help from Mister McGill on the tissue samples. Your team should have them by COB tomorrow, at the latest."

"Well, that's progress," she said.

"And there's also a list of names of people who got sideways with Hank Wallace," he said. "In fact, it should be available in my secure e-mail. Give me a moment."

He went over to the Agency computer console and held reveille on his e-mail. As promised, there was the list. He printed it out and handed it to Lansing. "In my opinion," he said, "It's not likely that any of these people would be up to homicide over an old grudge or professional slight. But . . ."

"Yes, indeed," she said, scanning the list. "Always the 'but.' People brood sometimes, and then act out in the most surprising ways. This will help. I'll get the tissue samples into the Bureau's forensic lab. They've got a poison expert there who's pretty damned good."

"You think poison?"

"The fact that whoever did the autopsy found absolutely nothing often suggests poison or maybe a chem-bio weapon of some kind. Or something simpler: like an injection of potassium chloride solution into a vein, for instance. That would stop the heart. When death occurs in humans, all the body's cells release minute bits of potassium chloride, flooding the circulatory system, and thereby masking the substance that killed him."

"Sounds like you know a thing or two about poisons," he said.

"Got an amazing tour of the Bureau's lab when I was sent over. That's where I learned that little tidbit."

He nodded. "You know what we call our own forensics lab in the Agency, don't you?"

She smiled. "I do indeed," she replied. "Let me ask you a question. This list doesn't have General Chiang's name on it. Do you think it's possible that his family might try to exact some kind of revenge on Wallace? Or you, for that matter?"

"All the way from China?"

She shrugged. "The word in Company circles was that a lot of people besides Chiang went down after the swan, both here and back in China. You might think about your own security, given that some unknown *Chinese* entity may have dispatched Mister Wallace."

Allender instantly thought about Yang Yi's not-so-subtle suggestion that he might be looking for something in a foolish way. It was strange that she would bring such a thing up, until he remembered that she worked out of the director's office, or Hingham's stable, as it was called. She would be privy to things that lesser lights at Langley would not. For now, however, he decided that she didn't know any more than he did, so he finished his Scotch. She finished her drink and then stood up. "Thank you for the drink and your time. I look forward to working with you."

He stood up as well. "Do you mind if I don't come in until midmorning?" he asked.

"God, no," she said. "That gives me time to get the day going without—um."

"Without having to babysit the visiting high pooh-bah from Langley, right?"

She grinned. " 'Babysit' is probably not the right word, but when you do come in, I hope to know where we stand, or at least where we think we stand."

He nodded. "I think there's more to this case than you know. For that matter, than *I* know. I promise you this: If I think that people in high places are screwing around in the serious-shit arena, I will warn you. Being on the director's personal staff has its perks, I'm sure, Rebecca, but if things go wrong, proximity doesn't necessarily mean safety."

Her face became serious. "Likewise," she said. "And thank you again. Which way to the Metro?"

After she'd left, he poured himself a refill. Now, that was interesting, he thought. He wondered if McGill had somehow entangled the "unlisted" spook in the Hoover Building into whatever he was up to. He headed out to the kitchen to see if he could heat up some leftovers in the microwave without making a mess.

After dinner he spent time online researching some red bamboo specimens and then decided to turn in. He made sure the doors were locked and then set the house alarm at the kitchen panel. He kept a five-shot Judge encased in one of the sturdy bedposts of his antique four-poster bedstead. It could fire either .410 shotgun game load or .45 Long Colt ball ammo. He'd opted for the shot shell. A few years back someone *had* tried to break in and the alarm had duly gone off. It had been so loud he'd been totally disoriented by the overwhelming noise and had barely been able to get the gun out, and by then the crook had fled. After that fiasco he'd had a moonlighting Agency tech come out and replace that feature with a set of small cameras in each major room, mounted directly across from motion-detector beads. If someone got in, Allender would be awakened by a soft but insistent chime from the headboard of his bed. The flat-screen TV in the bedroom would come on and show what was going on, and where. The system itself called 911, and the crook wouldn't know he'd even been detected until blue strobe lights lit up the front and back of the house. His personal action plan was simple: Get up, drop the steel bar across the bedroom door, get back in bed with the Judge handy, and await the cavalry.

It was two in the morning when all of that failed him. He awoke to the room's overhead light coming on to reveal three Chinese men standing at the foot of his bed. Two of them looked like army types: short, squat, powerfully built, and as stone-faced as temple dragons. They just stood there, five feet apart, totally balanced, arms at their sides, fingers curled in fighting readiness. The third man was different: younger, with a chiseled face, a prominent nose, and icy black eyes, and thin as a refugee who hadn't eaten in a long time. He looked vaguely familiar and he spoke in standard Mandarin.

"You are Doctor Allender of the CIA?" he asked in a high, angry voice.

"I am Doctor Allender, but no longer of the CIA. I have not worked there for some time. Who are you, and what do you want?"

One of the security types reached into his pocket and then threw something that hit Allender on the left temple hard enough to make him see stars and roll sideways. As he tried to sit back up he could feel a wetness on the left side of his forehead. He put up a hand, which came away red.

"Do not speak to me in that tone again," the younger man said as he advanced to the side of the bed and stood over Allender like a cocked pistol. "*I* will ask the questions. You will answer them."

Allender said nothing, realizing that he was having trouble getting his eyes to focus. Waves of pain began to engulf his head.

"Are you the same Doctor Allender who masterminded the plot against General Chiang Liang-fu which led to his execution?"

That's who this is, Allender finally realized. Chiang's son or son-in-law. He remembered him from the restaurant in Williamsburg. Younger-faced then, and softer, more prosperous-looking. "I am," he said.

The younger man nodded his head one millimeter, and then slapped Allender so hard that he went unconscious for a moment. When he opened his eyes, Chiang's son was leaning over him, his face six inches away, close enough that Allender could smell his rancid breath. There was something glinting in the air between them. Allender focused and saw a *hudiedow,* a two-foot-long antique Chinese fighting knife, being held right in front of his face.

"I am Chiang We-tao, first son of Chiang Liang-fu," the young man hissed. "As a result of your trickery, my father was taken back to Beijing and put in prison. He was court-martialed and then taken to the execution square at Ham Dong military prison. There they stripped him naked and then shot him in the kidneys with hollow-point bullets. They then used one of these"—he rotated the knife back and forth so that the blade reflected bright light into Allender's eyes—"to open his intestines onto the concrete. Then they left him there, to die in agony. For three hours he writhed on the concrete, mewing like a kitten. We were forced to watch. And then the carrion birds came. We were forced to watch that as well. That is what you caused, *Doctor*."

"No, that is what your barbarous government did, Chiang We-tao," Allender said. "I engineered your father's great embarrassment in order to neutralize his espionage efforts in my capital city. *He* caused your government to lose great face through his many sexual indiscretions."

The younger Chiang pressed the edge of the *hudiedow* vertically against Allender's lips. He could clearly feel that razor-sharp edge, and suddenly tasted salt. "Our whole family was imprisoned," Chiang growled. "We lost everything—honor, respect, our house— *everything*. My mother now works in a military laundry. *My* wife was taken away and is now some policeman's concubine. My father's brother, whom he hated, has taken over the clan. Can you guess why I am here?"

Allender didn't have to.

Chiang continued to stare at him, and then put the point of the knife under Allender's chin. "I hear they call you Dragon Eyes," he said. "I'm not impressed. My father's eyes were bleeding red holes once the birds began their feast. As yours soon will be when I pull them out—"

Then Chiang's face literally exploded in a spray of blood and bone, accompanied by the boom and pressure wave of a magnum pistol. Two more booms and then the room went quiet. Allender had to grab a pillow to wipe the mess out of his eyes and off his face. The stink of sudden, violent death permeated the room, framed by the bright smell of gun smoke and a copious blood puddle spreading out on the floor.

He looked to see who'd rescued him. It was Rebecca Lansing, or, more accurately, the large man dressed out in what looked like SWAT tactical gear standing next to her, an enormous pistol in his right hand, which was now hanging down at his side. Allender stared at her in utter incomprehension. Then he reached for his glasses as he saw the shooter, who looked vaguely Korean, react to seeing *his* eyes and begin to raise that huge handgun. Lansing, wearing an FBI windbreaker, patted the man's hand down. She was already on the phone, calling Langley for a wet-cleanup team. The two soldiers were not visible, presumably because they were dead at the foot of his bed.

Allender closed his eyes and sank back into the mess on the bed. He could feel two tiny cuts on his lips, which hurt out of all proportion to their size. He could feel the skin on the left side of his head tightening as the swelling rose. For a moment he longed to just subside into the sodden pillow, but Lansing was there now and urging him to get up. He gingerly swung his legs out of the bed and sat up while she steadied him. His head swam for a minute but then he stabilized and opened his eyes again. The almost headless remains of Chiang's son lay on the floor, leaking an amazing amount of blood onto the floor. Out of the corner of his eye he could see one pair of feet sticking out from behind the foot of the bed. The wall behind the bed was covered with spatter.

She led him gently into the bathroom, turned on the shower, and told him to clean himself up. As he stood in the shower, holding on to the soap holder to stay upright, he heard someone come back into the bathroom and then leave. When he got out ten minutes later there were clean clothes and towels piled on the sink counter, and his pajamas, along with the bathroom rug, had been removed. He dried himself off and then wiped the mirror free of fog. The cuts on his lips looked like two purple cracks. There was a visible goose egg on the left side of his head, but it was no longer bleeding. He felt a sudden urge to use the toilet and barely made it.

A half hour later he sat in his study with Lansing while a specialist scene-clean team sent over from Langley did what was necessary upstairs. The three bodies had already gone out the back door. Allender sipped on a glass of quality cognac, trying hard not to let her see that his hands were trembling. The *hudiedow* was sitting on the coffee table as if to remind him of how close this had been. The cuts on his lips stung with each sip of cognac, which wasn't doing much to assuage his headache. He touched the crusty lump on his head every few minutes.

"Well," he said, finally, when he thought he could trust his voice. "Thank you very much."

She nodded, but didn't reply, waiting for his next question.

"How did you happen to be outside when they came?"

She looked down but did not answer.

"Okay," he said. "Let me rephrase: What the fuck's going on, Rebecca?"

"Does the name Yang Yi ring a bell?" she asked.

"Yes," Allender said. "He appeared out on the Mall after McGill let me out of his car. We sat on a park bench and exchanged cryptic pleasantries."

"And you know who he is, right?"

"He said he was the number two at the MSS. I wasn't entirely sure, but it sounded right. It's been a while, as you know."

"Yes, that's who he is. He was here because General Chiang's son escaped from a penal farm in North Korea, of all places, mustered up a couple of his father's loyal faction guards, and smuggled himself into this country. He was on a mission."

"So he said," Allender said, unconsciously fingering his throat.

"I got a call from the Chinese embassy," she continued. "Me: the unlisted Agency liaison officer working at the Hoover Building. Would I please come to lunch at the Old Ebbitt Grill. Yang Yi, himself, wanted to talk to me."

"Wow," he said. He wanted another cognac but decided to switch to water.

"Yeah, wow," she said. "I called home, reported the request and asked for eyes, and then I went to lunch. He was businesslike and polite. Spoke pretty good English. Told me about Chiang Junior, and said that he was coming for Dragon Eyes, *and,* and this is the important bit, that they were pretty sure the son was already here in Washington."

"What did you say?" Allender asked.

" 'Thank you'?" she said. " 'I appreciate the warning.' Then he became somewhat reflective. For once, I had the sense to just shut up and listen. He asked if I thought the warning was worthy—that's the word he used, 'worthy'—of a return favor. I said yes."

"What did he want?"

"Don't know," she said with a wry grin. "But I suspect I'll find out one day."

"You certainly will," Allender said. "And I'm very grateful for your initiative. But why you? I would have thought that once you reported the meeting, McGill would have had Langley security people set up a perimeter here and wait for Chiang the younger."

"That's what I thought, too, but Mister Hingham, himself, told me to deal with it. He said that he would assign an expert to me who could handle whatever problem showed up. You saw him, and he lived up to his billing. So that's what I did."

That was almost unheard of, Allender thought. The director didn't order operatives around. Even the DDO went through channels. So who *was* this woman? "I guess I have to ask: Who are you, really, and, more importantly, who's your real daddy?"

"*The* director," she admitted. "As I've been telling you. I work out of the director's office. I'm one of a small handful of people Mister Hingham uses to work around the Agency bureaucracy when necessary. Or at least, that's how he explained it to me."

"Hingham said that?" Allender asked, incredulously. "That hardly squares with his reputation for being a total wuss. A director who goes through the motions, but never makes a decision, always has to 'think about it' whenever anyone presents a decision brief, and then delays until someone else finally frames a decision. Once the principal directorates figured him out, they pretty much gave up and went to McGill for direction on anything important."

"I understand that's his reputation," she said. "But for all his purported weakness, I happen to think that his 'China Will Rule' hobbyhorse drives him a whole lot more than people realize. Think obsession."

"Hingham of the Ivory Tower?"

"Have you spent a lot of time with him?" she asked. "He keeps the whole Agency at arm's length for a reason, I think. Remember who appointed him, and how much he is aligned with the idea of a new world order, one in which the US doesn't swing a whole lotta weight. The old hands automatically think he's a weakling. I'm not so sure about that."

"You don't say," Allender replied. "So tell me once more: You do not work for Carson McGill, correct?"

"Absolutely not."

"Which means you probably don't know."

"Know what?" she asked, sounding just the least bit exasperated now.

"That Hank Wallace *isn't* dead?"

To his immense satisfaction, her face went pale. "Are you shitting me?" she asked in a horrified voice.

"Not one pound, to quote our beloved DDO," he said. "So maybe your close association with Mister Hingham in that fancy executive suite may not be as privileged as you think." Then he pointed at the cognac decanter. "Help yourself."

"Yes, please," she gulped, but she had to wait for her cognac, because the chief technician came downstairs at that moment and asked her to come upstairs. When she returned she told Allender he'd need a new mattress and bed linens, but that the room was now forensically clear. She told him that she did open the windows, and that he'd need to give it a day or so. Maybe repaint.

Over cognac for her and water for him, they tried to figure out what to do. He revealed to her what McGill had told him and what Yang Yi had had to say to him, and that he thought it was maybe time for them both to go see the director. Rebecca wasn't so sure. She pointed out that the two of them did not have any verifiable facts as to Mr. Wallace's real situation. That wasn't the best foundation for calling on Hingham to tell him that his DDO might be bent.

"Well then," he asked. "Answer me this: How do we—you—deal with the Bureau? They think they're working a possible homicide. Remember, too, that tissue samples are supposedly coming."

Rebecca made a face at the mention of tissue samples. Allender understood, remembering what Commander Waring had told him. He told her about McGill's comment that Wallace wouldn't feel a thing. She groaned.

"What's McGill's motive?" Allender asked. "Personal advancement?"

"He's certainly known to be ambitious, although he hides it pretty well under that faux British spymaster façade," she said. "But, I think the Agency's old-timers would agree."

Allender got up and started to pace. Just like McGill, he reminded himself. He wasn't entirely stable on his feet but needed to move around. He imagined he could still hear those booming gunshots. "Hank Wallace suffered a stroke," he said. "McGill saw an opportunity. Hustled him off to Bethesda, put him in the presidential ward for secrecy, and then assumed Hank's job, oh, so temporarily, of course. The director goes along with that because the decision has been made for him. McGill has probably been grooming some pet toads in the Directorate of Operations, so he proposes one of them become the new DDO. Hingham needs to think about that. If Hingham eventually agrees, then he controls the two most powerful positions in the day-to-day work of the Agency."

"I shudder to think," Rebecca said. "Oh, shit: What if Mister Wallace wakes up?"

"McGill told me that his prognosis was poor. Here's the more interesting question: Is McGill capable of *making* that prognosis come true, if he has to? You know, go out there to visit the old man, wave a vial of some nasty vapor under his nose and flatline him? I've always thought McGill to be somewhat of a poser. You know, 'M' reincarnated at Langley sort of thing. The pipe, the Brit bullshit . . ."

"Let me tell you a story," she said, eyeing the decanter. He poured her another draft. "When I came back from LA I was stashed in Hingham's office while they figured out where I was going next. One day McGill came for a one-on-one meeting. I happened to be searching for a document in a file safe in the inner office. The director closed the door for their meeting, but they got into an argument and I could overhear them. State had sent a message that three Agency operators were about to be rolled up by some Afghan warlord. The nasties wanted to trade for someone we held in Gitmo. Hingham wanted to go ahead, but McGill was adamant. The three operators were NOCs and they'd known the risks. The director was horrified, from the sound of it. He asked McGill at one point what would happen to them. McGill said they'd probably be skinned alive, rolled in salt, and then be staked out in the sun to be eaten by scavengers."

"Lovely," Allender said. "But I forget myself: Islam is the religion of peace."

"Well, then McGill gave the boss a lecture in the 'hard realities of international espionage.' Pointed out that the West had been killing Afghans of all persuasions ever since nine-eleven. Three non-operational cover contractors against *thousands* of dead Afghans, he said. Think about that. Give them three grisly victories and they'll become overconfident. Then we'll kill thousands more."

She paused to finish her cognac. "I'd not been around McGill much before this, but this was definitely *not* the caricature people talk about in the cafeteria."

"What did Hingham finally decide?" Allender asked.

"Don't know," she said. "I could tell they were wrapping it up and didn't want to be spotted, so I left the office before he came out."

Allender sat back down. "So the notion of going to Hingham and spilling the beans is—what? Pointless?"

She just looked at him.

"How about going to *your* titular boss at the FBI—the deputy director, correct?" he asked.

She nodded. "He's a total straight arrow," she said. "He'd tell the Bureau's director and then the two of them would go to Main Justice immediately." She hesitated. "I guess I'm trying to think of a way to keep this goat-grab in-house long enough to fix whatever's going on, as opposed to having the Agency crushed under a tsunami of public outrage before anybody knows what McGill was—is—up to."

He smiled. "Spoken like a loyal spook," he said. "And I tend to agree. In fact, as you pointed out, neither you nor I *knows* that Hank is alive. I found out that McGill published the story at Langley that he's getting medical treatment at Bethesda. He may have just been damned thorough in building that cover story, good enough to fool one of the senior pathologists out there. It's not like I 'habeas a corpus,' as one of their pathologists put it. Truth be told, I'm thinking I need to go see for myself. You know, fool me once, shit on McGill. Fool me twice, shit on me for letting him."

"You go out there, McGill will find out," she said. "He said no more 'sleuthing.' Plus, McGill's got Mister Wallace in the one place nobody from the Agency can access."

He sighed and threw up his hands. "Okay," he said. "Tomorrow. First thing. You and I will go see Martine Greer. She has the power to get us into that presidential clinic, or, if not us, someone from the Secret Service. We tell Martine what we think we know. If Hank *is* alive, even if he's a gorp, then she can deal with the Bureau, and then they can go after McGill."

Rebecca closed her eyes and appeared to think about it. She's actually quite striking, Allender thought, observing her, but she's hard. An edged weapon. Melanie was more attractive. Just as hard, perhaps, but more of a woman.

"All right," she said. "I agree. But if there are any more incidents like this mess tonight, we're going to need outside reinforcements. When McGill hears about this he's not going to just sit still. He's going to start asking the same questions we've been kicking around."

"That's why I want to fold the chairwoman into the picture. Think of it as insurance. For that matter, maybe we can obtain some ammo of our own, regarding Greer herself."

"Jesus," she muttered. "Why do I feel like I'm stepping into a snake den?"

"Because you are?" he said, and then felt a wave of fatigue sweeping over him. She saw it and stood up.

"You need to lie down," she said. "Get some rest. Take a day off until that swelling goes down. Then we'll go see Greer."

"Sounds like a plan," he said, turning to go back upstairs. He put his right foot onto the first stair and then she was right there, steadying him all the way up and then down the hall to the guest bedroom.

"Thanks," he sad as he flopped down onto the bed. He tried to think of something clever to say but then began to drift off, but still conscious of the fact that she was standing right there and looking at him with something of a sympathetic expression on her face.

How the mighty have fallen, he thought.

NINETEEN

By seven thirty two mornings later, Allender and Rebecca Lansing were sitting on park benches near the Rayburn building, where Martine Greer had her offices. Being a committee chairman, she had two, one for her congressional district and a second one for the select committee. Allender pretended to read *The Washington Post* while inspecting every vehicle that came single-file down the ramp into the building's protected underground parking area. Rebecca just sat there, enjoying a beautiful morning and sipping on a Starbucks, while she kept an eye out for the portly congresswoman in case she showed up at the building's front entrance. Their plan was to see her go into the building and then try to catch up with her before the legislative day got under way and an appointment became impossible. If she came by car, their second objective was to see if she had anybody with her.

The day after the attack at his town house had been unpleasant. He'd still had a bad headache, accompanied by waves of nausea every time he tried to move around. The clean-scene people had found an iron throwing star embedded in the wall behind his headboard. He'd been lucky that it had hit him broadside and not with one of the deadly points. He'd stuck to water all day, staying off the booze in honor of that headache, and that had worked. By this morning he'd felt a lot better, and had celebrated by having some cognac with his morning coffee.

While he pretended to read, Allender called Commander Waring at the Bethesda forensics office and asked him to check on something. He told the doctor that there was a remote possibility of some kind of radiation poisoning associated with Mr. Wallace's condition. He asked Waring to find out if the keepers of the presidential floors had checked for that, because, if it was true, they might want to move him so as not to contaminate such an important facility. Alarmed, Waring said he would do just that. Allender had spoken as if the fact that Wallace was indeed there had been firmly established, and he was pleased when Waring hadn't questioned that.

At ten minutes until eight, Allender got lucky. When a 500-series Mercedes rumbled down the ramp, he spied Martine Greer's large face behind the wheel. Even more interesting was the fleeting glance he caught of a striking Asian woman, probably Chinese, in the seat next to her. The ramp was stop-and-go because each vehicle's driver had to insert a security card and get a look-see from an armed guard at the swing gate. As they passed, he called to Rebecca, "Let's go."

They hurried up to the main security lobby, showed credentials, CIA for him, FBI for her, and asked for an escort to Martine Greer's office. A uniformed FPS officer took them upstairs. On the way, Dr. Waring called him back. No radiation, and yes, they had checked—SOP. Allender thanked him, and then they entered Greer's office about one minute behind the congresswoman. Again they showed credentials, this time to a truly stunning blonde who gave Allender a momentarily peculiar look. He explained that they needed to speak to the congresswoman urgently before the morning routine got fully under way. Aides and staffers were hustling through the office, and Allender could see that the congresswoman's visitors' waiting room was already full. The young woman made a call, nodded, and then got up and took them back to Greer's inner office.

"Make it quick, Doctor, we have a roll call in twenty minutes," Greer said, standing behind her desk. Her AA was not there. She was inspecting a pile of point papers and folders even as she greeted them. She looked up and realized he wasn't alone. "Who are you?" she asked.

Rebecca told her, and the congresswoman nodded in recognition. "Yes, now I remember that name," she said. "So: Whatta ya got, Doc?"

"Hank Wallace is *not* dead," he announced. "He is instead in a comatose state out in the presidential suite at Bethesda. Your dear friend, Carson McGill, has been lying to you. And me."

Greer's eyes widened as she lowered the papers. "Say that again?"

He did, and then she sat down, indicating for them to take chairs as well. Allender had expected her to ask him how he'd found this out, but instead she surprised him. "How does this affect me?" she asked. "Refresh my memory."

Good question, Allender thought. "McGill told you that Wallace was dead with no apparent cause or manner of death. You then sicced the Bureau into whatever investigation was going on to find out why and how. Ms. Lansing here, who actually works out of the Agency director's office as the 'unlisted' CIA liaison officer at Bureau head-quarters, was assigned to lead the team doing that investigation. I was brought back from retirement to help with that effort from within the Hoover Building.

"My instructions from McGill were pretty straightforward: mud-dle up the Bureau's efforts in order to give the *Agency* time to figure out what had happened. At the moment, I'm pretty sure neither the FBI director nor the Agency director knows that Wallace is actually still alive. Everyone else at Langley, on the other hand, thinks Wal-lace is out there at Bethesda recovering from something. We're here to get an answer to that famous *Ghostbusters* question."

The congresswoman opened her mouth to ask what that was and

then remembered. She then did what any boss who hasn't a clue does: She asked Allender what did he recommend?

"I think you should call in the directors of the Bureau and the Agency and tell them what you've found out. Then have the FISA Court issue a warrant to arrest McGill and turn him over to a joint interrogation team to find out what the hell he's up to."

"What do *you* think he's up to, Doctor?" she asked.

"If anything, I thought he was trying to do something that would knock the director off his perch and then take the top job, but I have to say, that doesn't seem—what's the word—sufficient?"

She nodded. Her phone rang. She picked it up and said, "Five Minutes." Then she looked back at Allender. "Where does this put you guys?"

Allender looked at Rebecca and then back at Greer. "Way out there, in the cold and the dark."

"Tell her," Rebecca said.

"Tell me what?" Greer asked suspiciously.

Allender told her about the attack two nights ago at his home.

"Are you *shitting* me?" she cried out.

"No, ma'am," he said. "Now, I *was* the brains behind what happened to his father. It's just that—"

"Well, fuck yeah," she said, almost shouting now. "There's no way that could have happened without the Chinese embassy knowing that he was in the country!"

"Make the calls, Madam Chairwoman," Allender said. "There has to be more to this than a vengeful son."

Greer put her hands up in fists. "I don't need this shit right now," she groaned. "We're going into an election year. For once I've got a fight on my hands. And, a roll call in five minutes."

"Madam Chairwoman," Rebecca said. "Here's a chance to root out a scandal at the CIA. Take the lead. Rotten apple, exposed by Martine Greer, defender of Democracy. National news. Keeping the people safe. Think about it."

Greer stared at her between her fingers for a long, appraising moment. "Want a job, sweetie?" she asked, finally.

A half hour later, they sat in the food court at Union Station, having had an expensive but pretty good breakfast. Allender thought they must have made an odd pair, he with the weird glasses and she too pretty to be sitting with him. The waitress brought the bill, which Allender paid.

"Think she'll do it?" Rebecca asked, once the waitress had left.

"Her first question was instructive," he replied. " 'How does this affect me?' That's what will guide her. Your comment at the end there was right on the mark, though."

"And yet," she said. "An election *is* coming. Everybody's goosey about upsetting any applecarts. McGill has to be counting on that."

"There's something else," he said. "This morning, when I spotted Greer going down into the parking garage? She wasn't alone. There was this really pretty Chinese woman with her in the front seat. You see any Chinese women there in the office?"

"No-o, but, so what? Carpool? How many thousands of people work on Capitol Hill now? I don't—"

"Martine told me that someone in her home district has started a rumor that she's a closeted homosexual. She told me that's not true, but she's worried because her district is family-values, church, guns to the max."

"Oh, c'mon, *sir*. Two women riding in a car means they're flaming dykes? You can't be serious."

Allender didn't say anything for a long moment. It wasn't the homosexual angle that was bothering him, he realized. It was the fact that the woman had been Chinese. Since he'd come back on quasi-active duty, there'd been an awful lot of Chinese in his life.

Instinctively he began to scan the concourse, which was teeming with tourists headed for the tracks concourse or the Metro, and daily commuters headed the other way out into the city. He wasn't sure what he was looking for, except perhaps a familiar face. Rebecca noticed.

"Sir?" she asked. "Do we have a problem?"

"Tell you what," he said softly. "You get up and leave. Go to the restroom area, but cut back so that you can keep me in sight. And turn off your phone."

"Should I call my team first?"

"Not yet," he said. "I may be imagining things, but my Spidey sense tells me we're being watched, and possibly by more than one watcher. You packing?"

"Always," she said.

"Good. I'm not authorized to be carrying, but I happen to have a little Ruger LCR .38 with me. Sorry to alarm you, but go through the motions. You see me make a signal to one of the waiters, come back. You see me take my glasses off, get the hell out of here and call for backup."

"Gee, you sure know how to show a girl a good time," she said.

"Remember our 'date' the other night? They prefer doing that shit in a quiet place, but they're not above shooting up the whole concourse."

"Sir: Who the fuck is 'they'?"

"Chinese operatives," he said, looking harder now. "Collateral casualties in their country helps solve their overpopulation problem."

She took a minute, casually gathering her phone and a small purse, pretending to say good-bye while she powered down her phone. Then she left the café and headed for the doors to the Metro escalators. Allender pretended to relax and finish his coffee, while he continued to scan the tourists and the natives for anyone who seemed interested in Rebecca. He turned his own phone off as inconspicuously as he could. He was about to relax when he saw *two* people, not just one, move rather quickly, and it looked like they were trying to keep Rebecca in sight. One of them was a young, fit black man dressed in a brown UPS uniform, while the other was a Chinese woman decked out in loose-fitting running gear. The woman was talking frantically on her cell phone as she hastened after Rebecca. As Allender watched, the two nearly collided trying to get through the door to the actual ticketing concourse.

He'd screwed up by telling her to turn her phone off. He'd been worried about tracking, but now he couldn't warn her. He'd just have to hope she'd see them and react.

Then *his* phone rang.

WTF? he asked himself. I just turned that thing off. He picked it up and accepted the call, which had no caller ID.

"Preston Allender, what *are* you doing at Union fucking Station?" asked Carson McGill.

"Breakfast?" Allender responded, remembering now that he'd been carrying an *Agency*-issued smart phone. Of course they could turn it back on.

"Where's your date?" McGill asked. His voice had the tone of a man who's seriously angry but who's trying to keep things civil, at least for the moment.

"She's going potty," Allender said. "But you know what? I think she's actually being followed."

"Just like you are, Preston," McGill said. "Look up, and to the right."

Allender looked, found the ceiling camera, and wiggled his fingers in its direction.

"Cute," McGill said. "Telling Martine Greer that Hank's actually alive was *not* cute."

"But true, yes?" Allender said. "Or did your tissue-sampling people flatline him for you?"

"Oh, for God's sake, Preston. Stop trying to turn this into some kind of mystery movie. I don't want Hank dead. I've got other fish to fry. You have complicated that, however."

"Did I tell you that Greer's consorting with a young Chinese woman?"

"Not news," McGill retorted. "We were talking about *you,* Preston. I think you're becoming a liability."

"How's about I resign, then?" Allender said. He was still scanning the crowds in the station, this time looking for a grab team headed his way while he babbled away on his treacherous phone. "You come get all your toys and my secret decoder ring, and I'll go back to chasing my pretty veneers. It was you who called me, remember? And I think I said: 'Not interested.'"

"But you're interested now, aren't you, Preston," McGill said. "You want to know what game I'm playing at, don't you."

"No, not really, Carson," Allender said. "Break this off now and I'll subside back into the retirement ooze. You'll have to explain it to the Hooverites, but this retiree does not give one shit about whatever the fuck you're up to."

"I wish I could believe that," McGill said.

"Why not?" Allender asked. "It's not like I've got a dog in this fight. Speaking of dogs, aren't you the Deppity Dawg at the Agency now? Your problem is Martine Greer, not me."

"Go home and wait for my call, Preston," McGill said. "I need to red-team this problem and see what threat you and your girlfriend pose."

"*Girl*friend?" Allender snorted. "She's the so-called unlisted Agency liaison officer at the Bureau headquarters. She works out of the director's office. She's sure as hell *not* my girlfriend."

"That what she told you, Preston?" McGill said, softly. "Go home. I'll be in touch. Believe me, I will."

The phone went dead. He looked across the concourse to find his "girlfriend." She was nowhere in sight, and both the followers had also disappeared through that same door. He took off his glasses and rubbed his eyes. Then he put them back on. If she'd been able to see him, she should be on the move. He scanned the concourse

again, but saw only the normal flow of people through the cavernous hall.

He got up and headed for the Metro entranceway, looking hard
for either the young UPS man or the Chinese woman. As he slowed
to search the area he became an obstacle in the flow of human traffic, so he stepped to one side of the entranceway and then stopped.
Public restrooms were to his left; the double escalators to the Metro
underground were on the right. Between them was the hallway that
led out to the Amtrak waiting room. He pulled out his phone, which
had gone dark again, and pretended to check his messages while
standing flat against the wall. He scanned both sides of the hallway,
the one with the public restrooms and the other side. Then he saw that
there was a utility room of some kind on the opposite side from the
restrooms. Lying on the floor at the bottom of the door was what
looked a lot like Rebecca's gold-plated NRA pen.

He checked the ceiling for security cameras and counted four
tinted domes on the ceiling within visual range. If those two had
managed to capture Rebecca and drag her into a utility room, she
might be in real danger. He fingered the LCR in his coat pocket and
then realized if he pulled a gun out here there'd be a response force
coming on the run. Then he saw the solution: a heavy fire extinguisher mounted on the wall right next to the utility room door. He
walked casually over to the door and tried to open it as discreetly as
he could without rattling it.

Locked.

He then dismounted the fire extinguisher, waited for some people
to get by him in the hallway, lifted it above his head and brought it
down as hard as he could on the doorknob, which snapped right off.
A woman passing behind him yelped in surprise.

The door swung open to reveal three concrete walls covered with
fire main valves, riser piping, and hose racks. Rebecca was sitting on
the floor with her hands behind her head, while the Chinese woman
stood in front of her with a handgun. When the door opened she

didn't hesitate, turning and firing at Allender as he stepped through the door. The bullet hit the fire extinguisher instead, which spouted a cloud of white powder and CO_2 into the Chinese woman's face. She dropped her gun to protect her eyes but not before Allender had fired back, hitting the woman in the upper thigh. She screamed and then darted past Allender and out into the concourse, where people backed hurriedly away from the chaos in the utility room and the sound of gunfire.

Allender bent down to check on Rebecca, whose own firearm had been kicked under a hot-water radiator at the back of the room.

"I'm okay, but glad to see you," Rebecca said, trying to stand up but failing to get traction on the powder covered floor. "Where'd she go?"

They both heard a lot of thudding feet as the station's security response team ran past the utility room and down toward the track gates. Everyone else in the vicinity was either crouched down on the floor or trying to back through the doors leading to the main concourse. Allender helped Rebecca up, retrieved her weapon, and then pretended to assist her out of the utility room and over toward the Metro escalators. He pulled his Agency credentials wallet out and flashed it the huddling figures in the hallway, shouting, "Federal officers, don't move and stay down." No one challenged them as they made it to the top of the escalator, but as they stepped onto the sliding treads there was a double purple flash from the direction of the train-track gates, followed by the muted sounds of several people screaming.

They didn't stick around to watch but trotted down the escalator just in time to scan their fare cards and board a Metro train. It was going in the wrong direction for Allender's purposes, but it was leaving Union Station, which was just as useful right then. He stuffed his LCR and her weapon into his coat pockets as they boarded. A minute later the train slid out of the station and into the darkness of the tunnels. Rebecca sat next to him on the train, trying to discreetly slap the extinguisher powder off her arms and clothes. She was breathing hard but had kept her composure. She started to tell him what had happened but he put a finger to his lips.

They went two stations along the route, got out, did an up-and-over to the westbound track, and then took the next train to Metro Center, where they were able to transfer to one going to Dupont Circle. They hurried back to the town house. Allender sent Rebecca upstairs to get cleaned up and then went to find a Scotch. He, too, had white powder on his trousers and even on his hands, but didn't notice as he sank down into an armchair. That was when he started to shake.

I'm too old for this shit, he told himself.

TWENTY

An hour after they'd made it back, Rebecca reappeared in the tower study. Her clothes still showed faint traces of powder, but she'd been able to shower and generally recover from her experience in the utility room.

"Feeling better?" he asked as she plopped down on the sofa.

"Much," she said. "You look a little pale around the edges."

"Not trained for that shit," he said. "My hands can still feel that bullet hitting the extinguisher."

She nodded. "Training helps, but your instincts were spot-on. Thank you. I think we're even."

Hardly, he thought, but couldn't think of anything clever to say.

"I need to get back to the Hoover Building, though," she continued. "May I use the phone? Lost mine in the scuffle."

"Sure about that?" he asked. "We're still operating in the mushroom mode here. Did that woman want something specific?"

"She yelled at me in what I assume was Chinese, almost like she expected me to understand what she was saying. You know, like some tourists do—shout, like that's going to make the locals understand?"

He nodded. "But with gun in hand, right?"

"Yep," Rebecca said. "Jammed right into my side. Queasy-nine, standard issue in the People's Liberation Army."

"MSS, then," he said. "Interesting that she was operating alone."

"General Chiang have a daughter?" she asked.

"Not sure," he replied. "She got really excited when you got up from the table—blasting away on a cell phone while she hurried after you. There was another guy who seemed interested, too—a black man in a UPS uniform. I don't know if he was with her or someone else, or if he was even involved. And then I discovered that McGill had *me* up on a ceiling security camera right there at the table."

"Eyes everywhere, then," she said. "Probably out front as we speak."

"McGill scolded me for telling Greer that Hank was not, in fact, dead and gone. Said he needed to red-team the new situation. Told me to go home and stay there. That he'd definitely be in touch."

Rebecca shook her head. "I need to get to my team and synch up," she said. "The Union Station cops're gonna find my phone, so E.T. really needs to call home. You're welcome to come with me if you think a grab team's spooling up."

"I don't get it," he said. "I just don't get it. What the *hell* is McGill up to?"

Rebecca was on his desk phone by then. She told whomever she was talking to where she was and that she needed a pickup to get her back to the Hoover Building. Then she hung up.

"I've got to alert the Bureau to what went down at Union Station," she said. "Then I think we need to lay actual eyes on Wallace, assuming he really is alive. What are *you* going to do?"

"I'm going to stay put. See what McGill does."

"I can get you somewhere safe," she offered. "The Bureau's good at protecting people."

"What's the point?" he sighed. "I'm no operator."

"You sure looked like one to me when you popped her," she said. "Especially when you fired that extinguisher."

"Actually, *she* did that," he said. "When she shot at me and hit the extinguisher, instead. And she didn't hesitate for one instant. I opened that door and she opened fire. If I hadn't been holding the fire extinguisher chest high she'd have had me."

"I see," she said, and then got up and gathered her things. "It's probably a good idea for you to stay put, then," she continued. "I'm going to brief the deputy director at the Bureau. I assume McGill will be talking to Hingham as soon as he gets word of this latest incident. Did you see that flash, by the way?"

"I did," he said. "That woman I wounded took off down toward the tracks concourse. I wonder if she tangled with a third rail."

Rebecca made a face and then headed for the front door. Allender went with her. When he opened the door, a government car was waiting out front. "That was fast," he said.

"They're nothing if not efficient," she said with a quick smile, and then she was gone.

He went back to his study, sat down at his desk, and took the protective glasses off. "Eyes everywhere," she'd said, as he rubbed his. "Probably out front," she'd said, as if she'd known. He was seriously beginning to wonder about Rebecca Lansing, the "unlisted" Agency liaison officer dispatched from the Hingham's office. "That what she told you?" McGill had asked. He realized he didn't *know* the first thing about Rebecca, other than whatever legend she'd been spinning for him.

On the other hand, she'd certainly saved his ass from the Chiang crew. He could still feel the bits of bone, brain, and blood spraying over his face. But what exactly had brought her and her shooter out into the night and to his house at exactly the right time? As he recalled, she'd kind of brushed it off when he asked her, claiming Yang Yi had warned her. But why her? How would he even know who she was unless he'd asked someone inside the Hoover Building? And, finally, she'd said that that Chinese agent today had wanted something from her and apparently expected her to understand Mandarin. What did that tell him? He hadn't a clue. Maybe he needed another Scotch. He looked at his watch. Early, but his hands were still trembling. He realized that a lot of his so-called power at the Agency had been utterly useless when someone swung around in front of him and opened fire.

He wondered if he shouldn't just grab some clothes, his passport, one of his guns, and some emergency cash and then just get in his car and leave town. Nobody would expect him to do that, because they knew that *he* knew that Washington was one big surveillance grid these days. Silent drones everywhere, cell phone traps across the entire spectrum, every building with a security force on duty twenty-four hours a day. They could track his phone and probably his car. He'd have to get past a zillion surveillance cameras just to get down to one of the river bridges.

McGill had told him to go home and stay home. If he bolted and they had to chase him and pick him up, wherever they took him wouldn't be as comfortable as sitting right here, not to mention that McGill could decide to send some people who knew how to engineer a fatal accident. A year ago he would have dismissed the thought, but since coming back to work he'd faced two occasions where people were willing and even anxious to kill him. Maybe even three, if he counted McGill. Except it had been McGill who folded him into this circus. WTF?

For his entire career, he'd been the one in control. Now he was being pushed around a chessboard he couldn't see by people he didn't know, and it wasn't a pleasant feeling. He wondered if the people who'd had to come to see him once a year had felt the same way when he applied some of his talents to explore their thinking. Payback is hell, isn't it, he thought.

Another Scotch. Definitely. Then a shower and a change of clothes. Something to eat. Yet another Scotch, even. He got up, went into the kitchen, and tried to set the security system. The screen was blank and the system unresponsive. He swore and made a mental note to get a dog instead of a cat.

That night, after a dinner that involved microwaving a defenseless cardboard box filled with some mystery meat, he went back to the tower study to think. The phone rang.

"Doctor Allender," a woman's voice said. "We need to talk."

"Do you have a name?" he asked, although the voice sounded vaguely familiar.

"Virginia Singer," she said.

"And why do we need to talk, Ms. Virginia Singer?"

"I think you are in danger," she said.

Me, too, he thought. "From whom or from what?"

"Carson McGill," she replied. That got his attention. He sat up in his chair.

"What do you know of Carson McGill?" he asked.

"I'm getting out of a taxi one block from your house," she said. "Let me in and I'll explain."

"I'm not accustomed to letting strangers into my house, Virginia Singer."

"Tell you what, Dragon Eyes," she said. "Once I come in, you can ask me to disrobe if you really have to."

He was stunned. "Melanie?"

"It's Virginia for now," she said. "Open the goddamned door, please. I think there are eyes out here."

"You look—gorgeous," he said, as he let her in. "Princess Grace."

"Scary, isn't it," she said. "How're you fixed for gin?"

He laughed and took her into the tower study. She was wearing a silver-gray pantsuit and he thought she'd lost weight since the last time he'd seen her. Maybe it was part of the new persona. "I don't have Bombay," he said. "Tanq do?"

"Absolutely."

"Have to be straight," he said. "Tonic water's gone flat. Ice?"

"Please."

He handed her the gin, looked at his own wee dram and decided to hold with that. He then sat down. "Spill," he said.

"I saw you in Greer's office the other day," she began.

"Oh, right, yes," he said. "I saw you. Wondered at the time who you looked like, but, then, I was kind of busy."

"Me, too," she said. She told him about the Agency position in Greer's office, her training at the Farm, and then her assignment to "almost" tantalize Greer into initiating a homosexual advance.

"Almost?"

"It's complicated."

"Ah," he said. "*You're* the one." He then filled her in on what Greer had told him about the woman from the Agency coming on to her.

"Total bullshit," she said, shaking her head.

"Excuse me?"

"Her not being gay. She's a full-fledged bull dagger and she came on to me the second day I was there. In fact, on my first day there, one of the girls in the office warned me to watch out, that Greer was an absolute predator. You know Capitol Hill: hundreds of good-looking women everywhere. Those congressmen don't hire the fatties and the uglies."

"Wow," he said. "I believed her."

"She's a snake," Melanie said. "When I took on the assignment, I told my instructor down at the Farm that I wasn't going there literally, so they trained me up to being a woman who didn't know she was a lesbian. Apparently, that's like fresh liver to a catfish."

"Interesting simile, for a city girl," he said.

"I dated an outdoorsy guy for a while at school when I couldn't stand the academics anymore. He liked to fish the rivers around Boston, especially for catfish. He'd sell 'em in certain parts of town in return for weed. Regardless, she's still a snake. She invited me to lunch in their private dining room, and then to a dinner function at State.

I played the naïf, which apparently just whetted her interest. She'd stand too close, run a hand down my back while talking to someone else. I would blush and shiver, and then move away and do some bosom heaving."

He shook his head. "They have a course for this at the Farm?"

She laughed. "You should have seen the *guys* in training."

"All gay guys?"

"No!" she said. "All straight guys. Pretending. Walking that fine line."

"But why not—?"

"Yeah, why not? I asked that question. My instructor, Gabby Farrell, told me that that would mean the Agency was exploiting an employee's sexuality, which would be unfair."

"The Agency, exploiting an employee," he mused with a totally straight face. "What a concept."

"My thoughts, exactly," she said, glancing over at the bottle of Tanqueray. He saw the look and refilled her glass. A pain-filled year in LA will do that to you, he thought.

"So your assignment was to get Martine Greer into a compromising position and then 'out' her in some fashion?" he asked.

"Mister McGill said he would disclose my assignment in pieces," she said. "First, confirm she is what she is. Then, additional instructions to follow. That's where it stood when I saw you and the FBI lady come into the office. My turn: I thought you'd been mustered out."

He told her the story of McGill's original call and his being brought back in to "help" the Bureau while the Agency solved the mystery. He explained who Rebecca Lansing was as well.

"Mister Wallace is dead?"

"Not exactly," Allender said. He told her the rest of it.

"So all this started because of something Hank Wallace was up to?"

"That's the original story. Right now, I'm not sure about any of it. Of course, I didn't really have many dealings with Wallace when

I was active. He knew who I was and what I did, but I don't think the training directorate was high on his priority list. You know, counterterrorism über alles. When I got fired he did promise to warn me if he detected any funny business aimed at me after the black-swan debacle. Told me to remember what the seer said to Caesar about the ides of March."

She shook her head. Then she spotted the fighting knife.

"What is *that*?"

"That is a *hudiedow,* an antique Chinese fighting knife," he replied, picking it up. Then he told her about the incident upstairs, and how Rebecca had brought in the cavalry at just the right moment. "And then she called in an *Agency* team to do the wet cleanup."

"Let me get this straight: This Lansing woman is an *Agency* operative from Hingham's private stable working in the *Bureau* headquarters to find out how a senior *Agency* director has been offed? And you've been recalled to active duty to work on her team while surreptitiously slipping nuts and bolts into the gear train to run their investigation off the tracks?"

"Knew you were smart," he said. "It gets better."

"I think I need more gin."

He gave her a short splash before continuing. "So: today. After seeing Greer, Rebecca and I went to Union Station for breakfast and a kick-around." He told her about what had happened next.

"Both times, you—and Rebecca—and hostile Chinese?"

"Yeah, interesting, isn't it."

"This is the black swan," she said. "Coming home to roost."

"Well, Chiang's son certainly put it that way and there's no way that team could have come into the United States, made it to Washington, and got into my house without the embassy MSS office knowing, if not actively aiding and abetting."

"We-e-l-l," she said. "Getting into the United States these days isn't exactly difficult."

"Yeah, but: These guys weren't desperate wetbacks crossing the

Rio Grande. My guess is they came in through one of the West Coast
ports, but here's the thing: Chiang Junior escaped from prison over
there. The regime had executed his father and destroyed the family.
The regime's ambassador over here would not be helping someone
like that."

"So if not them, who?"

"Yes, that is the question, isn't it."

"Shit," she said. "I'm getting cold feet about this Greer assignment.
Tell me, when you first came back on board, McGill wouldn't brief
you on the whole mission, either?"

"No," he said. "Now: You said you thought I was in danger, and
presumably without knowing anything about what's been illuminat-
ing my life lately. What gives?"

"When I came back from LA, I got stashed in Hingham's office.
I then got my marching orders from McGill himself which is kind
of unusual. I'm a junior operative; he's the freaking DDO. So when
I saw you in Greer's office, I put a call in to his office. Got one of
his aides and told him I'd seen you in conference with Greer. He
listened and then said, disregard. I said okay and went back to work.
Same guy called back an hour later. Said it was a friendly heads-
up. Told me to stay far away from you, that you were radioactive, and
that measures were in motion."

" 'Measures were in motion'?"

"Too many B-grade movies, I guess, but the message was pretty
clear. That's why I called. Having heard what you've had to say, I
think I was right."

"How'd you get my number?" he asked, suddenly curious.

"I kept it," she said. "Was I wrong to do that?"

There were a thousand possible meanings behind that question,
he thought. "Absolutely," he said. "Terrible breach of professional
protocol. Junior operative stalking a senior Agency retiree. A really
senior retiree. And old. And decrepit, too. The universe trembles."

"That bad," she said, with a sly grin.

"Without a doubt," he said. "But I'm glad you're here. That shit today? The way that woman whirled and fired without a second thought? Chinese killers in my house, past all my security systems? I'm somewhat out of my comfort zone these days."

She hooted at his use of the term "comfort zone." Then her expression sobered. "I get that," she said. "We young spooks are at the very least subconscious adrenaline junkies, as I think you pointed out a while back. Your gig was more along the lines of a top-drawer mind fuck, which is not what you bring to a gunfight or a knife fight."

He nodded. "You get complacent when everyone around you agrees to be afraid. General Chiang's son put a different perspective on things when he described his father's execution. I'm glad you're here, Melanie."

She looked down and smiled. The phone saved him.

"Rebecca?"

"Doctor," she replied. "I know it's late, but we need to talk, and not on the phone. May I come over?"

"Certainly," he said.

"Twenty minutes," she said.

"That long? I would have thought maybe sixty seconds."

She laughed. "This time *I'm* driving."

It was more like a half hour when Rebecca showed up. Even after normal working hours, getting through downtown traffic could still be torturous. She blinked when she got a look at Melanie. Allender made introductions, and they all went into the study. Allender asked Melanie to tell Rebecca what she knew and why Carson McGill had sent her into Greer's office in the first place. Rebecca listened carefully but without any questions, which for some strange reason gave him the impression that maybe she already knew all of this.

"Okay," Rebecca said. "Here's the deal. I sat down with FBI deputy director Green after the incident this morning. At that time I didn't know that Greer had been lying to us. I did report the Chinese woman in Greer's car. He immediately made the same assumption you did—that the Chinese woman could be an operative for the MSS. I pointed out that she could also just be a car pool. As to Greer's sexuality, his response was 'who cares'. That said, the fact that she has been concealing it might give someone leverage, especially if she's facing a contested election."

"Well," Allender said. "McGill certainly has an interest. He threatened me after he found out that I'd told Greer Hank Wallace was probably still alive."

"Exactly," Rebecca said. "As I've told you, I'm based out of the Agency director's office. But: Having been seconded to the FBI, I feel as if my loyalty belongs to the truth, not necessarily to the Agency. *Especially* if the DDO is targeting a sitting member of Congress. Director Green flat-out asked me the question: whose side was I on with this cluster."

"And?" Allender prompted.

"I told him two things. One, if McGill has cranked up an attack on a congresswoman, even one as obnoxious as Martine Greer, he needed to be stopped and prosecuted. But, two: I can't imagine he'd do that without the knowledge and tacit approval of the Agency director."

"What'd he say?"

"He said that's what he thought, too, so he was going to order the Bureau to break off any further interaction with the Agency and convert the investigation to a major governmental corruption case. And if I wasn't comfortable with that, he would send me back to Langley, and the Bureau would go after McGill on its own."

"You understand the implied threat in that, don't you?" Allender said.

Rebecca nodded. "If I'm not part of the solution, then I'm part of the conspiracy. Yeah, I get that."

Allender took off his glasses and leaned forward to stare hard at Rebecca. "And which are you, Rebecca?" he asked softly.

She was obviously uncomfortable under that his stare but she held her ground. "I'm on the side of law and order," she said. "Are you going to ask McGill's operative here the same question? Who is she, anyway?"

Allender saw Melanie begin to bristle. "She came to me," he said, putting his glasses back on. "Tell me, what does the Bureau want from me, if anything?"

"They don't really know *what* you are or *who* you are," Rebecca said. "I think they want you to stay out of it entirely. Especially since McGill sent you in the first place."

"More than happy to oblige," he said. He turned to Melanie. "You want to work with the Bureau on this? You could be hugely useful to them if McGill still thinks you're *his* asset."

Melanie sat silent for a long moment, then turned to Rebecca. "Let me tell you who *I* am," she began. She described her education, her government career before the CIA, and then her brief career as a Clandestine Services officer, including an operation that later required her to undergo a little over a year of unpleasant cosmetic surgeries to look the way she looked today. "Then I was brought back to Langley, stashed in Hingham's office for a month, and then sent for training at the Farm for this Greer mission, and, yes, by Carson McGill. And for the record, Doctor Allender, I've never seen this woman at the Farm or at Langley."

Rebecca was taken aback, but then nodded. "Okay," she said. "Fair enough. I was never part of CS. I came to the Agency during the previous director's tenure. I got my undergraduate degree from Columbia in business administration, and my law degree from NYU. I then applied to the Bureau, went through the academy, and then was sent to the New York field office. My specialty was a hybrid form of forensic accounting—in other words, serious fraud. It was interesting work, but the Bureau was a little too stovepipe for me, so then I applied for a GS position at the Agency. I'm not an operative, per se, but with my Bureau training, I can mix operational experience with financial and legal analysis, which is why I'm now a GS-15."

"Impressive," Allender said. "Columbia. NYU. You must have come from a wealthy family."

Rebecca laughed. "No," she said. "Well, in a way, I suppose. My mother won the lottery in my sophomore year in high school. Took home six million. Divorced my deadbeat father and then told me the sky was the limit, as long as I worked my ass off. Which I did."

Melanie looked at her for a long moment. "Here's the thing, Wonder Woman," she said. "You say you work for the director. We both know that Hingham is nothing more than an idealistic dilettante masquerading as the director of the CIA. So I'm sorta curious: What do you do there?"

At that moment, Allender stood up. "Enough, ladies," he said. "This pissing contest isn't getting us anywhere. Rebecca, I think you should proceed on the side of the FBI. If this ever gets to the level of a national investigation, you want to be working for the investigators. My role in this mess is over, as far as I'm concerned. Melanie, I think you need to go to Congresswoman Greer in the morning and lay out the truth of why you were sent there in the first place. The DDO is a powerful man in the Washington intelligence hierarchy. Greer is equally powerful. When the elephants dance, it's best for the ants to get the hell out of the way. Ladies: I bid you good night."

Rebecca and Melanie exchanged hard looks and then got up. Rebecca hesitated and then asked Melanie if she needed a ride. Allender could see that Melanie wasn't that keen to accept any favors from Rebecca. "You two need to reach neutral ground," he said. "Say yes, Melanie."

"Okay," she said. "But—"

"Great," Rebecca interrupted. "I agree—we're not on opposite sides here. This whole thing might be a whole lot bigger than any of us knows, and that means that when it gets exposed, we peons will be the first ones thrown under the bus. C'mon. I don't bite."

The two women walked to the front door. Melanie gave Allender an "are you sure?" look over her shoulder as she followed Rebecca out. He mouthed the words "call me" at her, and then closed the door.

TWENTY-ONE

"Where do you live?" Rebecca asked as she drove her Volvo sedan up Connecticut Avenue. Melanie gave her directions and thanked her for the ride.

"Why are you suspicious of me?" Rebecca asked.

Melanie hesitated. If this woman was *not* who she said she was, she might end up saying something that could get Allender in trouble. More trouble. "Too many intersecting lines," she replied, finally, trying to keep it vague. "Two violent incidents involving Chinese operatives involving the both of you. Admittedly, I'm new to the operational world, but we discussed this during training. Coincidence equals alarm."

"Okay," Rebecca said, watching street signs now for her turn. "I get that. But technically, Doctor Allender is supposed to be working with me, the team leader at the Bureau doing the Wallace case, as a senior advisor. That would inevitably cause coincidences, don't you think?"

Melanie shrugged. She thought Rebecca was being evasive. "You asked," she said. "Next street, go left."

Rebecca appeared to give up on peacemaking, which suited Melanie just fine. She'd been unwilling to say that this woman just rubbed her wrong. Something not quite right. Spidey sense, to quote

Allender. She pointed to the apartment building coming up. "Just there," she said. "And I do appreciate the ride. I could have walked it, I guess, but . . ."

"Yeah, but," Rebecca said, pulling to the curb. "Not in this town and not at this hour. Even if you're carrying. Tell me, why did he call you Virginia?"

"Long story," Melanie said, opening the door and getting out. "It was just a cover name. Thanks again, and good luck with your case."

Rebecca wiggled her fingers back at her, gave a fake smile, and then drove off. Melanie headed for the entrance to the apartment building and then pretended to look in her purse for something. When she could no longer see Rebecca's taillights, she turned around, crossed the street, and keyed herself into her real building. Wanted to know if I was carrying, she thought. Ought to have pulled on her, except, if she was working the Bureau, she'd definitely be carrying, herself. And: She'd actually not heard Allender calling her Virginia in front of Rebecca.

She took the elevator to her floor, stepped out, and encountered three men standing in the hallway. They were all dressed in suits with coats unbuttoned, and their physical appearance strongly suggested security types. One stood by her front door, which was open, the other two were positioned nearby. She immediately clicked open her purse and reached inside, but the man nearest her put up his hand and told her whoa. "No reason for that, Ms. Singer," he said, which was when she noticed he was wearing a communications earbud and wire. "We're US Secret Service. Just go inside, please. Congresswoman Greer is waiting for you."

She gave each one of them a hard look, and then slowly removed her hand from the purse. All three immediately relaxed. She walked into her apartment, where she found the congresswoman sitting on the sofa and partaking of some of her Bombay gin.

"There you are," Greer said, putting down the drink. She looked over at the man by the door and asked him to please close it. Then she looked back at Melanie. "Sorry for all the cloak-and-dagger, sweetie, but I've called in the cavalry. Please, have a seat, and tell me what the *fuck* is going on with you, me, and that snake, Carson McGill."

Melanie gave Greer a look that said, What the fuck are you doing in my apartment, then went to the sideboard, got a rocks glass, and poured herself a slug of Bombay. The Tanq had been good, but not sufficiently long-legged. Then she sat down across the coffee table from Greer, crossed her legs, took a sip, closed her eyes for a moment, exhaled, and asked Greer who the people in the hallway were.

"You-nited States Secret Service, Ms. Singer," Greer replied. "Now, your turn: Who are you? Even better, *what* are you?"

"I'm an Agency operative," Melanie said. "Sent by Mister McGill to confirm whether or not you are a closeted homosexual, and whether or not you are in a lesbian relationship with an operative from the Chinese embassy."

Greer's face went white. Melanie leaned forward. "Because if you are," she said, "he probably intends to compromise you to the point where you are booted out of your congressional seat, and then prosecuted for allowing a member of a foreign intelligence service to get so close to you, so to speak, that one could reasonably ask why every one of your security clearances should not be instantly revoked and you brought to an undisclosed location for some serious 'debriefing.'"

"How *dare*—"

"Oh, please," Melanie interrupted. "Your entire staff warned me about you and your sexual proclivities. The word 'predator' was used, actually. And, for the record, I don't give a shit about your bedroom choices. This is business, Madam Chairwoman, national-security business, and I think you are now formally in a world of shit. Would you please leave now? Or do I have to call in *my* cavalry? Trust me, they're nowhere near as polite as those guys outside."

The congresswoman was obviously flabbergasted. Before she could protest further, Melanie got up and went out onto the balcony to enjoy her Bombay . . . She heard the large woman heave herself off the sofa and leave. But then she heard someone else come into her living room.

"Ms. Singer?" a male voice asked.

Melanie wished she'd brought her purse. "Out here," she said.

The man who'd asked her not to pull on them opened and then stepped through the door and introduced himself. "Sam Worcester," he said. "Secret Service."

She turned, smiled, and asked for his creds. He produced them. She examined them and then asked if he liked gin.

"Actually, yes, I do," he said.

They went back into the living room, where she poured herself a refill and he poured a tiny amount. They sat down.

"This is complicated," he began. He kept staring at her face.

She started laughing. "You have no idea," she said.

"Okay," he said. "You got me. But here's the thing. Do you know who Henry Wallace is?"

"You mean the gorped-up deputy director of the CIA whom you guys are holding out in Bethesda? *That* Hank Wallace?"

Worcester blinked in surprise and put down his glass. "Yes, that Henry Wallace," he said. "But not gorped up. Not dead, not even ill, no matter what word's gone out around Langley or in the Hoover Building. And not being held, either. Here's another thing: When Martine Greer contacted the Secret Service to find out what Mister McGill—and you—were up to, that word got back to Wallace, who is, if you haven't figured it out yet, under our protection at Bethesda. It was his idea that we play along with Greer and accompany her to a meeting with you."

"And break into my apartment? That his idea, too?"

Worcester frowned. "Would you have come home for a nightcap if you'd known Martine Greer was waiting for you, either down in the street or up here?" he asked. "This was the simplest and most discreet venue. You know that."

"Okay, for the sake of argument, I agree. Wait: 'Play along with Greer'?"

"So: Mister Wallace is not just sitting out there resting up from several years of being a senior spook. He's running something. It's got a weird name. Care to guess?"

"Does it involve a swan?" she said.

His eyebrows shot up in surprise and Melanie started to laugh uncontrollably.

"What?" he said. "What's so fucking funny?"

"You'd never believe it in a thousand years," Melanie said. "So, once more: I assume you've brought a message?"

Worcester regained his composure, and then, almost as if he'd just discovered it, slugged down his dollop of Bombay. "Just this," he said. "He strongly recommends that you and someone called Allender go to ground, preferably out of Washington, if possible, because what he's got running is going to get, to quote him, messy, possibly even 'wet,' if that makes any sense to you."

"Yup," she said. "Clear as a bell. Tell Mister Wallace message received. I can't speak for Doctor Allender, but this very junior Agency operative is gonna make like Houdini."

"Really? Just like that?"

"Just like that, Mister Sam Worcester. Now if you don't mind it's been a long day, and I've got plans to make and trains to take, as it were. Thanks for delivering the message."

He put the glass down, nodded, got up, and left the apartment, closing and locking the door behind him. Now, she thought: How to warn Allender without alerting any listeners? Then she remembered something he'd told her.

TWENTY-TWO

Allender sat at his desk in the tower study with all the lights off and the venetian blinds cracked open so he could see out into the avenue. By now he'd convinced himself that, one, he was little more than a pawn in some bureaucratic power play McGill was making, and, two, he couldn't trust Rebecca Lansing. Too many coincidences, and even Melanie had had doubts about her.

He heard his cell phone chirp from out in the living room. He decided to ignore it. Any more surprise visitors tonight and he was going to go downstairs and get one of his shotguns. Then he realized that the tone was not for a call, but a text. He rarely used the text function; in fact he found the smart phone most useful for getting navigation help when he was driving. He got up, spied the phone's window alight on the coffee table, and read the message: "Beware the Ides of March."

Whoops, he thought. He unlocked the phone to check the sender box. V.S. He didn't know anybody with the initials V.S. Wait. Virginia Singer. Melanie.

He immediately had questions but sensed this wasn't the time for phone conversations. He went upstairs to pack a bag. Then he went down to the vault to get some cash, his passport, his emergency travel valise, and a different handgun. He retrieved the phone and his car keys and left through the back door. He didn't bother with the alarm system, which was still defunct. He walked across the dark garden to the back gate, then stopped and listened for a minute. The alley seemed to be deserted. He walked back to the side door of the garage, let himself in, and got into his car, an older-model Mercedes diesel sedan. He put the key into the ignition and then stopped, wondering if he should turn it.

"Aw, c'mon," he muttered. Too many spy movies. He reached up and triggered the garage door, started the car, backed out into the alley, lowered the door, and drove down the alley to the side street. He made his way through downtown and across the Memorial Bridge and headed for Richmond, not even bothering to look in his mirrors for followers. Unless they wanted him to know he was being followed, he'd never see them, and it was much more likely that his car would be tracked, along with his phone. Shortly before midnight he took a motel room off the interstate and turned in.

The following morning he went to the lobby, got some coffee and a fat pill, and then asked where the guest computers were. Once into the motel's terminal, he sent a text message to Melanie's phone number, telling her to meet him where they had had their first dinner date, at 8:00 P.M. Then he continued down the interstate until he came upon a large truck plaza, where he pulled in for diesel and a pit stop. He was tempted to take off his license plate and park it on the back of a nearby semi, but remembered that he had a better plan once he got to the Farm. Two hours later he took a motel room next door to the Opus Nine restaurant. He got his key card, checked the room, and then drove out to the Yorktown battlefield park to just walk around and get some fresh air.

At 8:00 P.M. he was sitting in a corner table nursing a martini and examining the wine list. He heard a flutter in the dining room conversation and looked up. Melanie apparently had decided to reprise her Ms. Vanderbilt gig. She was dressed in a tight-skirted yellow linen suit that complemented her hair and the Grace Kelly look-alike features. He watched with amusement as some older couples flat-out stared at her face as if they were seeing a ghost. He wasn't staring at her face, and he realized she'd caught him checking her out. The maître d' came out of nowhere and seated her at Allender's table.

"That looks good," she said.

"Tanq marty," he replied. "I ordered you Bombay."

"God is good," she said as a waiter arrived and produced her drink. She smiled and they tipped glasses at each other.

He complimented her on her entrance and told her Minette would be proud. "You think you were followed down?"

"No need," she said. "Nobody follows anyone in a vehicle these days. The surveillance systems have moved way past physical bugs. Operations tracks the computer in the car if it wants to because the manufacturers are all collecting continuous maintenance and operating data via various Wi-Fi links. And since we're both employees, our vehicle entertainment systems have all been modified for real-time tracking and the occasional 911. Plus, if you step outside, Google Earth, or at least the NSA version, can actually see you. You want to hide, get on a submarine."

"Yeah, I'd forgotten all about that stuff. What provoked your get-out-of-Dodge warning?"

She described her own late-night visitor and the subsequent drink with the Secret Service guy.

"They have him under *their* protection?"

"That's what he said. Looks like you were right about Bethesda. Good thinking on his part, too. A presidential facility on a military installation."

"That would imply that McGill *didn't* do something to Hank Wallace, but that it's the reverse: Wallace is running some kind of in-house op against McGill."

"And using you—me, too, I guess—to do—what?"

"I have no fucking idea," he said. "Let's order. I'm starving."

After dinner they retired to the bar. She was apparently staying in the same motel he was in, so they could afford to relax, not having to worry about driving anywhere. She finally asked why he'd wanted to come down to the Farm.

"I wanted to get out of Washington," he said. "I'm convinced the Chinese are watching everybody involved in this little caper. I figured if I could get to the Farm I'd only have to worry about McGill."

"You think the Chinese still mean to take you out? For the Chiang thing?"

"Not sure, but I've seen more weapons pointed at me in the past week than I have in years, if ever, actually. All by Chinese, too."

"Logical conclusion," she admitted.

"You'd probably find that exciting. I don't."

She laughed. "Why would I find that exciting?"

"You're an operator," he said. "That's a volunteer profession. Sometimes dull, sometimes hair-raising work. An element of real danger, depending who your opposition is. We screen out the true adrenaline junkies, of course, but there has to be some element of Action Jackson in any good operative."

"I suppose," she said. "Like I said, I mostly tried out because I was bored."

"What's the usual cure for boredom?" he asked, gently. Then both their phones began ringing. They looked at each other and accepted the calls.

"This is Hank Wallace," a voice said, to both of them. "I trust you've had a good dinner at Opus Nine?"

Melanie nodded at Allender, indicating she wanted him to do the talking.

"We have," Allender replied. "Are you here with us tonight?"

"Regrettably, no," Wallace said. "I'm at one of those famous 'undisclosed locations' in an effort to stay healthy. I recommend you both head over to the Farm and stay there until I send further in-

structions. I have arranged entry clearance and there is secure trans-
portation outside your restaurant as we speak. Tomorrow I will have
a job of work for Doctor Allender. Go now, please."

The connection beeped off. They looked at each other, finished
their drinks, paid the bill, and went out front, where a black Suburban was waiting as advertised.

"This the grab, after all?" Melanie said, her brave façade cracking
just a little.

"After a fashion, I suppose, but I think this has more to do with
a threat from the MSS. As we know, they're here in the Williamsburg area. I'll get the driver to take us over to the motel for our stuff."

Allender opened the back door for Melanie, half expecting Carson
McGill to be sitting there, but he wasn't. Forty minutes later they were
cruising through the gates to the Farm.

The next morning they were sharing coffee in the breakfast dining
room when a young man brought a sealed brown envelope in and
gave it to Allender.

"Oh, goody," Melanie said. "Our decoder rings." She'd been enjoying the stares as other people came into the dining room and saw
a reincarnation of the famous actress having breakfast with the
dreaded Dragon Eyes.

Allender opened the envelope and scanned the contents. "Oh,
my," he said, finally. "This is going to be interesting indeed."

"Where we going?" she asked.

"To the dungeons," he said, closing up the packet. "I'm going to
do an interrogation."

"Anybody I know?" she asked, but before he could answer, her
phone rang. It was Martine Greer, demanding to know why she
wasn't at work.

"I've been recalled to another assignment," Melanie told her
smoothly. "They'll be sending my replacement shortly, I'm sure."

"Tell him or her to wear Kevlar, then," Greer declared. "I'm cranking up a proper shit-storm in the House this morning. Your bosses are gonna hate life."

"I think they already do," Melanie said, and closed the connection. She told Allender what Greer had said.

"Wow," he said. "That's going to rattle some cages at Langley. Headline: 'CIA Attempts to Sabotage House Chairman's Reelection. Homophobic Smear Campaign. Speaker Schedules Hearings.'"

"Smear? Not if it's true."

"Can you *prove* that she is gay?" he asked.

"She sure as hell came on to me, *and* other women in the office—"

"That doesn't *prove* anything," he said. "You could testify, and so could they, but they'd all lose their jobs, and you work for the Antichrist over there in Langley. Plus, accusing someone of being homosexual doesn't carry the clout it used to."

"It would in her district, or so she said."

"She's a Democrat. She'll get the DNC to crank up the smear professionals and totally demonize her opponent and then blame him for the whole thing. No, all this means is that McGill has dropped the first shoe."

"What's the second shoe?"

"That Chinese woman in Greer's car. McGill has set a trap, I believe." He looked at his watch. "Meet me out front in thirty minutes."

An hour later they arrived at the gates of what looked like a high-security prison, without a single bit of greenery in sight around its two-acre compound. It was enclosed by high chain-link fences surrounding a single long, windowless one-story cinder-block building. A grass-covered hill rose right behind the building. The grounds immediately around the building were surfaced entirely in gray gravel and there appeared to be an unusual number of utility and HVAC cabinets at the back of the building. The parking lot outside the compound contained several civilian vehicles, but no people were in sight when they arrived. Allender told the driver that they would call Dispatch when they needed a ride back to the residential building, and then walked up to a kiosk outside the gate. He pressed a button. A television screen came to life. A voice asked them to state their names and then hold their facility badges up to a scanner. A moment later, a warning buzzer sounded and the gate retracted. They walked up to the plain metal door and went right in. Inside there was a security lobby with a desk and a metal-detector portal. The guards were in casual clothes and not visibly armed. A large and totally bald black man waited to greet them.

"Doctor Allender, welcome back," he boomed as he offered a massive paw.

"It's good to be back, Deacon," Allender responded. "I think. This is Melanie Sloan from the CS. Melanie, this is Armstrong Battle, the director of this facility. She looks quite a bit different from when she came through the basic training course."

"I guess so," Battle said, shaking hands gently with Melanie. "This face I would have remembered. Let's go to my office and I'll fill you in."

Melanie massaged her right hand as they walked down a corridor to one end of the building, passing several offices where people appeared to be pushing papers, talking on the phone, or doing other office-drone things. There were no windows, and she felt that the building was amazingly quiet and kind of creepy. She was struck by the fact that Allender seemed quite at home here. As tall as he was, he was still a head shorter than the giant leading the way.

Battle's office took up the entire width of one end of the building, and while there were no windows in the walls there were large-screen display panels that gave a view of what looked a lot like vistas from Yellowstone Park. Battle saw her looking and explained that the panels could do day and night and display just about any panorama in the world. He sat down behind an enormous oak desk and gestured for them to take seats in a circle of armchairs positioned in front of the desk. Coffee was offered and declined.

"Right," Battle said. "Ms. Sloan, do you remember doing interrogation training as part of your CS syllabus?"

"Yes, I do, vividly," she replied. "But it wasn't here. It was—"

"Yes, yes, of course, it was in building six. Still is. This, on the other hand, is the real deal. All the admin and control rooms are on this level where we're sitting. Two stories down and tucked back under the hill behind this building is a suite of interrogation cells, ranging in ambience from a lawyer's conference room to something the Inquisition would have approved. Below that is a complex of cells which we modeled after the Lubyanka complex in Moscow, complete with those pretty, white-tiled rooms with a prominent drain in the center of the floor. Hence the building's nickname: the Dungeons. Ever hear of it?"

"No, I haven't," Melanie said. "You said 'real deal.' Does that mean—"

"Yes it does, Ms. Sloan," Battle interrupting her again. "It surely does. And Doctor Allender has been, over the years, the grand master of the edgier parts of our little fun palace. For reasons only he knows, he has asked that you be allowed to sit in, on the control level, of course, on one of his special séances. I have agreed to allow that, on two conditions. One, that you never speak of your experiences here to anyone, ever. And, two, that once you go into the control room you may not leave until the session is completed, nor may you speak. Agreed?"

"I guess I have to ask," she said. "Am I going to be watching people driving ten-penny nails into a subject's head?"

"No, no, it's ten in the morning. We don't do that kind of thing until well after lunch."

She cocked her head to one side and gave him an impatient look, knowing he was screwing around with her. He finally grinned.

"No, this is going to be done in what we lovingly call the Extrusion Room. It hasn't been used since the good doctor here retired, much to our sorrow."

"Who's the subject?" she asked.

"Agreed? Or not agreed?"

"Yes, agreed," she said. "Never tell and don't speak. Got it."

"Very well, Ms. Sloan. Never violate those conditions, especially the 'tell' part. If you do, we will find you and introduce you to the museum level. Now, Doctor Allender: Do you know who the subject is?"

"Hank Wallace didn't say," Allender replied. "He termed it a 'job of work.'"

"Ah, yes, I've heard that term before," Battle said. He fiddled with some controls on the console that was sitting on his desk. One of the eight-foot-high scenic panels went gray and then came back into focus. It now showed a gently lit room carpeted on both the floor and the walls, with a medium-sized conference table in the middle. There were two comfortable-looking, high-backed upholstered chairs, one on either side of the table. There was a single, oversized doorway with a window at the back of the room. The door had a sign on it that she couldn't read, but she did notice that the door lacked a handle. In its place was a simple brass plate.

Sitting at the table in one of the upholstered chairs was a woman dressed in what looked to Melanie like an oversized, sleeveless, white pillowcase. The woman was Rebecca Lansing, and Melanie thought she looked terrified.

"What. The. Fuck," she murmured, unaware that she'd even said it.

TWENTY-THREE

"The Secret Service brought her down here from Washington late last night," Battle said, returning the large screen to a pastoral scene. "We put her in a simple cell. This morning she was allowed to shower but then was given the white smock you see her wearing now. All of her other clothes were confiscated. She got breakfast in her cell and then was taken down to the interrogation suite."

"Has she protested or otherwise spoken?" Allender asked.

"Not to us. The Secret Service escort said she raised hell when they came for her, but once they strapped her into the backseat she stayed quiet all the way down."

"Okay, I'll need to make some phone calls first," Allender said. "Is Doctor Chen participating?"

"Ready and waiting, as is the surgical team. They won't scrub until you tell them to."

"Right," Allender said. "Melanie, could you please write up a timeline of all your activities since you first arrived in Greer's office? Line by line, time and date."

"On it," she said, looking for a legal pad. Allender thought she looked just a bit worried now. Battle probably shouldn't have used that word "surgical," he thought. Oh, well. He sat down at the secure-link console in Battle's office, and made his first call.

Forty minutes later he had what he needed. He told Battle he was ready. A moment later a man wearing medical scrubs appeared and motioned for Allender to follow him. They took an elevator down to the interrogation level, where his escort took him to the prop room. There he gave Allender a doctor's white coat, a face mask, a pair of latex gloves, and a boxed syringe set. The doctor's coat was white on one side, but black on the other. The fabric case was covered in transparent plastic wrap with a sterile label acting as the band. Inside were several needles, two syringes, packaged alcohol swabs, and three tiny vials of clear fluid.

"What has she had to eat or drink?" Allender asked.

"Breakfast this morning—a muffin and coffee. Nothing but a bottle of water since. One bathroom break, thirty minutes ago."

"And she's in the autorestraint chair?'

"Yes, sir. The remote is at the end of the right armrest on your chair. Once to restrain, twice to tighten, three times to relax, hold to fully open. It's a newer model, put in since you were last here."

"The backlighting panels are the same?"

"Yes, sir. Dark behind you, controllable behind the subject. We have the backlight profile for your, um—"

"Special eyes?" Allender said, turning to look the young man full in the face without his glasses on.

The escort smiled nervously, then looked away. "Exactly, sir."

"Okay," Allender said. "I'll call Chen in over the closed circuit when I need him."

"Very good, sir. Need anything else or are you ready to go in?"

"How long has she been in there?"

"Two hours, now."

"That should do it."

They went down the hall to the actual interview suite. The escort put his palm against a reader plate and the door clicked open, swinging into the room with a slight hiss. The room had been pressurized at slightly above ambient pressure. Once Allender went in, the escort brought his paraphernalia to the table, put two bottles of water on the table next to Allender's chair, then backed away and closed the door. Allender sat down, briefly touched the medical equipment, and then looked across the table at the totally surprised woman.

"You!" Rebecca said. "What are *you* doing here?"

"I might ask you the same question, Rebecca," he said. His chair was two inches higher off the ground than hers, forcing her to look up at him. "Or whatever your real name is."

"What is the meaning of this—this *out*rage?" she said, angrily. "Where am I? Why am I being held prisoner here? I want to call Langley."

Allender let her spout. He said nothing, just examined her with those amber eyes, staring at tell points in her face, the blood vessels on her neck, and then her hands, then back to her chest to gauge her respiration rate, all in order to take in each physical manifestation of how much stress she was under. He felt his ears crackle just a tiny bit as the air pressure inched up. Then came the sound of elevator machinery spooling up outside the room. The lights flickered imperceptibly, and the platform onto which both chairs were bolted dropped two inches before stopping and then slowly, almost imperceptibly, began inching back to their original position while the elevator noise reached steady state. His ears crackled again, with a tiny bit more force this time. Air came gently out of a continuous register all around the room to heighten the impression that the whole room was going down.

"Are we *moving*?" she cried, looking around as if to confirm what her senses were telling her. The chairs dipped again as the "elevator" spooled down; then it "landed," and everything went still.

"Not anymore," Allender said. "What we need to do here requires extreme security. That's best accomplished a hundred feet underground."

By now the temperature had also gone up a few degrees. She wasn't exactly perspiring, but her cheeks were starting to flush. To one side lights came on in the adjacent room. Rebecca looked. The window in the door was no more than a foot square, but Allender knew she would be able to see figures moving around in there, and at least one surgical spotlight on the ceiling.

"Let's begin with this," he said. "You told me you worked in the director's office. I've spoken to Wayne Corry, who is his principal admin assistant. He tells me he has no Rebecca Lansing in the system."

"When I was sent to the Bureau I was assigned a cover name," she said. "You still haven't told me why I am being held here. You're Agency, so you must know that all you have to do is call—" Then she stopped.

"Go on," he said. "Call—?"

"Operations, for God's sake."

"As in Carson McGill?"

"He's the DDO," she replied. "I'm just an operative. As you must know, operatives don't get their tasking from the DDO himself."

"Okay, who's your controller?"

"I'm not at liberty to tell anyone that, as—"

"As I must know, yes, got that. But you told me you didn't work for Carson McGill. Now you're saying you do?"

As they'd been talking, the lighting in the room had changed subtly. The wall behind Allender was going dark, while the wall behind Rebecca was changing to a hue that amplified the glowing aspect of Allender's eyes. Rebecca was trying not to make direct eye contact, which drew her gaze again to that little window. "Who are those people?" she asked. "What are they doing?"

"Do you work for Carson McGill?" he asked.

"I want this to stop," she said, her facial expression and the tension in her voice revealing that she was getting scared.

"Are you afraid of me?" he asked in a soft but menacing voice.

"No," she said, trying for a brave face.

"Good," he said. "So sit back, relax for a minute, and then we'll continue."

She took a deep breath, then straightened up in the chair and put her arms back down on the armrest. He hit the button. Four stainless-steel bands emerged from the chair like coils in a big spring. One went around her neck, one on each side clamped down on her arms, and the fourth encircled her waist. She gasped when she realized that she was fully restrained now, and then tried to stand up. He hit the button twice and the bands tightened enough to make her inhale with fright. She went rigid.

Allender pulled the fabric medical case closer, unzipped it, and opened it. A recessed pin light in the ceiling lit up the collection of needles and the syringe, making the needles glitter. He reached into the pocket of his doctor's white coat and pulled out the gloves and the face mask.

"What are you going to do?" she whimpered. "Please, let me make one call."

"Allergic to anything?" he asked, as he picked up one of the syringes and affixed a needle. "No? Good, because I'm going to give you an injection which will make you sleepy. Then we're going to talk some more, only this time I think you'll be a little more forthcoming."

"No," she said. "Please don't do that. I can't—I don't want—" She stuttered to a stop, her eyes fixed on the syringe.

He picked up one of the vials, stripped off the metal protective cap, and then pulled back the syringe's bolt handle about an inch. He pushed the needle through the rubber cap and pressed some air into the vial, then reversed the handle and drew up some of the clear fluid in the vial. He got up and walked around the end of the table with an alcohol swab in one hand and the syringe in the other. She struggled with the restraints but there was nothing she could do.

He stood behind her and swabbed the lower right side of her neck.

"Hold still, please," he said. "You don't want me missing my target here."

He gave her the injection and then waited; it took effect in fifteen seconds and she slumped in the restraints with a plaintive sigh. He went back to his chair and relaxed, but he did not remove the steel restraints. He took off the mask and the gloves, and then the white coat. He turned it inside out, and put it back on. Then he opened a small drawer under the table and took out a thin, black collar microphone, which he clipped on, leading the wire under his collar and down through the coat to the table port. He sat down and waited, sipping some water, until she mumbled something and her eyes fluttered. At that moment the control room darkened the room completely except for the lighting panels behind Rebecca, whose LEDs now made Allender's eyes glow like hot coals. With the all-black coat, the only thing she would see would be his face, floating like a specter above the table, framing those hypnotic eyes.

"What is your name?" he asked.

She blinked a couple of times, wet her lips, cleared her throat and tried to speak, but slurred her words. He could tell, however, that she'd been trying to say "Rebecca Lansing." Her eyes kept closing and then snapping back open. Control then cued the deep, almost subliminal organ tone. He could barely hear it, but he knew her sub-conscious mind could definitely hear it. Her head cocked impercep-tibly when the tone came on.

He keyed on the invisible mike. "What is your name?" he asked again, but this time the voice seemed to come from everywhere, with a slight reverberation. Several small speakers in the wall behind her uttered small, weird noises, giving the acoustic impression that some-thing large was creeping up behind her through an immense forest.

She turned her head to look behind her, which was when Allender slid his chair one foot to the right on the greased track underneath the chair. "Look at me!" he said, the word roaring out of the speakers. She jumped, badly frightened now as her senses tried to take in her environment. She looked to where he had been, and then jerked her head to the left. She was still having trouble focusing, especially now that Allender's face seemed to have detached from the rest of his body and was floating in midair. He widened his eyes to full power and listened to the stream of thoughts that were crossing his mind.

That were *not* crossing his mind, he realized. Shit. She's blocking. She's *faking*! She's not scared at all.

"What is your name?" the speakers hissed, this time from under the table. An air nozzle under the table blew a short jet of warm air against several strands of cotton mop cordage, which had been suspended from the underside of the table. She jumped when they caressed her ankle. She looked back at him and said no, but in a tiny voice. Allender pressed a button under the table. A hologram materialized at the opposite end of the table, surrounded by a pale green mist that evolved into the face of McGill. The face drifted in and out of focus, but it had Rebecca's undivided attention.

"Oh, go ahead, tell him," the face said, in McGill's distinctive voice. "It doesn't matter now."

"Wha-a-t?" she cried. "What are you saying? *What* doesn't matter?"

Allender slid his seat back to its original position while they held their ghostly dialogue. "They know," the hologram said. "They know everything. Spare yourself. I release you. Tell him what he needs to know so they don't hurt you. Or worse, much worse." Then the mists returned and the hologram dissolved into darkness.

Rebecca looked back toward where Allender had been, unaware that he had moved again. Her eyes flicked back and forth before settling on his face. For an instant he thought he had her, but then, as he'd almost expected, she settled back in the restraints and looked directly into his eyes.

"Nice try," she said. "Especially the hologram."

"Well, shit," Allender sighed. "And you're right—we did try. The easy way, I mean. Lights."

Normal lighting brightened the room, and then the door to the adjoining room opened on silent hinges and a Chinese man stepped through, dressed in surgical scrubs. Behind him the brightly lit room revealed itself to be a pre-op room. The Chinese man greeted Allender in Mandarin.

"Quite a show, I must admit," he said, examining the perspiring woman glaring at him from down the table.

"Usually does it unless you're facing a deep-training operative," Allender replied. "So: Get your team scrubbed. Take one kidney for now. We'll show it to her and explain that we're going to keep it viable for two hours, then send it out to the city organ-transplant center. If she won't talk after that, we'll take the other one and send her downstairs, hook her up to life support, and then do comprehensive harvesting. We don't have time to go through any more profiles with this one."

"Yes, Doctor," Chen said. "One hour, we'll be ready." He headed back into the OR suite.

Allender got up, shucked the lab coat and the gloves, put on his glasses, and started to walk out of the room.

"You wouldn't," Rebecca said, in flawless Mandarin.

Allender stopped long enough to suppress a smile. Then he turned around. "You're right," he said, also in Mandarin. "*I* wouldn't. But Chen will. The MSS killed his parents, so he's a bear when it comes to Chinese operatives. You're lucky it's going to be a kidney. His last one involved surgically removing the guy's eyeballs from their sockets and letting them dangle on his face so he could see him piss himself. Think about it."

He then did leave the room before she could say anything. The door to the operating area was still open, leaving her a great view of the preparations being made in there, including trays of brightly glittering surgical instruments. Allender walked to the elevator, went up two floors and then down to Battle's office, where he and Melanie congratulated him. "How in the world did you do the hologram?" she asked. "I swear, McGill was right there."

"Gave five minutes of video of McGill talking to a camera plus about a hundred scripts to an outfit in Hollywood that does those cartoon movies. Took 'em six months. We have an entire database of faces and short speeches like that, including over a hundred foreign spymasters. It's pretty effective, except with jihadis."

"What do you do with them?"

"You probably don't want to know that, Melanie. Deacon, I think she'll break on the table, but if not, I intend to have Chen put her to sleep, make the appropriate external incisions, and then establish some pain paths that would resemble a post-open-nephrectomy recovery. We'll bring her out, show her a 'kidney' in a dish, and then try again."

"What do you think she knows?" Battle asked.

"I've already made her as an MSS operative. Her Mandarin tells me she was probably taken as a small child, most likely in Hong Kong, and brought up Chinese in service to the State. She's Caucasian on the outside but all ChiCom inside. Their Section 70 has a whole stable of them. Closest thing to a perfect robot you're going to see, at least for the next five years. They call them dragon seeds."

"Are you saying that this woman is a mole in the DDO's office?" Battle asked.

"Worse than that, probably, but I'm still in the dark on some aspects of this mess. Remember, the Chinese are masters of the long game. She was probably sent for immersion training here in the States as a strictly supervised teenager right through college."

"And *this* is the person who was sent to assist the FBI in finding out what happened to Wallace?" Melanie asked.

"Supposedly sent by the director, but so far, at the admin-assistant level, we find out that they've never heard of her, at least under that name."

"And yet she had access to Agency assets when Chiang's son showed up," she pointed out.

"Which means?"

"She *has* to be working for McGill," Battle said.

"*That's* what I need to prove," Allender said. "I think she knows at least the outline of what McGill is up to, and that was the second thing Hank Wallace will need. Time is of the essence, because Congresswoman Greer is about to nuke the Agency on public media. Now: Where can we get lunch?"

Battle looked at his watch. "The roach coach should be here any minute. They've got sandwiches, hot dogs, soft drinks, stuff like that."

They met the food truck a few minutes later outside the building, in company with several of the employees. The truck looked like an oversized ice-cream truck, and it was doing a healthy business with one side opened for food service. Battle recommended the organic chili dogs. Allender just rolled his eyes and went with a plain ham sandwich.

They went back to the office and had lunch in Battle's small conference room. A television screen on one wall showed Rebecca still sitting there at the table, under restraint, and looking increasingly worried. They saw one of the escorts come in to check on her. She asked for water, but he declined, telling her nothing to eat or drink before general anesthesia. Dr. Chen's orders. The OR was out of the frame, but they could still see the bright white glow of the operating lights and hear muted conversations.

When Chen finally called, Allender went back down to the lower level. An escort in scrubs was waiting, and they went back to the interrogation suite, walked past the by now sick-looking Rebecca and into the preoperative suite. The actual OR was visible through glass walls in an adjacent room. Chen and his surgical team were waiting in the OR. Allender nodded to Chen and then went back out talk to Rebecca one last time before Chen got to work. There were two orderlies standing behind Rebecca's chair. Rebecca's face revealed that she was long past her "nice try" moment.

"As far as we are concerned, you are a spy for the People's Republic of China," Allender began, after taking off his glasses. "If our roles were reversed, I would be standing in an execution courtyard in front of a firing squad. Or, like General Chiang, facing disembowelment and then a lunch date with a pack of vultures. So: One last time— what is your name?"

She swallowed hard. Almost on cue, someone in the pre-op suite dropped a steel pan, causing her to flinch and look over at the door. Then she looked back into Allender's amber eyes. Fear and fatigue had finally broken down her mental defenses, so this time he could hear her: Mei Ling Won. He switched to Mandarin.

"Mei Ling Won," he said. She blinked in surprise. Allender wasn't entirely sure whether she'd said it or just thought it, but the fact that he knew it was apparently the final straw. The woman closed her eyes and collapsed in the restraints with a great sigh. One of the orderlies, suspecting they'd missed a suicide pill, immediately felt for a pulse then looked up at Allender and nodded. Still alive.

Allender reached under the tabletop and withdrew the restraints while the orderlies held her upright in the interrogation chair.

"Give her some water," he ordered. She opened her eyes and drank half the bottle when it was handed to her. Then she put it down and looked back at Allender.

"I don't know what exactly he has planned," she said. "But it does involve killing Henry Wallace. And by now, you."

"Carson McGill?"

She smiled at him as if he was a fool. "Who else?"

TWENTY-FOUR

Allender went back to Battle's office where Melanie was waiting. "Mister Battle's gone to wrap up the surgical team," she said. "And get Rebecca—or I guess it's Mei Ling—to a detention cell."

"Have we heard from Wallace?"

"Yes, sir, we have. His people have asked us to call a certain number when we have a result."

"Okay," Allender said. "Call that number, and tell whomever answers that I want a videoconference with Henry Wallace."

While Melanie was making the call, Allender went over to a small bookcase in one corner of Battle's office, pressed the spine of the Holy Bible. Two doors opened to reveal a well-stocked liquor cabinet. He poured himself a small Scotch and then sat down at Battle's desk. He'd come to the realization while riding the elevator up that this one had been a close-run thing. If Mei Ling had been Japanese she never would have broken, and some of the Chinese operatives he'd worked were that strong, too. The first surgery would have been a fake, of course, but if she'd kept on, he'd have had to tell Chen to actually take a kidney, and, if necessary, the other one. Shit, he thought. I'm getting soft in my old age. Chen, on the other hand, was probably frustrated.

"Sir?" Melanie called from across the room. "Their operator says they don't have video capability at their current location."

"Then tell them to get some," Allender said. "I'm not speaking to Wallace until I can both hear him *and* see him."

Wallace himself called back five minutes later. "O ye of little faith," he began. "Don't you recognize my voice? I'm told it's unique back at Langley."

"And so it is, Mister Wallace," Allender said. "But since I can't be sure where you are, I want a little more proof that you are who you're supposed to be."

"We're on a secure Agency voice link right now, are we not?"

"You, me, and who else? Carson perhaps?"

There was a silence on the line for a few seconds. "Okay," Wallace sighed. "I'll have to move. Stay right there."

Battle came back about then, saw Allender sitting at his desk, and asked what was up. Allender told him to get a videoconferencing terminal set up in his conference room.

It took an hour, during which Allender wrote out what had transpired in the interrogation suite and what he'd actually achieved. Obviously Wallace wouldn't have had Rebecca Lansing picked up if he didn't already suspect her, but Allender still could not figure out what the game was here.

The phone in the conference room rang, and then the flat wall screen at the end of the table lit up, revealing Henry Wallace in all his annoyed glory. Melanie and Battle took seats alongside Allender.

"Okay," he began. "Satisfied? And, no, there's no gun in my back." He reached a hand up to the camera on his end and swung it around the room, which appeared to be a large conference room. As best Allender could tell, there was no one else in the room with Wallace. "What did you find out?"

"That she is MSS, probably one of their Section 70, dragon-seed creatures. She told me that Carson McGill plans to kill you. And me, apparently."

"Does she know what he's up to?"

"She says she does not," Allender said. "Do you?"

"I have my suspicions," Wallace said. "But we need to smoke McGill out somehow. I'm hoping that when Greer unloads, that will do it."

"She hasn't gone public yet?"

"No, and that's another little mystery. Perhaps McGill's made her an offer she can't refuse."

"My sense of Chairwoman Greer is that she is not easily intimidated," Allender said. "Quite the opposite—I think that would make it worse."

"May not be intimidation," Wallace said. "Remember, she's a congressperson. Refresh my memory: Tell me how you got into this goat-grab in the first place?"

"It started with McGill telling me that you had been found dead of unknown causes at your home. He was supposedly keeping that news close-hold, but he told Hingham, who informed Greer. She, of course, didn't trust Langley to do anything but cover it all up, so she got the Bureau into it. McGill said he wanted me to 'assist' as a senior liaison officer between the DDO and the Bureau's team."

"'Assist'? As in lead them astray at every inconspicuous opportunity?"

"Yes."

"Okay, now walk me through the rest of it, by which I mean your involvement."

Allender did, ending with what Mei Ling had said.

"How dramatic," Wallace said with an expression that said he thought it was bullshit.

"What do we do with her?" Allender asked.

"Eventually, we'll hand her over to the Chinese embassy and formally thank them for her services to the Central Intelligence Agency and the FBI. Tell them that she's been extremely helpful, but that she probably needs a little vacation back in China just now."

"What will they do to her?"

"Same thing we'd do: Either give her a medal for her efforts, or, if they think she was turned, close her out. I could give her one last chance to expose her own network in return for the same thing we did for Ms. Sloan, there, but, the moment she was taken, I have to assume that network rolled itself up. Keep her there for now."

"All right; I'll have Deacon set that up."

"In the meantime, you and Ms. Sloan go back to your town house and await further instructions. I'll have people in place to make sure no more Kung Fu Pandas come calling. I think I know what Carson's up to, and it involves his endless pursuit of the top slot at Langley."

"Except for one open question, Mister Wallace," Allender said.

"What's that?" Wallace asked, sounding impatient now.

"He had an MSS operative working for him. That can mean one of two things: He knew she was a double, and it pleased him to make her expendable. The second alternative is too awful to contemplate."

Wallace just stared at him for a long moment. "There are days, Doctor Allender," he said, finally, "when you scare even me. Don't leave for Washington until your escort arrives. Once you get there, stay put. I may have one last job for you."

"I'm a retired interrogator, Mister Wallace," Allender said. "Not an operator."

"That's what you think, sport," Wallace said with a wolfish grin.

The screen went dark.

One last job, Allender thought. As in, Why don't you become the goat that gets staked out in the jungle to draw in the tiger. He looked over at Melanie and saw from the expression on her face that she was thinking the same thing.

Eight o'clock found them in the tower study trying to figure out what would happen next. A Secret Service SUV was parked out front and there were two agents standing out on the sidewalk in front of the house. Allender had seen another vehicle in the alley and two more agents patrolling back there plus a third in the backyard itself. They'd had to cool their heels in the Dungeons for two hours while Wallace got everything set up in Washington. The drive up from Williamsburg had been uneventful, with only a single pit stop for a bathroom break and a greaseburger.

"Uncle Hank must be expecting a full frontal assault of some kind," Allender said, peering through the front curtains one more time.

"Do we really know who those people are out there?" Melanie asked. "They could be there to keep us *in,* not someone else out."

Allender sat back down, took off his protective glasses, rubbed his tired eyes, and looked longingly at the Scotch decanter but decided against it. He'd been turning to a wee dram a bit too often these days. "If that were the case," he said, stifling a yawn, "it would have been easier just to keep us on the Farm. I've set you up in the guest room, by the way."

"Thank you," she said. "I'm more than ready."

"Yeah, me, too. It's been a long day. An interrogation like that one is always stressful."

"As in, this will hurt me more than it will you . . . ?"

"Something like that," he said, distractedly. "Once the sensory illusions have worked their magic, the subjects often get pretty loud."

"You mean screaming?"

"Up here," he said, tapping his forehead.

"You can actually hear what they're thinking?"

"It's complicated," he said. "It's a mixture of hearing, feeling, and subconscious sensing. And mental pressure, just for grins."

"A blessing or a curse, I wonder," she said.

"Just like these," he said with a tired smile, pointing now at his amber eyes. "My classmates in Taipei were apprehensive around me. If I'd been in an American school, I would have been the school freak."

She tilted her head to one side. "And that's why you keep your distance from women, isn't it," she said.

"Women are dangerous," he replied. "Let them get close, and they destroy the dragon-eyes mystique. Can't have that."

"Let women get close, they can do a lot more than that, Sir Dragon Eyes."

He shook his head. "I'm going up," he sighed.

"Chicken," she said to his back as he went upstairs. He clucked back at her, but smiled as he did. And kept going.

His bedroom, fully restored, took up one entire side of the house, including a part of the tower, which had been made into a sitting alcove. He took one last look out the front windows at the security cordon. Secret Service, he thought. How the hell did the Secret Service get into this mess? Then he remembered where Hank had come from before the CIA.

He got the Judge out of its hole, checked the loads, and put it on the bed beside him. He thought about getting a quick shower, but decided to turn out the lights and then lie down on the bed, still dressed, for just a moment or so. He hadn't been exaggerating about the mental pressure of the Extrusion Room. Maybe a little in the case of Mei Ling, because once he'd realized he couldn't read her—that she was blocking—he knew she was what she was. After that, all he had to do was raise the physical threat to the point where she folded or became a whole-body organ donor, but he could distinctly remember a couple of subjects whose mental strength had actually caused him pain.

And now here was Melanie Sloan beginning to circle him, Melanie of the new face but the same banked-coals sexuality. He tried to recall what she'd looked like when he'd forced her to stand naked in front of his desk. He couldn't quite do it, which, in itself, told him something about himself, that the man in him wanted the chance to paint that picture in his own imagination. Why? Because he wanted her. He opened his eyes at that thought. Was it possible she wanted him as well? If so, she'd be the first woman who'd managed to get past his scary eyes and semi-electric head. What had she said— she liked to ride the edge once in a while. Then he laughed at his capacity for self-delusion and drifted off to sleep.

TWENTY-FIVE

He awoke to the sound of urgent knocking on his door, and then Melanie was in his room. The night-light in the hall framed her in complete silhouette, and she was telling him to wake up right now. He sat up, scrambling to focus on where he was and who she was.

"What's the matter?" he mumbled, looking at his watch. It was five minutes past eleven.

"They're gone," she said in a low voice. "The Secret Service guys. They're all gone, front and back."

"You sure?"

"Yes; there's no one out there. We're wide open."

He swung his legs onto the floor. She was dressed in the same pantsuit outfit she'd been wearing downstairs, which meant she'd done the same thing he had: lain down for a minute and promptly gone to sleep. He instinctively reached for the Judge and then stood up.

"I'm going to go make sure," he said. "Wallace promised protection."

Together they made the rounds of the upstairs windows, front and back, his room, her room. There was no one out there except the occasional car going past as the traffic finally died out.

"*Shit!*" Melanie hissed. "So: What do we do? Fort up here or get out of town?"

"Can't get out of town—our cars are still down at the Farm. But I'm leaning to getting out of this house. One firebomb, the old girl will go like dry straw. I know—let's get to the Metro."

"At this hour?"

"It runs until midnight. We can make one of the last trains if we hustle."

"And go where?"

"Away?" he said in exasperation. He dropped the Judge, and then he and Melanie grabbed their cell phones and weapons, went out the back garden gate, and started trotting down the alley, guns ready. They paused at the alley entrance to the first side street. The night was clear but moonless. The streetlights along Connecticut Avenue glowed orange, but the side street was relatively dark. Both sides of the street were chockablock with closely parked cars, but, otherwise, there didn't seem to be anyone afoot.

"The alleys go two more blocks," he said. "Then we can cut over to Dupont Circle and the Metro. I'm not sensing eyes just now."

"Me neither, but any one of these cars could have someone watching. Let's boogie."

They got to the Metro station at 11:25 and hurried down the broken escalator. Neither of them had a wallet, but Melanie kept a Metro card in her cell-phone case. She went through the turnstile, then handed the card back to Allender so he could get through. At this hour, thirty minutes before the system shut down for the night, there was no one else on the platform. The air smelled faintly of ozone and old grease. The day's litter was still lurking in the corners of the platform.

"Which direction? Melanie asked.

"Doesn't matter. Any train will be headed out to the end of the Red Line for the night. We can regroup out there."

"You think Wallace is tracking our phones?"

"I sure as hell hope so," he said. "I think."

He looked anxiously down the tunnel and then back at the down escalator. There were security cameras everywhere, of course, but they wouldn't deter a professional grab team once they figured out where their rabbits had gone to ground. And somehow he knew they *would* figure it out. He didn't want to mention to Melanie that the Agency's phone-tracking devices might not be working sixty feet underground. Or, worse, the possibility that Wallace might not be their friend.

She'd shoved her weapon into her waistband and covered the butt with her jacket. His weapon was in his trouser pocket. The dark material should hide the fairly prominent bulge from security cameras. He fervently hoped. He felt truly exposed out there on the empty platform, with its circular lights embedded on the concrete floor. Then those lights began to blink. The air in the station began to pressurize as the final train of the night approached, stirring a faint breeze and then showing a rising glow of headlights. The litter at the back of the platform danced around in a circle of welcome. The four-car train squeezed its brakes hard and came to a stop right in front of them. The doors slid open, and two people got out. Allender and Melanie stepped into the third car from the end, which was now empty. The chimes rang, and then the doors slid closed. The electric motors ramped up, propelling the train out of the brightly lit station in a hum of power before rushing into the gloom of the next track segment.

Allender looked into the two adjacent cars, visible through the door windows of the intercar connection. No one else in either car. Wait. There was a single Metro cop sitting all the way forward in the second car, just ahead of them. He was leaning back into his seat in a serenely grateful, finally-off-my-aching-feet, end-of-shift pose. Outside, the car's overhead lights illuminated flashes of concrete tunnel panels on either side like empty frames in a black-and-white movie.

"Did we make it?" Melanie asked.

"Metro Center will tell the tale," he said. "Three lines converge there. If they're on to us, that's where they'll board. Listen, we may have to bail out in a hurry. Split up or stay together—what d'you think?"

Melanie gave him an amused look. "I don't even know who 'they' are. Call me Velcro."

The train began to decelerate for the next station. It was now 11:40, so this would definitely be the last train running the Red Line and the last station before the Metro Center complex, where it was possible to access three of the system's lines in a maze of bridges, platforms, and stairwells.

The outside lit up as the train rushed into the station and shuddered to a stop. The doors hissed open. The Metro cop looked up for a moment, then resumed his downtime. The gongs chimed for the door's closing announcement. Then, to their alarm, two teams of three Chinese men each rushed the doors into the cars on either side of their car. They timed it so close that the doors had to rebound, provoking an angry response about standing clear of the doors from the train's announcing-system robot.

The doors closed again, and then the train lurched forward toward Metro Center. The Chinese men were all dressed in dark suits, of all things, complete with ties. They dropped into seats from which both teams could stare into the car between them through the connecting door windows.

"Now what," Melanie growled, unconsciously clearing her weapon from her waistband.

"Lots more people at the next stop, even now," Allender said. "We get off and look for Metro security."

"Like *that* guy?" Melanie asked, pointing to the dozing guard in the next car ahead. The Chinese weren't even looking at him. The train had reached max speed now and was screeching through the big dogleg turn that led into Metro Center.

"You got a better idea?"

"Yeah. Let's wait for the train to stop and then start shooting into the cars on either side. *Then* run for it. That ought to get the Metro security system energized."

"We can't do that," he said. "Too many civilians might be getting on. Besides, right now those guys're just some Chinese businessmen riding the train."

"Sure they are," she muttered between clenched teeth. "Six businessmen on the Metro at midnight? Mei Ling said McGill was going to kill people. She's a Chinese operative. Makes sense that's who he'd use."

The train's speed had leveled off. They'd start slowing in a minute. Melanie had racked her weapon and was concealing it in her lap. The Chinese appeared to be staring blankly into space.

"Okay," Allender said. "Train stops, we get up, get off, and head for the station security office. It'll be near the fare-card machines and the turnstiles. See what those guys do. If weapons come out, then we'll have to wing it."

"There's six of them," she pointed out.

"Well, hell," he said. "You're the trained operator. You figure something out."

Melanie checked her phone and made a face. The train began to decelerate, accompanied by a lot of clacking and sparking as the wheels crossed multiple tracks and switch points, each one generating a blue-white flash beneath the car. Finally the train entered Metro Center and came to a stop. Allender looked at the Chinese teams, who remained motionless. The doors chimed and then opened.

"Let's go," he said. They got up and stepped out of the car. Perhaps a dozen people stood on the platform, most of whom looked like they'd been out on the town. Allender spotted the station security office and started in that direction, but Melanie grabbed his elbow. The doors on the train behind them chimed and then slid shut. All six Chinese "businessmen" remained seated. None of them paid the least bit of attention to Allender or Melanie, who was now trying to conceal her weapon in the crook of her arm. The train's brakes exhaled and the cars jolted into motion and then hummed out of the station, accelerating into the dark tunnel beyond. Now they were alone on the platform.

"WTF?" Melanie murmured, looking around the station to see what she'd missed. Then Allender thought he'd spotted movement up on the escalators.

"Let's go," he ordered urgently. "Go *down,* to the next platform."

"Wha-at?" she asked as she joined him in a quick trot toward the short escalator leading down to the next platform. He didn't answer, but took the sliding steel stairs two at a time. She nearly fell trying to keep up with him and he had to grab her at the bottom. This platform was also empty, but Allender realized that it was just a transfer platform: no turnstiles, no station office, no Metro personnel.

Then he heard excited voices up above.

Excited *Chinese* voices. "*Shit!*" he cursed, and then headed toward the end of the platform.

"What are we doing?" she called as she chased after him.

"Into the tunnel. *Now!*"

"Are you crazy?" she said. "We can't do that."

He got to the end of the platform, sat down on the concrete lip, and jumped down to the track bed. He turned around and helped her do the same. Then, still holding her hand, he lunged into the tunnel.

"What if a train comes?" she shouted at him. "There's nowhere to go!"

"That was the last train," he said over his shoulder. "Now keep quiet. We need to listen."

They ran another hundred feet and then stopped. There were two tracks in this tunnel, glinting softly in the light from the dirt-covered fire-tight light fixtures mounted every fifty feet. Four rails for the trains, two center strips for the six-hundred-volt power running down between the rails. They could still see a white glow from Metro Center, but the tunnel was strangely quiet.

"What are we listening for?" she whispered. Then they both heard voices coming from the direction of the station. They started trotting farther into the tunnel, their feet crunching softly in all the dirt and trash on the floor. By this point the only light was coming from the wall fixtures, and some of them weren't working. They kept going, trying to maintain distance from their pursuers without making any noise. The breeze in their faces felt good, until they both realized what that breeze meant.

Allender scanned the darkness ahead, looking for an alcove or any other kind of space notched into the tunnel wall that would get them back away from an oncoming train. The distance between the outer rails and the wall was no more than five feet.

"There," Melanie cried out. "On the other side."

Allender saw it, too. A firefighting station, with hose racks, a valve bank, a man-sized CO_2 bottle mounted on a dolly, and a refrigerator-sized locker labeled BREATHING APPARATUS. The fire station was set back into a notch in the tunnel wall. It would be tight, but better than being so close to the tracks that the suction would be strong enough to pull them under the cars. But first, they had to get across the four tracks and their power strips.

The breeze was stronger now, and a distinct humming filled the air. They could no longer hear any voices behind them. They looked at each other for an instant and then stepped carefully across the tracks and their six-hundred-volt "third rails." This was no time to trip over one of the concrete crossties. Allender flattened himself between the locker and the valve bank, while Melanie stood next to the CO_2 bottle, facing the wall. A white glow began to fill the tunnel as the train approached. The bow wave of air being compressed by the speeding train was strong enough to force both of them to hold on tight as the train's twin headlights, on high beam as it approached the station, lit up each crack and crevice in the concrete walls. Then with a roar it was right there, and then in the next instant gone, a whirlwind of trash and dust spinning angrily in its wake as its twin taillights vanished around the wide curve leading into Metro Center Station.

Allender touched her shoulder and they took off again, still trying to make as little noise as possible.

"Thought you said that ours was the last train," she said, puffing a little.

"We went down a level, remember?" he said over his shoulder. "This isn't the Red Line anymore."

"Which line is it?"

"Don't remember," Allender replied. After another minute it was obvious that Melanie was running out of steam, so he slowed it to a fast walk. This part of the tunnel looked like all the rest of it, with the only illumination coming from the wall lights. Allender looked for a call box, but the walls were covered in bundles of large aluminum conduit, encased in decades of grime. He checked his cell phone. If it could have laughed at him it would have. The tunnel continued to bend around to the left. It was gradual, but definitely curving. Then suddenly they saw what looked like lights in the distance. Allender stopped to see if they were moving.

"What?" Melanie asked, obviously grateful for the stop.

He pointed ahead. "Lights."

They stared into the distance, but the lights appeared to be stationary and all on the left side. It was hard to tell, because the tunnel curved to their left.

"Maybe there's a call box there," he said. "We have to get out of these tunnels before they start repositioning trains for the morning commute. You okay?"

"Gotta cut back on the gin," she said, bravely.

He nodded, then cupped his hands to his ears and faced back the way they'd come, listening for voices. If their pursuers hadn't found an alcove, they would have much bigger problems than two *laowai* to chase. He heard nothing except the ticking of the rails relaxing after the train's passage.

"Good," he said. "Let's go see what those lights are all about. Maybe there's even a fire escape."

They went another three hundred yards and then stopped again. The lights, which were all dim blue, seemed to frame a gate of some sort. Fifty feet ahead of the gate they could see a set of rails curving off the main line and heading under those gates. In the far distance shone a penumbra of more lights up on overhead signal towers but facing away from them. There were several equipment panels mounted on the walls nearby, and Allender thought he could see security cameras above the gates.

"See those cameras?" he said. "Let's get down into their field of view, maybe trip some alarms and get some help."

"Right," she said, and they resumed their jog down the track toward the junction. Allender felt a breeze begin to build on the back of his neck, but it died down after thirty seconds. When they reached the gates they slowed to a walk, both of them looking up at the security cameras to see if any of them were turning to have a look. Then a bank of much larger white lights framing the gates snapped on, blinding both of them. For a horrible instant Allender thought a train was coming right at them.

"HALT!" boomed a loud male voice. "You are *not* authorized to be here. Turn around right now."

Allender put an arm up in front of his eyes and held his credentials case out in front of his face. Out of the corner of his eye he saw Melanie do the same thing. "Federal officers," he shouted. "We need—"

"You must turn around and go back the way you came. Do it now. Deadly force authorized. You have fifteen seconds."

Allender could now make out human shapes behind those intense lights. They appeared to be taking stations behind the gates. He could see rifle barrels sticking up above their heads, and then, suddenly he couldn't.

"Five seconds. Deadly force authorized. We *will* shoot you. Move. *Now!*"

Allender dropped his arms and turned back into the tunnel. The lights stayed on, intense enough that he thought he could feel the heat from those blue-white bulbs on his neck. Melanie trudged along beside him and cursed softly.

What the hell did we stumble onto, he wondered. He closed his eyes for a second and saw two bright red circles burned into his retina. They walked back up the tracks for another hundred yards before the white glow behind them finally subsided.

"Now what?" Melanie asked. "I can't see shit."

"I guess we go back to Metro Center," he said. "Try again to contact some security people."

"Ours or theirs?" she asked. Then they both heard something coming from behind them. They searched frantically for cover, but this section of the tunnel had no alcoves or other places to get back from the tracks. A glow of headlights rose behind them, but without the sudden burst of wind that one of the trains would produce. They flattened against the nearest wall as the machine came into view.

It wasn't a train, but something smaller and going much slower. The driver's station was a boxy cab up front, fully lit inside, and they could see the driver looking down at his instruments as the car approached. Greenish light reflected from his face, as if he was staring at computer screens. On the body of the vehicle they could see what looked like maintenance men, wearing jumpsuits, safety glasses, hard hats with helmet lights, and large gloves, hanging on to the railing of a platform on the back. Pulses of greenish lights came from underneath the vehicle as the vehicle drew abreast of them, but it was obvious the driver hadn't seen them drawn up against the concrete wall as the vehicle rumbled by. In another moment, it was just a set of red taillights headed up the tunnel toward Metro Center.

Allender realized he'd been holding his breath the whole time, and now exhaled as he eased off the cold concrete.

"I don't think they saw us at all," Melanie said, trying to brush the dust and dirt off her clothes.

Allender looked up the tunnel. "I think you're wrong about that," he said.

Melanie looked. Four figures were walking back down the tunnel toward them, spread out two to a side of the main-line tracks. Instead of tools they appeared to be carrying submachine guns, held flat against their chests.

She didn't hesitate. She drew her weapon and then went down on one knee and assumed a two-handed shooting position, but Allender stepped in front of her and put his left hand down in front of her weapon.

"Don't be stupid," he said, quietly. "There's four of them with automatic weapons. Put that away."

The men had stopped when they saw her kneel, but now they continued to walk toward them, still holding their weapons at port arms. Melanie lowered her weapon but didn't put it back in her waistband. The man on the far right pushed his safety glasses off his face and stepped forward. Melanie gasped when she saw he was Chinese.

"Doctor Allender," the man said in Mandarin. "You must come with us."

"Who are you?" Allender asked.

"We are from the embassy of the People's Republic of China," the man replied. The two men on the other side of the tracks had now moved to get behind the two Americans. "We have been sent by your agency, actually, to bring you to Langley."

"That is absurd," Allender said. Then he heard the bolts on the two submachine guns behind him being retracted to the firing position.

"It might be absurd, but that is why we are here in this tunnel. Why you are here in this tunnel is a mystery, but you have two choices. Come with us or die here and let the morning commute grind your bodies into a red paste."

"What's he saying?" Melanie asked.

"Nothing you want to hear," Allender replied. "We have to go with them. He says they're taking us to Langley."

"Oh, bullshit," she growled. "I'm ready to shoot it out."

"Please, Doctor Allender?" the man said. "Put your weapons down on the concrete and just come with us? You know that is what you are going to do, yes?"

Allender nodded. "Put your gun down on the floor and then keep your hands in sight," he told Melanie. He fished his own weapon out and did the same.

"Ah, very wise," the man said. He barked out some rapid-fire orders and then they were all walking toward Metro Center, the leader in front and the other three behind them, still spread out in firing positions. Allender saw the leader speaking into a tiny radio as they walked.

"We get to Metro Center, I'm going to start screaming," Melanie said. "*And* I have a hideout strapped to my left leg."

"Just stay alert for now, okay?" Allender said. "If there's a crowd of Metro people at Center, then we might have a chance. But it's after midnight and the whole system is shut down except for maintenance people, and they're going to be in the tunnels. That driver probably didn't even know he had 'passengers.' "

If the leader of the grab team had overheard them, he gave no notice of it. The glow of the lights of Metro Center were in view now, and they could sense that the three guards behind them had closed it up. All three were on their side of the tracks now, and walking close enough behind their prisoners that Allender could feel their presence. Their footsteps were almost in unison as they crunched their way through the gravel. They saw the leader pull his safety glasses back down over his face and then slide a yellow fabric sleeve over the front half of his submachine gun. A casual observer could no longer tell what he was carrying, but Allender knew that gun could still do its job if it came to it. Now that there was more light they could see the words Metro Track Maintenance embroidered across the back of his jumpsuit.

"I'm not getting into any car with these fucking guys," Melanie muttered, as the glow grew more apparent. "I'll take the three behind us. You've got the fearless leader ahead of us."

"Mel—" Allender started, but it was too late. Melanie gave an earsplitting shriek, whirled around, and lunged at the three guards walking close behind them. She managed to knock two of them sideways. As they tripped over the outside rail and then went sprawling onto the power rail, both of them began to literally cook as six hundred volts split them open like overfired sausages. The third guard recovered himself after bouncing off the wall, but was so shocked by what he was seeing that Melanie had time to kick him in the groin and then smash his head against the tunnel wall. He collapsed in a bloody-faced heap.

The leader hadn't hesitated, either. When he saw what was happening, he swung the bagged submachine gun's barrel in Allender's direction and pulled the trigger. Nothing happened, so he snatched at the slide to cock it, but the slide got caught in the fabric and his second attempt failed as well. Before Allender could do anything, he heard three cracks from a pistol behind him and the leader doubled over, dropping his weapon, then subsided into mortal stillness over a rapidly spreading pool of blood. Behind them the horror show on the rails had progressed to the blazing-barbecue phase. Melanie flew past Allender and grabbed up the leader's weapon, shucking off the fabric sleeve. The slide closed with an authoritative click. She handed him a snub-nosed hammerless .38 as she went by.

"Okay," she said, breathlessly. "*Now* we go to Metro Center. You okay?"

Allender had trouble finding his voice and could only nod. One of the bodies behind them began to spatter flaming bits onto the tunnel ceiling. That scene shook him out of his momentary paralysis and into motion to catch up with Melanie, who was already striding determinedly up the tunnel. He jammed the pistol into his coat pocket and hurried to catch up, glad to get away from the horrible smell that was filling the tunnel behind them. In the distance, way behind them, he thought he heard a siren.

Melanie stopped fifty feet short of the tunnel's threshold into Metro Center Station, the submachine gun at the ready and carefully sweeping the cavernous station. Only some of the overhead lights were on, and the platforms on either side were empty. The up-and-over escalators had been shut down, and the glass-walled safety-officer booths on either side were dark. They were now deep in the station, with two more lines joining the maze, one running above them and yet another below. They went to the end of the platform on their side of the tracks and clambered around the locked gate to reach the platform. Allender expected police officers to come trotting down from the station above at any moment, but the silence remained unbroken save for the soft whoosh of the ventilation systems. He could see several cameras around the station, but none of them seemed to be panning in their direction.

"We need to go up one level," Allender said. "Back to the Red Line platform. That can get us to the street."

"How did those guys know we'd be down on this level?" she asked. "The last sighting would have been from those 'businessmen' on our train."

"I can only assume they've got the entire system covered," he replied. "Those businessmen could have gone on to the next stop beyond Metro Center, gotten off and into the tunnels, and simply walked back to Center. You go first—you've got the weapon that counts. I'll be behind you. *Wa-a-y* behind you."

She grinned like a pirate and then they went to the motionless up-and-over escalator and from there on up into the next level. Jesus, he thought. She's enjoying this. He thought about pulling the hideout gun she'd given him, but in a dispute featuring submachine guns there wasn't much point, so he kept it in his pocket. When they reached the top of the second escalator they stopped to look around. To their surprise, there was a four-car train parked down toward the end of the platforms. Its windows were all dark except for the destination banner on the end car, which read OUT OF SERVICE. Allender had expected a night-shift workforce—cleaners, machinery maintenance, fare-card-money collection teams—but there wasn't a soul in sight and only half the overhead lights were on. None of the escalators were running, up or down.

They searched for a way to make a phone call, checking their cell phones and then looking for emergency telephone boxes. Allender saw a door that looked like the security office he'd been in at Union Station. He walked over and tried it. Locked. Melanie checked the Red Line tunnel in both directions, but nothing seemed to be stirring. A cool breeze came down from the extended escalators leading up to street level, but Allender knew there were large expanding metal gates at the entrance to all the Metro stations. It was after one in the morning. They were stuck here until the morning-commute personnel came to work. He realized he was tired and thirsty.

"Now what?" Melanie said, leaning the gun against one of the concrete benches and then sitting down.

"No point in walking to another station," he said. "Strange, though. I really expected a night shift."

"I expected some 'businessmen,'" she said. "Something's wrong."

At that moment they were both startled by the sound of one of those big metal gates being rolled back up on the street level. The sound echoed in the escalator channel, which sloped nearly seventy feet. Melanie picked the gun back up and laid it across her lap. Allender stared hopefully up the escalators, expecting the night crew. Instead, two men appeared at the top of the down escalator and began to walk down. The slanting tunnel containing the escalators was not lit, so they were halfway down before their faces appeared. He was surprised to recognize the first one: none other than

J. Leverett Hingham, the director, looking impeccable even at this hour of the morning.

"Good Lord," Melanie muttered. "What's *he* doing here?"

But by then Allender was trying to wrap his mind around the identity of the stocky figure descending behind Hingham, because it was none other than General Chiang, or, if not him, his twin brother.

TWENTY-SIX

"Okay, what the fuck?" exclaimed Melanie, cradling the submachine gun and standing up. Allender was too surprised to do or say anything. *Chiang? Alive?*

Hingham reached the bottom of the escalator, taking baby steps as the motionless steel panels flattened out into the floor. Chiang was grinning like the proverbial Cheshire cat right behind him.

"Doctor Allender," Hingham said, warmly. "Fancy meeting you here. Recognize this fella?"

"You're supposed to be dead," Allender said in Mandarin.

"Appearances can be deceiving, Doctor," the man replied.

"You two must stop talking in Chinese," Hingham said. "It's rude, if nothing else."

He'd stopped about ten feet from Allender but he was eyeing Melanie, who had turned her body so that the gun covered their two visitors, even though it wasn't raised right at them. "Young lady, there's no need for that," he continued. "I sent some messengers to bring you two in for a chat at Langley. Something must have gone wrong, because my friend here called and said we'd probably have to go ourselves if we wanted to get this done."

"Your 'friend'?" Allender said. "The Chinese MSS station chief in Washington is your friend?"

Hingham waved his hand elegantly. "If I've told you once, I've told you a thousand times, the dominance of China is a foregone conclusion. I've expounded on that thesis to anybody and everybody who'd listen and even some who wouldn't for damned near ever as you well know. I even told the president that when I took the job, and, frankly, I think he tacitly agrees with me."

"I believe that's called treason, Mister Hingham," Allender said.

"Not really, Doctor," Hingham replied. "All I've ever done is facilitate the inevitable congruence of national interests between us and China. The only area I focus on personally is mitigating the unnecessary tussle going on between the Agency and the MSS."

"That is also treason," Allender said. "And don't your responsibilities extend a little farther than China?"

"Not in my view," Hingham replied, appearing to enjoy their discussion. "I've not shared any sources and methods or given them reams of top-secret material. As to all those Middle Eastern conflicts, ISIS, al-Qaeda, the Iranians—they are of little interest to me. I know the rest of the Agency has its hands full with those problems, but, since, in my view, those are all problems which we created, I choose to concentrate on the future."

"What do you mean by 'mitigating,' then?"

" 'Neutralizing' might be a better word," Hingham said, proudly. "Whenever that aging dinosaur, Henry Wallace, dreamed up yet another fanciful operation against the MSS here in the United States, a little bird would fly, and that would be that. Nothing more. Which is why your little black-swan gambit provoked such a harsh reaction, because no one had had the courtesy to inform me."

"Harsh reaction?" Allender said. "Wait until people find out who you've been playing footsie with, Hingham. 'Harsh reaction' won't begin to cover it."

"Who's going to find out, Doctor Allender?" Hingham said, his voice colder now, as if he was finally getting down to the real business at hand. "*You* going to tell them? I think not. But in case you still don't get it, I need you to go with Chiang, here. He wants to share his thinking with you, apparently. For the moment, however, please sit down."

Chiang was standing back from this discussion, his hands in his suit-coat pockets like an Oriental version of Churchill, a barely controlled smile distorting his face, which died away when Melanie quietly raised the submachine gun and pointed it directly at Hingham.

"Hey, now, boys and girls," she announced. "I've got an idea for a harsh reaction."

"Oh, please," Hingham said, rolling his eyes, and then he raised his head and looked behind her. Allender looked to his left, down the platform toward the tunnel. Standing there were four Chinese men dressed in the same Metro Track Maintenance jumpsuits as the previous crew, complete with hard hats. They had workbags draped across their hips which obviously contained some kind of a tool that had a pointed end. Like a submachine gun. He'd never heard them approach. He checked the other end of the station. Four more standing there, too, like white ghosts against the darkness in the tunnel behind them. They weren't posturing in a threatening manner, but the tops of those bags were open. They all had the look of soldiers about them.

"Melanie?" Allender said.

"Sir?" she replied, her voice sounding a little unsteady.

"Put the gun down, Melanie. On the floor. Now, please."

"They can't shoot without hitting each other," she pointed out, ever the tactician.

"Well, you know what?" he said, sitting down on the bench. "I don't think there's going to be any shooting tonight. Just put it down, please."

Melanie stared hard at Hingham, and then at Allender. Then she put the gun down and joined him on the cement bench.

"Because you've decided to just go with us peacefully into the capital night, correct?" Hingham asked, obviously relieved. Chiang positively gloated.

Allender, still watching Melanie, didn't answer. He sensed that she was itching for another fight, like the one she'd won so conclusively earlier.

Hingham shrugged and turned away to talk to Chiang, who started calling out orders to his people in the station. The two teams came forward, while Chiang got busy on a radiophone. Two of the Chinese went trotting up the escalator. Hingham just stood there, looking entirely satisfied, if not proud.

"I can pick that thing up and grease the first group before anybody could react," Melanie muttered to Allender. "Their weapons are still in those bags."

Allender put a hand on her knee and shook his head again.

"These people aren't here to *talk* to us," she protested.

Allender leaned toward her. "No, they're not, but I think that everything that's happened tonight has been staged. It's just too neat. Too pat. We're warned that something's really wrong at Langley. Told to go home and wait. One moment we have Secret Service protection, then we don't. We make a run for it, but we have no wheels. So we run for the Metro. We go one stop and then a Chinese squad gets onto the train. We bail out at the next stop, Metro Center, but they keep going. We go into one of the tunnels and run into a bunch of guards who force us to go back. We encounter yet another team. We get by that little problem, come back to Metro Center, and find it completely empty. No security reaction to people being down in the tunnels. No reaction to an unscheduled dim sum on the third rail, which should have at least set off smoke alarms. I know it's one-something in the morning, but there should be people here. This doesn't read."

"Just goes to show you how well these people are organized, doesn't it, Doctor," Hingham said, with a triumphant sneer. He'd come up behind them and overheard what Allender had been saying. "Think about it: In our own capital city, they can go anywhere and do anything. Can you imagine an American team doing that in Beijing? *That's* what I've been talking about all along: China. A *billion* of them. China is invincible. America is in decline. There can only be one end to all this. Now, enough chitchat. Chiang, if you please?"

Chiang stepped forward and motioned for his two teams to surround their captives. Hingham stepped out of the way, as if to supervise. The leader of one of the teams drew Chiang aside to tell him something, and Allender saw the general's face darken. He swung around and stared hard at Allender and Melanie.

"Perhaps we should just end this little drama right here and now," he growled in Mandarin.

Wait a minute, Allender thought. That's not Chiang. That voice is all wrong.

At that moment, the station reverberated with the ding-dong sound of the "doors opening" chime on that dark train. All the lights in the station flared to life, as well as the lights in the cars of the train, revealing about a hundred SWAT officers in full gear, who poured out of the cars and filled the platform without a word being spoken. The Chinese snatch teams grabbed their weapons but then looked to Chiang, who sighed and then gave a barely noticeable shake of his head. Their hands fell back to their sides.

Hingham's eyes, however, were out on stalks at the sight of the police. A police captain materialized in front of Allender and Melanie. He asked them both to come with him. He took them back on board the first car of the train, which was when Allender realized there was a Metro driver in the front compartment. The captain motioned for them to take seats and then waved toward the front of the train. The doors closed, and then the train's motors hummed to life and the cars accelerated into the tunnel. Allender's last glimpse of Metro Center was a scrum of black helmets, NVG goggles, and batons. Hingham, Chiang, and his helpers were somewhere in the middle, but no longer visible.

The train rushed through the tunnel and right through the next station without stopping. Allender was reassured to see people in that station doing what he'd expected the night shift to be doing. The next stop was Dupont Circle. The train slid to a stop, the chimes sounded, and the doors opened. The captain motioned for them to debark, and then he escorted them up the escalator and all the way to Allender's town house. When they got there they met some of the same Secret Service people who'd been there before they'd made their run standing at the front door. Some of them had uncomfortable expressions on their faces as Allender walked by them. Melanie's glare might have had a bearing on that.

The captain did the handover, said good night, and left. They went inside, where they were met by a supervisory Secret Service agent.

"Doctor Allender?" the supervisor said when he spotted them. "Mister Wallace is inbound in about ten minutes. He wanted to make sure you were physically and safely back here."

"Physically, yes. Safely? I'm not sure. You guys going to hang around this time?" Allender asked.

The agent nodded. He started to explain, but Allender waved him off. If Wallace was coming, they'd find out what the hell had been going on. He told the agent they'd be in his study.

"I need a drink or six," Allender said. "And then I want some god-damned answers."

"Heard that," Melanie said, dropping into a chair. "Should we rearm ourselves, in case Mister Wallace is not forthcoming?"

"To do what? Shoot it out with the Secret Service?"

"No, to kneecap Wallace into telling us what this is all about in case he gets all coy on us."

He shook his head, went to the decanter tray, and poured two substantial Scotches. He thought about putting his glasses back on but then said to hell with it. He handed his bloodthirsty companion her Scotch and then took a solid draft of the smoky whiskey and sat down.

"You do think we're going to get an explanation?" Melanie asked.

"I hope so," he said. "Although technically, you're his employee and I'm just a temp. He could cite national security, thank us for our deep interest in national defense, fire me and maybe even you."

"Lovely," she said. "Now I do want a weapon."

"You were pretty impressive tonight. I keep forgetting you're a real operative."

"We're trained above all else never to get captured," she said. "As soon as their leader turned his back on us I knew I could take them. I wasn't prepared for what happened after they fell onto the tracks, though."

Allender nodded. He thought he could still smell the aftermath on his clothes.

"Seeing Chiang was a shock, too," Melanie said.

"I'm wondering if that *was* Chiang," Allender replied. "There was something—"

They heard noises at the front as a Secret Service agent admitted Henry Wallace, accompanied by none other than Carson McGill, into the house and pointed them toward the tower study. Allender put his glasses back on.

"Got any more of that?" Wallace asked, eyeing Allender's Scotch.

"Only if you're going to tell all," Allender said, getting up to retrieve some more glasses. "Why isn't *he* in custody?"

"Preston, my dear fellow," McGill began. "Good to see you, too. There's much you don't know yet."

"Glad to hear the 'yet,'" Melanie snapped. She looked ready to attack McGill.

"Then it's showtime," Allender announced. He looked meaningfully at McGill, but apparently it was Wallace who was going to tell the tale.

"This all started when someone told us that Maxine Greer had a

Chinese girlfriend," Wallace began. "The girlfriend part wasn't the surprise. The Chinese part was, because the 'someone' recognized her as being a member of the MSS stationed at the embassy here in Washington."

"Who was the someone?" Allender asked.

"The Agency guy assigned as liaison between Greer's office and Langley," Wallace said. "The one who got 'sent home,' for being little more than just a spy for the Agency, as Maxine put it? Which was, of course, his exact job description. Thing was, he'd been on the black-swan operation, where he'd been briefed on all the faces we could expect to show up as General Chiang's security detail at the hotel that night."

" 'We'? I thought you'd been cut out of that entire operation."

Wallace sighed. "As if," he said. "Carson here is fully capable of going behind my back, of course, but he most definitely did not cut me out of that particular op. And that's because Chiang wasn't the real target that night. Now, here's your chance to impress me: Can either of you guess who was?"

Allender thought hard. He'd been asked to come up with something that would irreparably damage the MSS network here in Washington. Chiang's loose zipper had provided the perfect opportunity. So, if he hadn't been the target, then who?

"I think I can," Melanie said, surprising him. Wallace raised his eyebrows at her.

"The real target was Hingham," she said. "And tonight, you achieved your objective, didn't you?"

Wallace looked over at McGill as if he'd just won an interesting side bet. "Very good, Ms. Sloan," he said. "Can you connect the dots?"

She shook her head. "Above my pay grade," she said. "Besides, I want to hear your version."

"Good thinking, Ms. Sloan," Wallace said, looking over at Allender. "Then I shall continue. The problem was indeed Chinese in nature, which is why we needed to construct something of a Chinese box in order to get our arms around it. Carson?"

McGill leaned forward. "Your involvement resumed when I called you that day to bring you back on active duty. Remember?"

"Yes. You said that Hank here was dead, under mysterious circumstances."

"And what else?"

"That your real problem was that he had been running a swan, but you didn't know who the swan was."

"Exactly so," McGill said.

"And none of that was true?"

"*Not* exactly."

"Let me give you some background, Doctor," Wallace said. "You were in the training department, and you were most valuable in the matter of current assessment of our training staff, as well as in the fine arts of interrogation. What was your sense as to what the Agency spent most of its efforts and energy on?"

"The war on terrorism," Allender replied. "The defeat of intelligence efforts mounted against the United States. A resurgent Soviet Russia. The development of global espionage networks of our own. I suppose those are the main lines of effort."

"Yes, all correct," Wallace said. "Those are the efforts that occupy the headlines and most of our day-to-day work and budget. But there's also a long-range, not-so-well-known mission, and that involves China."

"Our director's favorite country," Melanie offered.

"I don't know about favorite, but it certainly is his major preoccupation. As he is fond of saying, ad nauseam, China's triumph on the world scene is inevitable."

"We heard some of that tonight."

"So I'm told. He has a point. China does pose a special threat to America, and for one main reason: They are *here,* and in great and growing numbers. In our universities. In our labs. In our high schools.

In our dot-com tech world, our hospitals. I'm not saying every Chinese person you see is a spy for China, but: China remains a harsh Communist dictatorship. If the MSS contacts a postdoc scientist working at JPL and asks him for some information, they'll begin with the news that his mother and father back in Beijing are currently in good health and there's every hope they'll stay that way."

"Subtle."

"Isn't it. But the point is that they'll never have to invade the US of A; they're already here and, in terms of scientific and technical progress, we're probably dependent on them."

"So what's this long-range mission?" Allender asked.

Wallace hesitated. "Yes, that is the question, isn't it. Carson here and I disagree somewhat on the answer."

"Hank wants to interdict totally the theft of America's premium intellectual property by the Chinese," McGill said. "I want to attenuate it, because in my heart of hearts, and as much as it pisses me off, I think the director's thesis is correct. We'll never stop them entirely, and eventually, they will rule the world. I think the mission is to slow that prospect down."

"You're saying that Hingham was actively helping them?" Allender asked.

"'Actively' is the key word. He was in the sense that he strangled that part of the budget used to deal with Chinese espionage. Was he giving them secrets? No. Was he in contact with the MSS? Yes, but not at secret drop boxes around the city. It was more like a discreet lunch with the counselor at the Chinese embassy. Where they'd play chess and discuss history and the long-range trends in human enterprise. All very intellectual and academic."

"But not actionable?" Melanie asked.

"Precisely," McGill said. "Good choice of words. Not like catching him handing over state papers. Hence the second swan."

"Wait a minute," Allender said. "Are you saying that the black swan was not an operation in its own right? That it was an opening phase of a larger op?"

Wallace nodded. "You were told that *your* objective was to crash the MSS infrastructure here in town by taking down Chiang Liang-fu in a highly public and embarrassing manner. Which it did. A welcome bonus, but not the main event, as you were led to believe."

Allender looked at Melanie. "Yes," he said. "We both believed that. So Chiang was, what? Just a precursor? You're saying that Hingham was the objective?"

"You will recall that his reaction to the Chiang affair was to—?"

"Exile me into early retirement, among other things."

"Exactly."

"So why didn't he fire you two as well?"

"Believe me, the thought crossed his mind and some shots crossed our bows," McGill said, with a wry grin. "But I convinced him that the Chiang business was a necessary slap in the face, that we had to demonstrate from time to time that we could if we wanted to. A matter of maintaining respect. They'd call it face. He probably considered the trade-offs, and then let us get away with it, mostly to protect Rebecca Lansing."

Allender looked at the two bureaucrats sitting there like a pair of satisfied cats, trying not to look quite so pleased with themselves. "And Rebecca, or Mei Ling, was *his* controller?" he asked.

" 'Controller' imputes active espionage," Wallace said. "She was his back channel to the MSS in the sense that she encouraged his crusade to acknowledge China's ultimate superiority to America. Throw in some artful adulation and maybe even some social privileges, and she could keep Hingham on track. She was exceptionally competent, and, unfortunately, an unplanned-for surprise."

"Talk about penetration," Melanie said.

"It was all about China," Wallace said. "I agree. We should have known. By the way, she was the second dragon-seed agent the MSS has managed to get into the Agency."

"Doctor Allender mentioned dragon seed down at the Farm," Melanie said. "Is that for real?"

"The MSS have a list of countries throughout the world where they want to achieve agents in place of the same ethnicity of the ruling majority of the population. In other words, a native Japanese for Japan, an Arab for Saudi Arabia, a Persian for Iran, or an American Caucasian for the US. They obtain a baby of the required ethnicity, usually from secretly vetted parents in order to enhance their chances of getting a smart child."

"Obtain?"

"Kidnap, usually," McGill said. "Or they buy them. The Chinese have long been in the baby buying and selling business. Then they raise that child entirely within the Chinese version of the *nomenklatura* in Soviet Russia. Is there a Chinese term for that, Preston?"

"It's the *zhiwu mingcheng biao* system," Allender said. "The gold-plated political layer in the Communist Party. In ancient times, we'd have called them Mandarins."

"Precisely," Wallace said. "They get sent to special schools and are indoctrinated from infancy through adulthood in the philosophy, morals, and lofty goals of the Chinese Communist Party. They make some of them into intelligence officers, teaching them a specific second language from the age of two right through their operational training. They get sent to the appropriate embassies, purportedly as family members of embassy staff, to become culturally colloquial. By the time they're in their early twenties, their legends are impenetrable. Consider Lansing's case. She was a graduate of Columbia University and NYU Law, and could speak English with a New York City accent."

"She told us her mother won the lottery," Melanie said.

"Her 'mother' was the MSS, doing what the Chinese do best."

"Taking that very long view," Allender mused.

"They have the people, and they have the time, don't they," Mc-Gill said. "Her assignment was to get hired by the Agency and then work her way into the director's office, which she did. It didn't hurt that she and Hingham shared the same worldview, although I doubt he initially knew she was MSS. Certainly neither Hank nor I ever suspected. She was one of those best-and-brightest officers, attractive, whip smart, and eagerly intellectual, just the type to appeal to a snob like Hingham. And being female, she helped with the gender-equality initiative."

"How did you get on to her?" Allender asked, before Melanie could pounce on that comment about gender equality.

"When she killed General Chiang's son," Wallace said. "We knew, of course, that Hingham had sent her to the Bureau, and that she would be your POC once we folded you into the op. We did *not* know that Chiang's son was in the country, or that he was planning to kill you in revenge for what happened to his father."

"And?"

"And, if we didn't know that, how did *she* know that? When we couldn't answer that question, we started pulling scabs until we figured it out."

"It had to be through Yang Yi," Allender said.

"Yes. But her meeting with Yang Yi was not for a warning—it was for instructions, as best we can tell. As in, Don't let Chiang the younger do a revenge murder on a CIA officer while we're still spinning silk over Hingham's dewy eyes."

"But *nothing* happened to his father," Melanie pointed out. "We saw him, tonight, alive and well."

"Actually," Wallace said, "you saw his older brother, Chiang Ho-liu. He took over the Chiang faction once his brother was executed. He apparently made the case to Yang Yi and the Central Committee that *he* ought to go to Washington to put the MSS network back together. General Chiang's immediate family was flattened, of course, but many of their operational people already in place here in D.C.

were still here and partisans of the Chiang faction, so that kinda made sense. The quickest way to recover from the disaster in the hotel, so to speak. His arrival in Washington was the defining moment, because he knew, of course, that the MSS had an agent in place in Hingham's office."

"That would be some amazing leverage," Allender said.

"Yes, indeed," McGill said. "He called a meeting with Hingham in a restaurant in Old Town Alexandria. Because of our suspicions about Lansing, we were by then up on Hingham and, wherever he went, there we were. He never suspected because he never went anywhere without minders. They made a deal, to which we listened: Hingham agreed not to obstruct the reconstitution of the MSS network in Washington in return for Chiang's silence on the delicate matter of Rebecca Lansing. All part of the inevitable victory of China over the decaying Western countries, a notion for which Hingham was already an apostle. We then had Chiang, the brother, picked up, discreetly, of course, and we made an even better offer: We would allow Chiang to reconstitute his operation in Washington in return for his facilitating our takedown of Hingham."

"Why would he do that?"

"Because we now had video of him suborning the director of the CIA to commit treason. If we ever made that public here in the US, the entire Chiang faction, having embarrassed the Central Committee once again, would be crushed once and for all."

"But if you did make that public, wouldn't that take care of Hingham for you?" Melanie asked.

"They were doing what Hingham often did, couching their discussion in academic terms, with lots of BS about the inevitable currents of history and the manifest destiny of such a great nation as China. Even if we released the video, we'd have had to dress it up with a lot of analysis, which meant it wasn't iron-tight. Plus, there was no guarantee that this administration would have let us even do it."

"Not to mention that it might have made the both of you look like fools," Allender pointed out. "For 'allowing' an MSS sleeper to live in the director's office."

"Ahem," Wallace said.

"So what happened? He agreed?"

"He did. But that still left us with the problem of Hingham. All we had was talk. We needed to force him to make a move. To *do* something."

"And there we were."

"Yes, precisely," McGill said. "There you were. The original loose ends."

"And all the smoke and mirrors about Hank being dead or Hank being in a coma—that was to induce me to play Sherlock?"

They both looked at him and smiled. "Hingham panicked when we had Lansing picked up," Wallace continued, "He'd figured out you guys were suspicious of Lansing, so he had to *do* something to take you and Ms. Sloan off the boards. And that was our objective all along: not to light up what Hingham *thought*, or agreed with, or predicted, but to catch him doing something—like trying to capture you and Ms. Singer, here, in the bowels of the city."

"And the Secret Service?"

"That's the Agency from which I came to Langley, remember?" Wallace said. "I couldn't use Agency assets, of course, or Hingham would know."

"And why use me to interrogate Lansing?"

"Why not? You're probably the best interrogator in the business, plus once you broke Lansing and told me, you would realize that somebody pretty high up in the Agency—Carson, here, or possibly even Hingham—would be after you. When you discovered that your protection had been withdrawn earlier tonight, you bolted. Chiang the brother had eyes on you. He got word to Hingham, who consented to a grab team of MSS operatives. Now, why *he* decided to personally come to the scene is puzzling."

"Because Melanie took out the first team they sent after us," Allender said. He described the fight and how Melanie had pretty much single-handedly taken the entire Chinese team on and won.

"Bravo," McGill said. "We didn't know that."

"By the way," Allender said. "We ran into something really strange down there. A track that switched off the main line and went into a heavily guarded tunnel. The guards there threatened to shoot us both unless we got out of there."

"Ah," McGill said. "You ran into the White House stub. That's a piece of track that leads from under the White House Situation Room to the main-line system. In the event of a nuclear emergency, they can hustle the president down to the stub, where there's a train always waiting. They can take over traffic control of the entire Metro system from there and divert every train in the system, and then get the president out of the city to one of several secret helicopter launch sites at eighty miles an hour, underground. I'm a little surprised they didn't just shoot you right off the bat."

"Well, I can explain that, Carson," Wallace said. "Those were Secret Service protective-detail guards. Once you ran for the Metro, I'd briefed them to look for you, and run you off if, in fact, you showed up. We couldn't know where you'd end up, but because the entire Metro system is part of the National Emergency Action network, there are Secret Service people throughout the network. I was just covering all the bases."

McGill looked over at Wallace. "Listen to you," he said. "You'd think you'd been a spook yourself."

"Well," Wallace said. "Sometimes I get it right." He looked at his watch and yawned. "Enough fun for one night, I think. Doctor Allender, your Agency thanks you for a job well done. For what it's worth, I'm going to take a shot at the director's job, and if that happens, Carson, here, will move up to Deppity Dawg. We'll need a new DDO. Interested?"

Allender laughed out loud. "Absolutely not," he said. "But you might think about letting me have a séance with Hingham down in the Dungeons."

"Why?" McGill asked sharply.

"Because you're both assuming that Hingham was just a naïve puppet in the MSS chess game. What if he wasn't? What if Lansing wasn't the only dragon seed? Hell, what if goddamned Hingham was a dragon seed?"

McGill's eyebrows shot up at that unlikely thought. He looked over at Wallace as the two of them got up to leave. "Okay," Wallace said. "I think maybe we should do that. I may even want to watch. We'll be in touch."

Allender got up, too. "One last question for Carson: When you originally called me out of retirement to help with the Wallace mystery, you said that Hank had been running a swan."

McGill started to smile, but didn't say anything.

"You said that you could brief me into whatever you did know about the bogus mysterious death, except for the identity of the swan. So: Who the hell was the swan?"

"Why, Preston, my dear fellow," McGill said, with a big grin now. "That would be you, of course."

TWENTY-SEVEN

Allender sat down and finished his Scotch, while Melanie looked at him with an amused expression on her face. "You have really interesting friends," she said finally.

He just shook his head. "I guess if you're going to be a chess piece it's good to have Hank Wallace as your player. Damn!"

"Is the Agency ever going to reveal any of this?"

"Are you kidding?"

"What about Greer? How will they keep her quiet?"

"They'll tell her that Hingham was removed for sanctioning a political smear on a sitting congressman and that the top brass at the Agency had to lie to her in order to get enough evidence to remove him. And, by the way—would she like to hold a public hearing on the matter, a year before the election? No? We thought not. We're so sorry for any inconvenience. Even sorrier about your friend."

"I'm not sure she's gonna let it go that easily," she said.

"Her question to us when we told her that nothing she'd heard so far was true was very telling, in my opinion—'how does this affect *me*'? Her own reelection was a whole lot more important than any national-security issues."

"She should be prosecuted for allowing MSS to get close to her," Melanie pointed out.

"Probably won't be," he said. "The Agency has some pretty good leverage on her right now, just as she has some on the Agency. That might lead to a much better relationship."

"You're getting pretty cynical in your old age," she said.

" 'Old age' being the operative term, secret agent," he said. "Now I need a hot shower and then some sleep."

"Me, too," she said, and then gave him an extremely direct look. Tired as he was, that look did not escape his notice. "Melanie," he began, but she interrupted.

"It's 'Melanie' now and forever, especially since you called me 'Melanie' in front of Chiang version two. And why not? You know I like you."

"I'm too old and I'm too weird," he said. "Ask anybody."

· She gave him an arch look that said this discussion wasn't over. He fled upstairs. Standing in the hot shower, he resisted the urge to kick himself. Why not, indeed. He'd hidden behind his amber eyes for almost his entire lifetime, and now here was a woman who didn't really care about that or the fact that he was much older than she was.

He came out of the bathroom dressed in a bathrobe and rubbing a towel through his hair. Then he stopped. All the lights were off. The only light in the room came from the bathroom door. Melanie was in his bed, her own head wrapped in a towel. She was grinning at him. He stared at her for a moment and then walked over to the bed. He was astounded to find that he didn't quite know what to do next. She solved it for him.

"Disrobe," she growled in a positively awful rendition of his own voice.